THE
WEAVER OF PLOTS

THE
WEAVER OF PLOTS

A Novel

David Orsini

THE
WEAVER OF PLOTS

Copyright © 2020 by David Orsini
First Edition Quaternity™ Books 2020
Quaternity™ Books
ISBN 978-1-943691-27-2
Cover Design by James Buchanan

Other Books by David Orsini

The Woman Who Loved Too Well
The Ghost Lovers
Schemes, Disguises, and Traps
Vanishing by Degrees
The Subtleties of Seduction
Bitterness / Seven Stories

CONTENTS

Part One: Charlotte   11

Part Two: Other Points of View   245

Part Three: Afterward   353

"I was kept fast bound, not with exterior chains or irons, but with my own iron will. The enemy held my will, and of it he made a chain which fettered me fast."
—Saint Augustine of Hippo

PART ONE

CHARLOTTE

PART ONE

CHAPTER ONE

Charlotte

Wednesday Afternoon, 4 October 1967

Looking Back to Wednesday Afternoon, 4 June 1952

And a Few Months Before That Day

The letter from Noah Blake arrived when she was not expecting it. The postmark and the sender's address told her that the letter had been mailed from Noah's office within the Blake and Tanner Steel and Aluminum Corporation in the Manhattan section of New York. Here, in Greenwich, Connecticut, seated in the comfortably upholstered home office where she had written many of her novels, she placed the letter on the desk before her. She did not care to open it. Whatever message Noah was sending to her, she would not enjoy reading. He had sent the letter fifteen years too late.

Instead of reading the letter, she looked out of the sun-misted panoramic window as a way of deflecting her attention. The two ancient elms stood, as usual, giant-like and apparently invincible, fifty feet in the distance. The night before, an autumn windstorm had torn away most of their russet leaves. Deprived of the vivid colors, the trees retained, nonetheless, a gnarled magnificence. To her imaginative eyes, they were rugged sentries that had, thus far, withstood the battering winds and the pelting rains and all the other adversarial elements of Time. The lessons they offered about survival lay, wordless and emphatic, within their bruised stolidity. From her fleet knowledge of trees, she knew that they could feel. She regarded them as sensate, living beings. Trees did express anger, loneliness, and pain. But their language was known mainly to themselves and to scientists and well-schooled foresters. She envied the apparent stoicism of these two elms outside her window and their disdain of any emotion-laden human language that could express their anguish and their pain.

She knew something about being stoical. The thirty-seven years that she had lived had taught her to be stoical. She had not always been so. There was a time when she rebelled against her pain and anguish. In that long-ago period, she had lashed out at the persons who had betrayed her. She had meted harsh punishment to the man who had betrayed her and to the woman who was his accomplice.

Noah Blake was that man, and Olivia Tanner was the woman. The sight of Noah's letter brought them back to her, even against her conscious will. After all these years, she still loathed the two of them. Her view of the stalwart elms, often a consolation, could not push away her new awareness that Noah and Olivia still existed. Nor could her gaze into the faraway distance at the cloud-capped horizon and the blue-green radiance of the sky dispel her wakened memory of them.

She did not need to open Noah's letter to remember who he was and how he had betrayed her. His name in the upper left corner of the envelope did that. It did more than that. It startled her. It revived the memory of him and of Olivia that she had repressed for so many years.

Now those ill-fated years came swiftly back to her.

Only afterward, long after everything was finished between her and Noah, would she admit to herself that she did not have to carry the snub-nosed revolver inside the secret pocket of her purse. Prodded by her tattered hopes and by her stubborn belief that Noah still loved her, she had made the six-hour drive from her parents' summer home in Newport, Rhode Island, to the house in Saranac Lake, New York, where Noah was staying—without her and without even a token promise that, in spite of his overbearing father, he would stand beside her. In the uncertain days that were waiting for her, he would be her advocate. He would make things right.

She had often travelled on highways alone at night. Sometimes, she drove three hundred miles from her Pembroke College dormitory on the Brown University campus to Poughkeepsie, New York, because she needed to talk out her problems to her best friend, Laura Madison, who was a senior at Vassar. On other nights, she made her way through the four-hour drive to her aunt Eleanor's summer place on Lake Champlain in Vermont. Always, she arrived in early morning, when the glow of a new day and the loyalty of her childhood friend or of her compassionate aunt promised her refuge from her disquieted awareness of Noah's indifference.

Never before had she carried the Colt Cobra revolver that she took in secret from an inadvertently unlocked cabinet in her father's gunroom. On that night in early June of 1952, she told herself that she was taking the revolver to protect herself from the gang of drug-addicted thieves who lately had been forcing drivers off the road and robbing them of their cars, their watches and jewelry, and their cash. Carrying the revolver was the sensible thing to do. It made her feel secure. It made her believe that she was not alone. If somebody trapped her, if some thief threatened her wellbeing, the revolver would be her advocate.

She had not expected to fire the revolver. She had fired it again and again, though not at any highway thieves. Those thieves had not rampaged the highways that night. Yet she had been involved in a shooting. For years afterward, she struggled to push that scene way back into the hidden corners of her memory. Now, fifteen years later, while she sat, solitary and conflicted, in the spacious room in the south wing of her large colonial home that she used as her office, the memory of that night—and of almost everything that had happened between her and Noah before that night—broke through her resistance. Even her memory had come to steal from her. Against her struggling will, it stole her uneasy peace. It took away her makeshift security. It dispossessed her of her willfulness, her arrogance, and her malice. Sullen and reluctant, she confronted its truth without flinching. She was used to thieves. Through all of her life, they had stolen from her.

"Be careful," her father had told her only two months before she became involved in the shooting episode at Saranac Lake. "Thieves have a way of coming back."

In March of 1952, shortly before her graduation from Pembroke and as she was leaving one of the campus libraries where she had been studying, she had been robbed at gunpoint by a tall, youthful man wearing a black ski mask. He had stolen the eighty dollars that was in her purse and a diamond watch that her parents had given her on her sixteenth birthday. She had noticed the nearly imperceptible tremor in the young, awkward hands of the robber as he quickly placed inside the deep pocket of his long black coat the cash and the watch that she had, without any resistance, held out to him. He had used his left hand to scoop the cash and the watch from her. His powerful right hand, with the slightest tremor, kept pointing the Smith-Wesson revolver at her heart. Although his face was mostly covered, she saw the intense, blue eyes peering at her from the openings in his mask and the sensual, chapped lips that suggested hunger and discomfort. She noticed, too, the silver wedding band that he wore on the fourth finger of his left hand. She remembered that, just before he hurried away, he had spoken to her. His curt voice had a raspy edge and his eyes gleamed with the desperation of a man who had never robbed before.

"I'm sorry," he said.

Her heart stirred with pity for him. She did not care about the watch or the eighty dollars. In that moment, she wished that she could have done more for him.

How remarkable it seemed to her now, so many years later, that she had felt pity for this thief. The anguished years that had pursued her soon after that night used up all of her pity for thieves and for everyone else.

Noah Blake had been the wiliest of the thieves. He had stolen her heart. He had played with her obsession for him. Without ever saying the words that could intensify the bond between them, he had led her to believe that he loved her. During two of their Brown University years, they had shared each other's life and each other's bed. Then, after she told him that she was carrying his baby, he turned away from her. Even her most impassioned entreaties failed to move him. When she begged him to stand by her and to protect her from the disgrace that would fall upon her as an unwed mother, he closed himself off from her.

"Get rid of it," he told her a few days after their graduation.

His husky voice sounded hard and unyielding.

He was packing for his summer stay at Saranac Lake, before he moved on to his graduate studies in London. They were in the second-floor bedroom of the townhouse that his parents had bought for him because it was located in the affluent east side of Providence and because it was near the Brown University area. His father regarded the purchase as a wise investment. His mother, with her team of interior decorators, had burnished each room with warm, earthen colors that, she said, enhanced the masculine vitality of her son's life style.

At first, Noah's words about terminating her pregnancy confused her. She did not want to believe that he had said those words.

Observing her confusion, Noah threw out those words again.

"Get rid of it."

His hardheartedness frightened her. She struggled to maintain her self-control. She wanted to mollify him. She sought to guide him to the path on which she was beginning a new journey.

"Everything will be all right," she said, "once we are married."

He laughed at her words.

"Marriage is not in my plans."

She was following him discreetly as he moved from room to room gathering the summer clothes and the athletic equipment that he was bringing to Saranac Lake. She kept her voice low and anchored her petition to a matter-of-fact remark.

"I thought that the baby might change your mind."

He paused to observe her carefully. There was no love in his eyes. There was only a momentary flash of contempt. She felt her ghost hovering by her. Her breathing quickened as she struggled to maintain her composure when she heard the blunt words that her remark drew from him.

"Not in a million years," he said. "I've always made my life an adventure. I'm not going to be chained to a baby."

Though she took care to keep her voice low, she made her words sound more insistent.

"The baby is part of you—your flesh and blood. Whether it is a daughter or a son, you are the father."

He left his packing now and placed himself before her. Gently, he clasped her shoulders and held her in his gaze. He was trying to be patient. He wanted her to understand how it was with him.

"I'm not willing to be anybody's father. And you are not ready to be a mother."

In that moment, the gentle touch of his hands upon her shoulders thrilled her beyond measure. She needed that gesture of his acceptance. So profound was her need, that his touch brought grateful tears to her eyes.

"I'll be a good mother. You'll see."

She wanted to believe that her tears stirred him in ways that may have surprised even him. She told herself that, in that moment, his softer feelings were struggling against his ingrained hardheartedness. But, looking back now, so many years later, she had to admit that his disdain of any sentimental responses had not left him. She saw with clarified realism that her petitioning manner had appealed to his narcissism. Usually, Noah yoked his feelings to a cold detachment that gave no quarter to clinging females or to the burden of unwanted babies. But, on that afternoon, only a week before the shooting occurred at Saranac Lake, he had treated her emotion-laden words with a brief show of warmth. He hugged her and kissed her forehead, the way a father might kiss the forehead of his seven-year-old daughter who had been left disappointed by a school-friend's betrayal.

The gesture solaced her. She would not permit herself to notice then how effortlessly he linked his next words to condescension and to indifference. Nor did she perceive his subtle arrogance.

"You are daydreaming," he said. "You are like a child playing house with her dolls."

She wanted to say more. She wanted to reassure him. She thought that she could change his mind.

"I'll be a good mother because the baby is from you. I love everything that is you."

A slight frown touched his brow.

"I don't love you in the same way. You know that. From the beginning, I told you how it is with me. I don't want anyone to tie me down. You have been my pal. You have been the good-natured girl that I have casually romanced. You have been a terrific bed partner, too. You are one of the girls that I may remember when I'm middle-aged and looking back."

Still she petitioned him.

"I thought my loving you would make a difference."

He met her gaze directly. His voice was more tense now and emphatic.

"It hasn't."

"Though you never told me so, you acted as though you loved me."

"Sure, I did. I have always had a loving feeling for you. I've had that feeling when everything has gone right for us. Maybe, we were with my best friends at a party and you made a favorable impression. Maybe, you cheered me up when I'd had a tough day on the hockey rink. Maybe, you made me look good when we were discussing the novels of Faulkner at an afternoon tea with the university president. But I have never loved you the way that you want me to love you. I've never been in love with you."

He pulled away from her. She told herself that, possibly, he was ashamed of his words. He was having a difficult time dealing with his feelings. But now, fifteen years later, while recalling what happened in that hour, she noticed what she had not then comprehended. His inability to feel deeply about anything or anyone isolated him from her dilemma. Her love for him, obsessive and prevailing, had subverted her common sense. She could not bring herself to admit that the condescending hug and the sympathetic words that he had offered her fed his vanity. On that uneasy afternoon, when she was trying to salvage their relationship, she saw his swaggering manner as a mere fault line in his life-loving and adventurous nature. She believed that, if she were submissive and loving, she could draw him to her will. He would understand that the bond they had forged with one another was valuable and even extraordinary.

With the three lovers who had been part of her life before Noah, she had never been so submissive. Her self-possession and her strong-minded nature had always anchored themselves to a steely courage and to a keen-minded awareness of her value as a woman. She was no innocent. By the time she was seventeen, she had witnessed the world's follies with a knowing cynicism. She had withstood the often subtle and sometimes obvious tyrannies of the three men who had passed through her life during the two years that followed. They had been drawn to her enthusiasm for fast living and to her discreet sensuality. All of them had declared their love for her without understanding what authentic love required from them. They had confused their sexual desire for her with the more profound expressions of love that are generated by honesty, fidelity, and empathy. She had never loved any of them, though she had learned a great deal about men by observing the ambivalent individuality of each of her lovers.

She had also enjoyed being the object of their desires. She had played the game well. She had effectively teased their carnal dispositions. Never did she pursue these men or allow them to chip away at her self-worth or her independence. On the contrary, it was they who pursued her. She had held them in thrall to their prurient appetites. Even the most self-centered of her three lovers confessed his need of her. Such confession empowered her. She had a healthy appreciation of her success with men. Whenever she opened herself to their vigorous copulation, she enjoyed mating her body with theirs. She received the lovemaking of these men as proof of her influence over them. The rawness and the urgency of the sex brought her much pleasure, because in her relations with them apart from the bed she had maintained her autonomy. She would not permit herself to be their plaything—a puppet on strings manipulated by their devious propensities or by their brooding masculinity.

She thought herself to be very clever in her relations with men. But then, in the first week of her sophomore year at Pembroke, she fell in love with Noah. His success as a goalie on the hockey team, his superb showing for the swimming team, his Dean's List status, and his freewheeling personality made him one of the most popular men on the Brown University campus. She did not love him first of all because he was the scion of a wealthy family. Her own family was wealthy. Nor did she love him especially because he was extraordinarily handsome. She loved him because he chose to live on the cusp of danger and because he flouted society's lock-step conventions and got away with it. They were both rebels. They belonged to each other. But he regarded her in a different way. She was a passing fancy. She was a pal. She was a temporary sexual partner. He made passionate love with her, but he did not love her.

He stole her heart without giving her any of his love. His refusal to make an abiding commitment to their relationship goaded the anger and apprehension that, for the most part, she had quietly learned to suppress. His not loving her challenged her belief in her womanly powers. It diminished her self-worth. Against her better judgment, she became acquiescent and pliable whenever she was with him. Yet never did she tell herself that he was unattainable. She continued to believe that she could win his love. Her desire to possess all of his love became an obsession that in this very moment, as he was preparing to leave her on that June day in 1952, drove her forward with even more willful urgency.

Before he could turn from her to resume his packing, she took hold of his big, masculine hands. She pressed her lips lightly against them.

Then she implored him further.

"We still have time. Nothing need be finished with us."

He watched her fold her hands over his own. The cold-hearted resolve that had come like an ally to observe him prodded him forward.

"But we are finished, Charlotte. Those are the rules that we set for ourselves when we started living with each other. We promised that we would go our separate ways on graduation day. We said that, on that day, all promises and debts between us would be cancelled."

Her memory of that promise dismayed her. Her words grew more excited.

"They can't be cancelled. I'm going to have your baby."

He met her outburst with a firm dismissal. Yet never did he raise his voice. He merely repeated the words that she did not want to hear.

"Get rid of it. We are done, girl. We are finished."

He turned away from her and continued the packing of his suitcases.

She hovered near him. Her voice hardened. Her words were accusatory and vehement.

"Your father turned you against me. He's never liked me. He wants you to marry Olivia Tanner, because of a corporate merger."

He looked up at her and laughed.

"I'm not marrying anyone, not even Olivia Tanner."

She moved closer to him now. The words hurried out of her, incisive and condemning.

"You will marry her. You will do what your father wants you to do, because you do not want to lose your inheritance and because you will have Olivia's fortune, as well. You are a taker. Even with your father's money to back you, you are a wily hustler. You never give anything that might cost you something. Yet you always win the game."

Noah held himself still. The slight frown returned, but it touched his brow only for a moment. He would not permit himself to be angry. Instead, he anchored his reply to an amused flippancy.

"Thanks for the character reference," he said. "I'm not sure, though, that I'll include it in my résumé."

She moved nearer still and caressed his handsome face. Her voice was once again soft and yielding.

" I love you in spite of your faults. I love you for all the good things that I see in you."

Her words did not touch him, as she had hoped. His face wore a determined expression, and his words were calm and straightforward.

"Then keep those good things in mind and walk away from me. Walk out of my life."

A giant wave of panic was rushing to overtake her.

"Not yet, Noah," she pleaded. "Not yet. I'm not ready to live without you."

He resisted her new show of emotion. He wanted her to suppress her feelings. He wanted her to face the facts of her situation.

"You can't cling to me any longer. You'll have to make your own way without me. But you need to get rid of the baby."

She saw no escape from her dilemma. She had to choose Noah or their baby. Desperate now, she summoned the words that might keep Noah and her together.

"What if I do get rid of it? Can we be together again, even for a little while?"

A new interest in her peered from his eyes and touched his face. He saw the tremendous sacrifice that she was willing to make for him. But he still resisted her petitioning manner.

"It's not going to work, Charlotte. Besides, I'll be in London."

She hurried to say the words that would convince him of the rightness of this new plan.

"I can be there, too. I won't get in your way. I just need to be near you."

For a few minutes, he pondered her words. But his momentary hesitation did not alter his decision to break away from her.

"Stop believing in romantic daydreams and happy endings," he said. "It's over between us."

Once more, the giant wave of panic came rushing upon her. Her breathing came faster. She felt her body swaying and suddenly she was falling to her knees. As if she were far away, she heard herself crying out to him.

"Don't leave me, Noah! Don't leave me!"

He grabbed her roughly and, after guiding her to a standing position, began shaking her. Tears were clouding her eyes, and her sobs were growing heavier

"Get hold of yourself," he said. "Let's end everything in style."

At that very instant, they heard two of his hockey mates barging into the first-floor entrance to help him pack his suitcases into the trunk and rear seat of his Bentley.

One of the friends yelled out to him from the bottom of the stairs.

"Hey, Noah, buddy, we are here to help you get packed for your new adventure!"

She stifled her sobs and, after wiping away her tears with a silk handkerchief that had the letter C embroidered in one of its corners, turned away to peer out the window. She heard the two friends running up to the top of the stairs. By the time they reached the threshold of the room, she had recovered her demure appearance. She turned back to Noah and joined him in greeting them.

But a tension, both palpable and urgent, stayed in the room.

The two friends, big-boned and hardy handsome, noticed her flushed appearance and Noah's tight, brooding expression.

"Are we interrupting something important?" the taller of these friends asked.

"Not at all," Noah answered him. "Charlotte has been helping me finish the packing."

If the friends saw through Noah's raspy explanation, they gave no sign. They were his hockey mates. They shared a strong bond with him. In a crisis, they helped one another. But they kept out of each other's romantic entanglements.

For the next half hour, they helped Noah finish packing and, right after that, carry the luggage into his car. She helped, too, with the less heavy items. The two friends were riding to Saranac Lake with him. Their families also had summer homes there.

Then, while his friends waited in the car, Noah came back to say "goodbye." She would be staying here in the townhouse for a few more days, before she drove on to her parents' summer home in Newport.

"We don't have to say 'goodbye,'" she said. "It doesn't have to be over for us. I won't get in your way. I promise."

He did not answer her right away. He held himself very still while he observed her, as if for the last time. Then, with no hesitation, he spoke the words that he needed to say.

"Let this be 'goodbye'," he said.

He caressed her face and kissed her lips. It was a casual kiss. It was a kiss without any profound feeling.

"Try to remember the good times that we've had."

Before she could speak, he turned and hurried away.

She followed him out through the doorway and called to him.

"This isn't 'goodbye.' I love you too much for this to be 'goodbye.' You can't walk out of my life. You can't!"

She followed him to the Bentley, but he did not pause to look back at her. Tight-lipped and dismissive, he placed himself in the driver's seat and closed the door. His two friends looked away, too embarrassed to observe her.

She began banging on the car window, while new tears clouded her eyes and deep sobs heaved up from her throat.

"You can't leave me, Noah! I won't let you! I can't live without you! I can't!"

The car hurried away, leaving her behind as she went on crying out her anguished words.

Wild with fear and anger, she chased the car along the otherwise empty street.

"Do you hear me, Noah? I won't let you leave me!"

The car quickly disappeared from her view. Yet she went on chasing it as she frantically called out his name.

"Noah! Noah! Noah!"

Other cars began hurrying along the street. Five or six pedestrians, some of them her classmates or neighbors, were milling on the sidewalk now, alarmed by her wretched cries and her air of desperation. She was still crying out Noah's name when she became vaguely aware of them and of a tall, silver-haired man with cragged features who had suddenly approached her and had grabbed her by the arm. He had hurried into the street and was pulling her out of the path of the oncoming traffic.

She recognized him as one of her neighbors. He was Roger Kenyon, a retired university professor who had shared conversations with her about Shakespeare, Montaigne, and Dostoyevsky.

"Let's hurry onto the sidewalk, Charlotte," he said, in a voice that was both firm and calm. "Your friends are there, waiting for you."

Even as he guided her to the safety of the sidewalk, she kept her head turned toward the place where Noah's car had disappeared. She went on screaming.

"I won't let you leave me, Noah! You'll find out! I'll never let you go!"

Then she fell silent.

For a moment, the friends who had gathered on the sidewalk did not move toward her. Instead, they observed her carefully, as though they were awed by her and by her cries of desperation. Days afterward, she remembered their wary stillness and their complicated regard of her. She would not permit herself to imagine how she appeared to their inquiring eyes. But now, with the accuracy of self-awareness, she looked back to that afternoon and saw who she was. In that eerie scene, as she was screaming her grieving words to Noah, she was an angry woman who was calling out a dark prophecy to the lover who had spurned her.

PART ONE

CHAPTER TWO

Charlotte

Wednesday Afternoon, 4 October 1967

Looking Back to Saturday Morning, 7 October 1950

"I'll never give Noah up," Charlotte kept telling herself in the days that followed his leaving her, right after their graduation from Brown in 1952. "There will be no life for either of us without each other."

Over and over, she told those words to herself, as if she were weaving a spell that controlled Noah's destiny and her own. But it was not a spell that she wove. It was a plot to bind Noah to her forever. She had devised the plot two years earlier, at the beginning of her junior year at Pembroke College in Brown University. At that time, Noah was only a casual acquaintance. His steady girlfriend was Olivia Tanner. There was a rumor on campus that they were going to be married.

Already, her obsession with Noah had begun to overtake her. Whenever she was observing him from a distance or sitting near him at a party, her heart beat faster. His voice was deep and resonant, and his body moved with well-honed sensuality.

She was determined to steal him away from Olivia Tanner.

Seated here alone, forlorn and bitter in her home office seventeen years afterward, she remembered that morning as if it were even now unfolding before her apprehension for the first time. Her memory, with unforgiving exactitude, showed her once again the stratagem that she had devised on that Saturday, the seventh of October in 1950. She was certain of the date, because it was Noah's twentieth birthday. He was spending this autumn semester in England at The University of Cambridge. He had won a prestigious fellowship that enabled him to study international law there with notable professors and to serve as an administrative assistant at a law firm in London. His semester at Cambridge was a preface to the years of study after his Brown University program, when he would be working toward combined law degrees at Harvard and at Cambridge. By accepting the fellowship, he had abandoned his spot as a formidable goalie for the university hockey team. He had also abandoned Olivia Tanner.

Olivia had never before been abandoned. For the most part, she concealed her dismay behind the artificial decorum that her mother had taught her to invoke whenever she had to confront an untoward situation or a life-altering crisis. But there were days when her resentment at Noah's absence reached a fever pitch. It was then that she turned to *her*—Charlotte Scott, whom she called her closest friend. Complaining about Noah's absence became a petulant habit.

"It's selfish of Noah to leave me alone here for the entire semester while he is having a grand time in London."

To placate Olivia, she had chosen careful words that defended Noah without revealing her love for him.

"I do not imagine that Noah is having 'a grand time.' He probably spends all his time studying. Besides, he is doing this for both of you. He has left you and his friends so that he can build something special for his future with you. When you are married, you will be grateful that he made this sacrifice."

Hearing those words, Olivia would grow calm again.

"I suppose that you are right," she said. "But I do not enjoy attending campus parties and all the other social occasions without him. I do not like being the girl who has no escort."

That was the moment in which she initiated the plan that could push Olivia out of Noah's life. It was exactly at that moment that she activated the plot to make Noah her lover. It was a plot that she had been devising for many months. Steven Bennington, her casual boyfriend for this semester, would be involved in the plot without knowing it. His pairing with her was essential, because, together, they convinced Olivia that she had no special interest in Noah, even though she had often been in his company. Always, of course, one of her boyfriends was with her. And Olivia.

Any other woman would have chosen Steven over Noah. Steven remained untainted by the narcissism that marred the character of most of the men that she knew. Tall, brown-haired, and muscular, he knew how to bank his fires. Yet he was always direct, and he knew how to make her feel that she was the most important person in the room. On more than one occasion, she felt a tinge of regret that she could not love Steven with the urgency that fuses its powers with authentic collaboration and to long-lasting fidelity. She felt this way right after he had made passionate love to her during a New York weekend, perhaps, or while they were skiing with smooth precision in Vermont, or when he was conversing knowledgeably with a group of their friends about politics, sports, or jazz. But the feelings for Noah that she carried in the secret recesses of her heart would not allow her to love Steven.

During this particular semester, while Noah was in London, Olivia had sometimes joined Steven and her at a concert or a play on the university campus or at a nightclub in Boston. Surrounded by the many admiring friends who chatted with her at the concert's intermission or danced with her at the Boston nightspot, Olivia usually managed to enjoy herself. But Noah's absence cast a cloud upon her enjoyment. In the days that followed, she would complain once again about the unfairness of her situation and about Noah's indifference to her loneliness.

"You don't have to be alone," she told her on that October evening in 1950, all the while weaving the intricate fabric of her plot. "Steven's roommate isn't going steady with anyone. He has sometimes joined us to make a foursome when one of my girlfriends from Vassar or Radcliffe spends a weekend here. Now you can be the girl, and Steven's roommate can be your escort."

Olivia brightened when she heard her sisterly words.

"That would be wonderful," she said. "Of course, Steven's friend would have to understand that I am Noah's girl."

"That will not be a problem," she assured her. "Steven's friend is not looking for a steady partner. He plays the field without getting too involved."

"That suits me fine," she said. "He and I can have a good time without any romance or drama."

"You will not be with him alone. Steven and I will also be there. You will have your escort, and you'll be the belle of the ball."

She remembered how easy it was to win Olivia's trust. As her roommate, she had cultivated the role of an always-accommodating sister. She had not protested when Olivia had appropriated the southwest corner of their room in a Pembroke dormitory, even though that corner offered the bright light and comforting warmth of the sun as its rays streamed through the window. She accepted with equal composure Olivia's ignoring her own impressive wardrobe and "borrowing" her newest dresses, slacks, sweaters, and jackets. She also had a habit of borrowing the notes she had taken at important lectures that Olivia had chosen to miss because she was meeting a friend from Bryn Mawr in Philadelphia or spending an extra day in New York at her parents' home on Sutton Place.

"You are a true sister," Olivia would tell her in a too-lighthearted voice that made her show of gratitude sound shallow. "You always come to my rescue."

"I am happy to be your rescuer," she invariably answered her. "You would help me if I were in trouble."

"You will never be in trouble. You are very competent in everything you do. And you are so patient with me. I might live for a hundred years and never be half as patient as you are."

"I wouldn't have you any other way. You are fine just as you are."

Upon hearing these words, Olivia always smiled. With easy alacrity, she consented to these words. They were her due. She was, after all, Olivia Tanner.

Now, looking back during this October afternoon in 1967, she perceived once again the young woman who Olivia Tanner really was. She was pampered, selfish, and vain. She was also a great beauty who had won the admiration, if not the heart, of Noah.

Olivia had been right to commend her for her patience. She had, indeed, been very patient. She had made Time and Chance her friends. She had been waiting for the day when she could unravel the plot that would push Olivia out of Noah's life. When Noah returned from London, she would make certain that he turned to her, not to Olivia, for comfort.

For six weeks, she had waited to initiate her plot. Now she was ready to make her move.

Steven Bennington was going to help her advance her plot, without realizing that he was doing so. He was no fool. In fact, he was far more street-wise than many of the men on campus. During his childhood, he had known poverty. He had lived through the financial struggles of his hardworking parents. But he had also observed his father's ruthless determination to turn his hamburger and hotdog business into a global restaurant chain that served fifty million customers daily in one hundred countries across thirty thousand outlets. Now the Bennington family was very rich. Steven, their first-born son, was enjoying all the privileges that his family's wealth brought him. But he was no weak-willed heir who had allowed his easy life to soften him. As if he did not trust the good luck and savvy deals that had brought his father a fortune, Steven carried with him a tough guy persona. Nobody could push him around or take him for granted. His hockey and swimming mates respected his toughness. They saw in his steely willfulness a man like themselves.

When she began her relationship with him, Steven made clear what he expected of her.

"You and I will have a good time if you don't cross me. Don't let me catch you with any other man. If I do, I won't go easy on either of you. When I grow tired of you, you will be the first to know. There will be no tricks or lies. Maybe, we will grow used to one another and stay together for the entire school year. If you ever want to pull out of our arrangement, just lay it on the line. I'll understand. I'll respect you for your honesty. I'll know that you are not trying to put something over on me. Nothing lasts forever— not when you are as young as we are and have a whole life waiting to be lived around the globe."

"I'll play fair with you." she said. "I like knowing where we stand with each other. I like your directness. I like your realistic sense of the world. You and I want the same things. We crave new experiences and new people. We search for adventure, and we won't let adversaries get in our way."

She enjoyed being with Steven. She felt easier knowing that she did not love him and that he did not love her. She regarded her temporary bond with him as a freewheeling experiment. Nobody was going to get hurt. They would have a good time and then go their separate ways.

Nevertheless, in this matter of negotiating her plan to win Noah Blake, she had to tread cautiously. She must not rouse Steven's suspicions or inadvertently reveal her interest in Noah. Thus far, all had gone well. Steven believed her when she mentioned that she wanted to dispel Olivia's melancholy by pairing her with an eligible man from their university. For a brief hour or so, there flashed across her mind the thought that she might place Steven on Olivia's path. Amoral and devious, Olivia would have no scruples about stealing Steven away from her. But Steven might become aware that she wanted to break apart Olivia's romance with Noah. He would not allow her to use him so that she could begin an affair with Noah.

Still, she was using Steven, though he did not know it. In Olivia's eyes, Steven was her ardent suitor. Never had Olivia suspected that she was planning to steal Noah from her.

But she alone could not accelerate her plan. She needed to choose a man other than Steven to lure Olivia away from Noah. The man needed to be wily and manipulative. To win Olivia's favor, he had to be both popular and sensual.

Here, at Brown University, she knew many men who were sensual and popular. She also knew as many men who were wily and manipulative. This more cynical group of men could easily propel the success of her plot. But she had forged a lasting bond with only one of them. His name was Rick Blanchard, and he was willing to be her accomplice.

The name of Rick Blanchard stirred her memory. The essential morning that she shared with him in Newport came swiftly back to her, while she sat pensive and stoic in her home office seventeen years later. Noah Blake's letter still lay unopened on the Chippendale desk before her. But it was not Noah's matter-of-fact voice that she heard in her retrospective musing. Nor did her memory show her his athletic physique. She could hear Rick's husky voice, though, and she saw his naked body once again, as if it were the seventh of October in 1950.

"You are one smart hustler," he was telling her as he reached for a cigarette from her gold case on the table near the bed they had shared during the night. "You know how to spot vulnerable people, and you know how to use them to your advantage."

He reached out again to take hold of the gold lighter and bring its flame to his cigarette. Only then did he speak more of the words that told her what he thought of her plan.

"From the way that you have described her, Olivia Tanner is very vulnerable. Her boyfriend has gone off to his studies in Europe and left her alone."

He leaned into the array of pillows behind him and watched the smoke wafting in ringlets from his cigarette. She lay next to him, carefully studying his enigmatic face that concealed more than it revealed. She wanted to be certain of him. She wanted him to tell her that he would make her plan work. During a free weekend from their university obligations, she had drawn him to her family's waterfront property in Newport, Rhode Island. They were alone. All the summer people had left the area. There was no one around to witness their intimacy or to overhear the callous words of her scheme.

Her instinct told her that Rick was the right man to carry her scheme forward. Her hunting instinct told her. That instinct had served her well. It was a power within herself that she kept hidden. It cautioned her to be wary and influenced her to be cruel. By means of it, she knew when to subdue her predatory impulses and when to activate a risk-taking plan. With Rick as her wingman, she could steal Noah from Olivia. The plan would also serve Rick well. He would win Olivia and become part of an immensely rich family.

Keen-minded and affable, Rick had paved a smooth path into Ivy League circles. Now he hobnobbed with the wealthy boys who might become power links that accommodated his desire to be as rich as their fathers and just as influential. His expertise as a defenseman on the university ice hockey team and his strength as a middle rower on the crew team solidified his popularity with other men. His dark-haired good looks and his brawny torso made him a favorite escort of East Coast debutantes. Though many of these girls enjoyed sleeping with him, none of them wanted to marry him. Rick came from a conventional middle class background. His father was a police chief in a small New Hampshire town, and his mother was an elementary school teacher. He was the first-born of their four sons. Guided by his parents' strict rules and by his own ambition, he had worked diligently to maintain his status as an honor student in a public school and as a formidable athlete. Several scholarships had made Brown University possible for him. Good grades and an equally impressive performance as an athlete were the harbingers of a successful future on Wall Street.

Marrying into a wealthy family would make his way easier.

Rick was a cool huckster. He had learned most of the subtle tricks for promoting himself. He had a savvy awareness of the ways that he could exploit his friends' good will. He was adept at making these friends believe that they owed him something. More than a few times, he provided alibis for wealthy hockey teammates who were cheating on their girlfriends. Patient and guileful, he showed a fine arts sophomore whose father was a Hollywood film executive how to navigate his way through the intricacies of calculus. He had cultivated a knack for making his friends look good at a campus party or on an ice rink or in an academic setting. The friends whom the world had not yet made cynical admired him for his selflessness. Even the friends who suspected that his conduct was motivated by self-interest admired him. They saw him as a blood brother. Like them, he was willing to sell himself to the world for a high price.

"We are all hucksters," he told her shortly after they had begun their secret affair.

They may have been spending their winter recess from school at a ski resort in Switzerland. Possibly, they were enjoying an autumn weekend in New York. More probably, he had made that remark there, in that bedroom within the secluded summer home in Newport that her parents had left in her keeping while they were traveling on the West Coast. Wherever she and Rick were, they were there in secret. That was part of the arrangement they had made with each other. They would not allow their sexual need of one another to subvert their plans to marry wealthy partners. She might have chosen Rick as her husband. She respected his razor-sharp perception and his refusal to be sentimental about anyone or anything. In so many ways, they were compatible. But her father would have disinherited her if she married Rick. He wanted her to marry into a family as wealthy as his own.

Though it was not a part of their arrangement, she had given Rick thousands of dollars. He had never asked for the money, but he was willing to accept it.

"I know my value," he told her. "I come with a high price-tag."

Of all her lovers, Rick was the most satisfying. Not even Noah would always give her the pleasures that Rick offered her. It was no fault of Noah's. Her obsession for him sometimes made her a tense partner in bed. She felt that she was not good enough for him. She worried about whether she would please him. But lovemaking with Rick was sheer ecstasy. Their mutual passion became a raw and thrilling experience. Always in secret, they continued to sleep with one another for many years after Noah and Olivia came into their lives.

"The important thing is that *I* know your value," she told Rick on that morning in Newport during the autumn of 1950 that sealed their complicity. "Right now, you are priceless. There isn't a price high enough to pay you adequately for what you are doing for me. But the reward for your service works both ways. Each of us can win the prize that we want. You will have Olivia and her money. I will have Noah Blake."

Sated and relaxed after a night of making love with her, Rick asked her to tell him once again the details of her plan. They were leaning side by side against the pillows. The silken sheets only partially covered their young bodies. His bare chest accentuated his ruggedness. She remembered, too, as though she were watching a vaguely familiar apparition of the young woman she used to be, that her firm breasts enhanced her sensuality. Taking a drag on his cigarette, Rick kept peering at the circles of smoke wafting away from them. But he was listening attentively. The words that she spoke and his tough-minded consent to them sealed their complicity.

"Noah will be in London for three more months," she explained. "That will give you plenty of time to persuade Olivia Tanner that you are the exciting man that she needs. Right now, she is angry because Noah has accepted the fellowship that keeps him away from her. She wants to avenge herself against his carelessness. She wants to show him and all their friends that she can be as freewheeling and as hardhearted as he is. She is looking for a man like you. Your timing couldn't be better."

"I've met her kind before," Rick said after he took a drag on his cigarette. "I know how to handle her."

"You will have to be careful. Olivia Tanner has been around. She is nobody's fool."

"I'll be careful," he answered her. "I'll be clever, too. I'll make her forget Noah Blake."

"I'm counting on that. "

"I'm counting on getting me a rich girl who thinks that she is clever. I'll make her world spin faster. She will know that she is getting her money's worth."

He kissed her lightly and hurried out of the bed. With swaggering nakedness, he made his way to the cobalt blue robe that he had left on the arm of a wing chair the night before. After he wrapped it around his athletic torso, he turned to glance at her once more. It was an ambiguous glance. Yet the glance told her that he accepted her for the devious woman that she was. With the cigarette dangling from the left corner of his lips, he looked like a hard-bitten guy who had fought a few battles on meaner streets. She was pleased that he was on her side. She watched him even after he turned away from her. Barefooted and loose-limbed, he opened the French doors and moved on to the terrace. For a few minutes he stood there, self-assured and proprietary. With studious regard, he was surveying the sun-hazy beach and the blue-green waves of the ocean. The autumn breeze that floated across the room to play upon her senses was warm and inviting. She wondered what Rick was thinking at that very moment. She imagined that, as he observed the azure expanse of the sky and the white, jagged cliffs in the far distance that towered over the spume-fed waves of ocean water, he was anticipating the ways that he could seize the day for his own purposes and all the other days that were to follow.

PART ONE

CHAPTER THREE

Charlotte

Wednesday Afternoon, 4 October 1967

Looking Back to October & November 1950

All of those months came swiftly back to her, as she sat before the Chippendale desk in her home office seventeen years later. The letter from Noah that she had received only a few hours earlier remained unopened. She might, reluctantly, allow her memory to impose the ghosts of the past upon the strict order of her present life. But she was not yet ready to permit Noah to reenter her life through his letter. For a few more minutes, at least, she wanted him to remain a ghost. Lovers die in different ways. They might be victims of a killer or an accident or terminal illness. Or they may be closed out of one's memory. They may die in that way. She had willed herself to forget Noah. It was in that way that he had died to her.

She had not called Noah back through her own volition. His letter was bringing him back to her. It was stirring her memory of the young man he used to be during the long-ago time of their university days. Without really knowing who he was at the start of their relationship, she had fallen in love with him. She had devised a plot to win him away from Olivia Tanner, a girl as selfish as he was and as willful. Yet Noah and Olivia were meant for each other. She could admit that now, so many years after they had gone out of her life. In the autumn of 1950, though, she had initiated a plan that would break their romance apart.

Rick, her sometime lover, drove the plan forward.

At first, he responded to Olivia in an understated and platonic manner.

"I am here to help you enjoy yourself," he told her on more than one occasion. "I am helping Noah, too. He's a hockey mate and my good friend. I know that he would want you to have a good time while he's away in London."

"Let's see what happens," Olivia said, uncertain of just where these friendly dates with Rick might lead her. "Let's find out whether we can have a bit of fun together."

In the beginning, she and Steven stayed in their company. They acted as chaperones. Steven was not happy about the role he was playing in order to protect Olivia from the gossip of friends and acquaintances who had heard that Noah might marry her if she remained faithful to him while he was away.

"Charlotte, I don't like the setup," Steven told her on one of the evenings that they would be dining with Olivia and Rick. "I don't like being used as a decoy."

He had noticed Olivia's increasing warmth toward Rick.

"Olivia's no innocent," he said. "She's been around. She knows the score. She doesn't need us to protect her. She is smart enough to stay out of trouble. If she decides to cheat on Noah, she will know how to cover her tracks."

She chose her next words carefully. She wanted Steven to believe that she was Olivia's loyal friend.

"You are judging her too harshly," she said. "She misses Noah. She is lonely. You and Rick and I can help her to get through this period without Noah."

"When did you decide to play Goody Two-shoes? I like the authentic you. I prefer your hard-edged realism."

"You are making too much of this situation," she said. "I simply want to help a friend."

"I have a feeling that there isn't anything simple about this charade."

"You may be right," she answered him. "It all depends on Olivia."

Olivia was instantly drawn to Rick. She liked his manly assurance. She admired his playful flirting and the suggestion of muted passion beneath that playfulness. She appreciated his calculated irony, and she was vaguely touched by his willingness to remain celibate while he made himself an object of her desire. She did not hold his lower middle class background against him. Nor did she begrudge him his inordinate interest in material things or the interest he took in her father's business success.

"Some day I am going to be as rich and as powerful as your father," he said. "That's a promise."

On more than one occasion, Rick suggested that she invite him to her parents' penthouse on Sutton Place. He wanted to meet her father. He wanted to find out what he had to do in order to become a part of The Tanner Steel and Aluminum Corporation.

"Is that why you are being so kind to me, so that you can meet my father?"

"I do want to meet him. He can give me a few tips about making my future work for me. Besides, I'm supposed to be your pal, not your boyfriend."

"You are using me."

"That is what people do," he said. "They use one another. They play games."

"Is that what we are doing?"

"Of course. All the best people play games."

"Does anyone ever get hurt?"

"Not if they are smart. Not if they know how to play the game."

The four of them, on recess from university obligations, were spending a few days in New York. They had visited art galleries and had seen a few plays on Broadway and a musical. They had heard a terrific jazz combo at a nightclub in Greenwich Village. They had enjoyed a ride through Central Park in a horse-drawn carriage. Through the influence of Olivia's father, they found themselves being photographed for the cover of *Time Magazine.* A leading journalist for that magazine made them the subject of her article about the social activities and career aspirations of Ivy League students. Many photographs accompanied the article. One photograph showed the four of them looking charismatic and lighthearted in tuxedos and gowns at an evening gala held at Carnegie Hall. The caption referred to them as "two romantic couples." Another photo showed Rick and Steven lifting weights at a private men's club. A third photograph centered on the four of them riding Arab bays on a horse farm in Rochester, New York. A fourth and more revealing photograph showed Rick planting a kiss upon Olivia's right cheek after they won a kayaking race on Lake Placid during a very warm October afternoon. The *Time Magazine* photographer who had accompanied the four of them on their trip to Lake Placid had asked Rick to bring a romantic subtext to the photograph. Calculating and ambitious, Rick refrained from making the kiss sensual and suggestive. True to the subdued role that he was playing with her, Rick made the kiss polite and understated.

It wasn't long before Olivia changed the rules of their relationship.

"I will have a good time if you stop pretending that you are my brother," she told Rick.

"I'll be happy to stop acting like your brother," Rick said. "Ever since I met you, I have wanted to be your lover."

It was the last evening of their week in New York. They were staying at The Waldorf Astoria. They had been dancing in a glamorous ballroom to the intimate melodies of Cole Porter, Jerome Kern, and George Gershwin, while a demure blonde and a dark-haired Latino sang of the kind of love that comes once in a lifetime.

Olivia and Rick had exchanged their remarks right after the music had stopped. She and Steven, who had been dancing near them, overheard the remarks. She remembered that in that moment Steven had made eye contact with her. He did not need to speak. His eyes told her what he was thinking. Olivia had forgotten about Noah. She had fallen in love with Rick Blanchard.

When the four of them returned to their table, Olivia looked radiant. She was brimming with new happiness that exhilarated her beyond measure.

"I have never felt this way before," she said. "Tonight has been perfect."

She glanced at Steven and her with genuine appreciation.

"You are my special friends," she said. "I'll always be grateful for what you have done for me. You have brought into my life the only man that I was meant to love."

Rick was beaming, drawing himself to her exhilaration with the nearly imperceptible slyness that eluded Olivia's gaze and that her own eyes detected. Rick was no fool. He had won the prize that he wanted. Olivia was his link to the big time. There was a special kick to the words that he now offered her. She, Charlotte Scott, his occasional bed companion and scheming partner, knew Rick well. The words that he spoke were a casual affirmation of the bond Olivia had made with him. She, not self-absorbed Olivia, noticed the menacing intimation beneath the levity.

"Now you are stuck with me, baby," he said. "I'll never let you go."

Steven also caught the ring of menace in those words. When they were alone together in their hotel rooms later that evening, he disclosed his misgivings about Olivia's relationship with Rick.

"They are using each other," he said. "Rick wants to use Olivia and her father so that he can team up with the power brokers. She wants to use Rick to avenge herself against Noah. She is trying to convince herself that she has really fallen in love with Rick. But there is a dangerous edge to Rick. If she finds out that she doesn't love him and tries to leave him, Rick will give her plenty of trouble."

Steven's words did not displease her. It was about time that somebody treated Olivia roughly.

As though Steven's words were a prophecy, the next weeks unfurled bitter and angry scenes. She had been present when Olivia brought Rick to meet her parents in their New York penthouse. Olivia had invited her there as a way of maintaining the propriety that her parents demanded. Olivia's traveling with a young woman from her own social class was acceptable and even reassuring. Her bringing a young man who was not of their class was an altogether different matter. Mrs. Tanner made certain to place "young Mister Blanchard" in the east wing of the penthouse, far away from the southwest wing where her "willful daughter Olivia" and "the very likable Charlotte Scott" shared adjoining bedrooms.

The very likable Charlotte Scott, indeed. She had fooled Mrs. Tanner, as well as her husband. She had fooled Olivia and, for a time, she would fool Noah. Her deviousness broke all the moral rules and eluded hesitation and remorse. In that long-ago year, she took secret pleasure from subverting the plans that the Tanners had been making to marry their daughter to an impressive young man from their own class. Belonging to the same class did not curb her desire to overturn Mrs. Tanner's inbred snobberies and to steal away the only man that Olivia would ever love.

How swiftly that November morning in 1950 was coming back to her, here in her home office so many years later. She could hear Mrs. Tanner speaking in that cultured voice of hers that tempered its displeasure with precise diction and reasonable assertions. The clipped speech was a genuine expression of the person that Mrs. Tanner's privileged background had taught her to be. Yet, the genuineness notwithstanding, the voice had made artifice and snobbery companions of long acquaintance.

"You have disappointed your father and me," she told her daughter earlier that morning, when Olivia, as excited as she was impulsive, declared that she was going to announce her engagement to Rick Blanchard.

Rick had just left the apartment, on his way to a game of squash at an exclusive men's club with Chad, the youngest of the three Tanner sons. Easy-going and unpretentious, Chad had found in Rick a soul brother. Beneath their gentleman's demeanor, they were street-wise and adventurous. They knew how to manipulate all the rules that might thwart their rebellious natures or inhibit their autonomy.

With Rick away from the apartment, Mr. and Mrs. Tanner protested with strong-willed emphases Olivia's talk of her engagement to Rick and their plans to marry soon afterward. The news had surprised and dismayed her parents. If they did not stop her, she would surprise and dismay the thirty-two guests whom they were hosting that evening at one of the glamorous dinner parties that the Tanners sometimes held in their penthouse on Sutton Place. Every one of those guests had imagined that Olivia would eventually become engaged to Noah. The union of a Blake and a Tanner maintained and enhanced the social order that Olivia's parents and their kind represented with exclusionary rigor. The Blanchards were not part of that order. The old guard families perceived them as working class. In spite of their upright behavior and their commendable vocations, the Blanchards were mavericks. They were interlopers, no matter how many civic virtues they had acquired and how many doors of opportunity were opening to them.

"You are not giving yourself time to really know this young man," Mrs. Tanner said. "And you know even less about his parents."

"I know all that I need to know," Olivia answered her. "I know that I love him very much."

They were enclosed within the privacy of the music room, where canvases by Pierre Bonnard, Edouard Manet, and Berthe Morisot adorned the walls and where an array of red, yellow, and white roses in an Art Nouveau vase by Emile Gallé collaborated with the splendor of the Steinway French Provincial console piano. A twenty-foot cloud ceiling, parquet flooring, and gilded antique *boisserie* paneling and columns were other French Classic emblems that suggested a refined luxury as well as the prestige of the persons who lived here. From her seat at the piano, she could see past the columns into the exquisite ballroom. She also saw the second-floor mezzanine that overlooked the music room and the ballroom. That mezzanine led, beyond her here-and-now seeing, to the master suite that had French doors opening to picturesque views of Central Park.

She was no stranger to luxury. Her father's inheritance of South African diamond mines and Texas oil refineries brought him immense wealth. She had enjoyed all the privileges that came with that wealth. In fact, she could not imagine a life without wealth. The spirit-driven idealists might disdain wealth, and the shop-worn have-nots with their borrowed moral platitudes might preach against it. But she had experienced the powers of wealth. She respected those powers. Yet, unlike Mrs. Tanner, she refused to become a prisoner of the rigid social codes and the entrenched prejudices that would keep her from experiencing life as a freewheeling experiment.

Already, as a sophisticated twenty-year-old woman, she was learning to play with the world. She kept testing herself. She kept testing others and finding out how far she could go with them in the sometimes risk-laden games that she played with them. She was discovering who she was. Early on, she had made a promise that she would never lie to herself. She would make no excuses for her coldhearted betrayals of lovers and friends, her cynical plots against adversaries, and her unsentimental regard of the rules that would appropriate her freedom. With well-honed wiliness, she was fashioning a persona to her liking. She was *that* Charlotte Scott and not any of the other Charlotte Scotts that her parents or her teachers kept persuading her to be. Disguise and deception were her stocks in trade.

The game was on, even more thrillingly. Here, at the Tanners' New York penthouse in that conflicted autumn of 1950, she kept weaving the plot that would win her the love of Noah, even as it left Olivia Tanner abandoned by the man that she really loved and in the thrall of a man that might do her harm if she crossed him.

On this specific morning, Olivia was upstairs, enclosed in the privacy of her father's study while her parents questioned her about her surprise engagement to Rick Blanchard.

"I can't understand why they are making such a fuss," Olivia had remarked just before she rose from her chair in the music room to confer with her parents. "Couples become engaged every day."

She made no reply to Olivia's words. Instead, she continued to play a Chopin nocturne and waited for Olivia to say more, with her spoiled-daughter petulance.

"I will not change my mind, no matter what they say. I'm going to marry Rick."

Having said so, she hurried away to the meeting with her parents.

Demure and reflective, or seeming so, she had been playing another Chopin nocturne when Olivia hurried into the room a half hour later, still complaining against her parents.

"They are treating me as if I were a child. They won't allow me to live my own life."

At that moment, while she was seated at the piano, still playing the nocturne as Olivia lamented her fate, she saw Mr. and Mrs. Tanner making their way into the room. So, she quickly left Chopin. With temperate words and gentle voice and with the certainty that the Tanners would hear her, she counseled Olivia as though she were a loyal and prudent friend.

"Your parents want what is best for you. They don't want you to make a mistake. They'd prefer you to wait a while before you think about marriage."

"You are so right, Charlotte," Mrs. Tanner said, as she and her husband took their places at the curved window seating area. "You think the way we do—not only the way Robert and I think, but the way everyone who belongs to our circle thinks."

Mrs. Tanner had breeding. She had beauty, too. Even at forty-four, with the assistance of cosmeticians, couturiers, and hair stylists, she personified a carefully crafted youthfulness and an inherent elegance. Her brown eyes and auburn hair, her slim figure and flawless skin, and her genteel manner allowed her in her middle years to keep at bay even the subtle traceries of time. Her bond with the artificial kept at bay, as well, any relationship that sought to be profound and that acknowledged the harsher realities that lay, inveterate and threatening, outside her class. She had been in Mrs. Tanner's company on only a few occasions. But she knew her well. She recognized her type. She imagined that, eventually, despite her temporary show of rebellion, Olivia would become just like her.

No, she—Charlotte Scott—had never shared Mrs. Tanner's prejudices or her husband's disdain of so-called ordinary people. But, with calculated mischief and deep-seated contempt, she had persuaded Olivia's parents that she viewed the world as they did.

Because she meant to rouse her daughter's remorse and apprehension and because she chose not to resist the spark of malice that flared against that daughter because of her disobedience, Mrs. Tanner echoed her praise of "the very likable Charlotte Scott."

"You have impressed Robert and me most favorably. You know the importance of following the rules. Olivia is very fortunate to have a friend like you."

As if, by the mention of his name, his wife was urging him to speak, Mr. Tanner brought to this moment the no-nonsense pragmatism that was anchored to his self-assurance and his immense affluence.

"We don't want you to fall into any traps, Olivia. We don't want you to make a mess of your life before you've really begun living it."

Mr. Tanner was tall, brawny, and loose-limbed, even at forty-five. It was not difficult to imagine that his early morning workouts at the gym primed him for his Wall Street exploits. In subtle ways that he had mastered years earlier, he bonded his physicality with arrogance and intimidation. Decades ago, his father had parlayed a lumber and coal company into The Tanner Bank and, eventually, into ownership of aluminum, steel, and shipbuilding corporations. This Mr. Tanner, Olivia's father, had turned those holdings into global enterprises. Behind his back, his competitors called him a ruthless behemoth. But they envied and respected his power.

Being an unsentimental man and chary of compromising even a pennyworth of that power, he was finding his patience tested, here in this opulent music room that had been created to solace every person who entered it. On this Saturday morning, he found no solace here. Instead, he had to deal with a foolish daughter whose infatuation with a blue-collar upstart might embarrass and even cast a shadow upon the merger of the Tanner and Blake Steel Corporations. The rumored marriage of his daughter Olivia to Kendall Blake's son Noah had enhanced the news that Robert Tanner and Kendall Blake were merging their formidable corporations. Wall Street considered the merger very important. On the day that he and Kendall announced the merger of their companies, investor enthusiasm across the globe surged by ten percent.

She was not a Tanner or a Blake. She was a Scott, and her family was their equal. She was well aware of her own father's greed and treachery as he pushed his way into one business success after the other.

"Being rich isn't enough," her father had told her, because he wanted her eventually to take her place beside her two brothers as the leaders of his business empire. "You have to be richer each day than you were the day before."

Robert Tanner did not share her father's liberal views about women as power brokers. He preferred women to be submissive and to defer always to the will of successful men. From her place at the piano, she saw how stern he had made his otherwise attractive features. She saw, as well, that he was not going to permit Olivia to cast a shadow upon his corporate merger.

"Think, girl! Think!" he cautioned his daughter with blunt words and no-nonsense authority. "You are making a big mistake. Rick Blanchard isn't the right man for you. He's a poor boy from nowhere, in spite of his university credentials. He's using you. You're his ticket to the big time."

With a tremulous voice that meant to disarm her father and with her hands clasped into a beseeching gesture that might recall for him the childlike innocence he sometimes associated with her even now, Olivia defended her choice. She knew enough about her father not to appear defiant. She was disguising her defiance. She was the loyal daughter petitioning his understanding. She was feminine and powerless. Her blue eyes were misty with tears. The gentle touch of her hand upon her father's arm was another disguise of her rebellion.

"Rick is not like that, daddy. He's going to be a success on his own terms. He *is* right for me,"

Mr. Tanner, adamant and self-controlled, answered her with matter-of-fact certainty.

"Not when I say he isn't."

"Please don't say so, daddy," Olivia sobbed. "Please."

She drew closer to him so that he could fold his arms around her and comfort her, as he had often done when she was a little girl.

Mr. Tanner did not resist this outward show of the bond he shared with her. But, for him, it was merely a careful display of that bond which, after all, was revocable if Olivia behaved in a willful and imprudent manner.

"Pull yourself together," he said. "We have a problem here, and you must do your part to resolve it."

Olivia offered her father no new conciliatory words or the promise that she would accede to his demands. Instead, she went on sobbing.

As calculating as he was perceptive, Mr. Tanner interpreted his daughter's tear-blemished performance as a stratagem for dissuading him from the only sensible resolution of this problem involving Rick Blanchard.

"Postpone the engagement to this Blanchard fellow. Don't make any announcement at the party tonight."

"I can't do that, daddy," Olivia said, still a tearful supplicant, yet more apprehensive now because of her father's blunt directive. "I promised Rick that, tonight, I would tell everyone we are going to be married."

"Postpone it," Mr. Tanner said, "if you want to go on being my daughter."

Olivia grew very quiet. Whatever words she might use to coax her father to change his mind failed her.

How clearly she heard her own words now, while that meeting in the music room kept unfolding its complications as though they were newly wrought and had not yet imposed their penalties upon the Tanners as well as upon herself.

"I'd better leave," she had said, gentle and solicitous while addressing her words to Mr. and Mrs. Tanner. "You'll want to talk things out among yourselves."

Mrs. Tanner, who—with cool-headed judgment and muted approval—had been observing her husband's unsentimental handling of a wayward daughter, responded as she had anticipated.

"On the contrary, Charlotte," she said, understated yet concerned, "Robert and I want you to stay here. We'd like you to talk some sense into our daughter."

"I'd like to help, of course. But I wouldn't know where to begin. I've never become involved in my friends' romantic problems."

"A very wise policy, my dear," said Mrs. Tanner. "But for Olivia's sake, make an exception this time. You are her best friend. You can help her to see things more clearly."

Politic and sensitive or seeming so, she did not resist Mrs. Tanner's petition. But she was careful not to violate her contrived friendship with Olivia. Mrs. Tanner would respect what appeared to be her loyalty to her daughter, and Olivia would continue to trust her. Believing so, she cast a worried glance at her troubled friend and spoke heartfelt words that would satisfy both mother and daughter.

"I want for Olivia what she wants. I want her to be happy."

From her place near her father and for only a moment, Olivia beamed with gratitude.

"Thank you," she said, her sobbing words struggling through a low whisper.

Calculating friend that she was, she now initiated the plan that would gradually make even more trouble for Olivia and her parents. Rick, spurred on by his renegade hostility, would become more deeply implicated, and eventually Noah, motivated by self-protection and ambition, would become involved as well.

Now she made hesitation her ally.

"I do think, though, that…well, I probably don't have the right to say it."

She quickened Mrs. Tanner's interest.

"You must say it, Charlotte. You owe it to Olivia and to us."

Confronted by Mrs. Tanner's appeal, she nodded her assent. At the same time, by glancing at Olivia, she showed that she was willing to defer to that weeping daughter's judgment.

"Do you want me to say what I think?"

"Yes."

"Be fair to Noah. He's coming home for the holidays. Wait until then to talk over things with him. Find out how you feel once you see him again."

Her words gave Olivia pause. This spoiled heiress, whose only authentic feelings were directed to her own interests, was wondering whether it would be more advantageous, after all, to be married to Noah. The problem stymied her.

"I don't know," she said, pensive and confused.

Mrs. Tanner nudged her a little.

"You will make your father and me very happy."

Mr. Tanner, still blunt and proprietary, pushed her forward.

"Do it, girl. Do it. You have it in you to do the right thing."

Frightened of the consequences if she disobeyed her parents, Olivia wavered.

"Maybe."

It was at this precise moment, when Olivia stood uncertain and fearful before her parents and before her, that she—the demure-seeming Charlotte Scott—wove another intricate design to her plot to destroy forever Olivia's relationship with Noah. She was collaborating with The Fates or with Blind Chance, perhaps, or with her own capacity for wrongdoing. She was counting on drawing one or all of those powers to the intrigue that she was devising.

Olivia was the unsuspecting linchpin of the intrigue. Her telling Noah about her romance with Rick would effectively end the possibility that Noah was going to marry her. Men such as Noah were never interested in being runners-up in any competition or in being the dubious objects of a girl's second-guessing.

With these thoughts in mind, she hurried to say the words that were going to weave this new, intricate design to her plot.

"Rick will understand if you postpone the announcement of your engagement. I think that he really loves you. He wants you, but only if you are certain that you don't love Noah."

"I am certain."

"How will you feel when you see Noah again? Give yourself a chance to pass that test. Wait until he comes home in December. Tell him about Rick."

"What will I tell Rick? I promised him that we'd announce our engagement at the party tonight."

Mr. Tanner came into it again. His words were still matter-of-fact, but less brusque.

"I'll talk to Rick. There won't be any problem."

"Thank you, daddy," Olivia said. Her voice was tremulous, and her manner infantile and acquiescent. Her parents recognized her little-girl apprehension and were pleased. Her demure response was, in their eyes, a sign of daughterly obedience.

But she, Charlotte Scott, who pretended to be her loyal friend, felt contempt for her. In spite of her ingrained selfishness and her occasional flares of willfulness, Olivia lacked the courage to be an authentic rebel. Her happiness required safe perimeters. She dared not violate the inbred codes of her class or alienate herself from her formidable parents.

Yes, in that long-ago hour, she viewed Olivia with disdain. She also pitied her. She would not be able to push Rick out of her life, even as a conciliatory gesture toward her parents. Rick would not let go of her. Nor did she want to give him up. Though she had at first regarded him as her plaything—an interim lover whom she could easily abandon once Noah returned—her feelings for Rick had grown intense and even obsessive. They were also intertwined with her fear of him and with the riffs of pleasure anchored to that fear.

Here, while confronting her parents, she was being torn apart. She wanted their acceptance and the comfort of her promised inheritance. But, without forfeiting those rewards, she needed to break free of her parents. Even more so, she needed the unbridled sensuality and the spark of danger that Rick had brought into her life. She wanted a man who, even more than Noah, was willing to break the rules and get away with it. She wanted to break the rules with him.

The game was still on. Rick was going to move faster now.

Believing so, she—Olivia's disingenuous friend—offered her new, congenial words.

"You see," she said, "doing the right thing isn't so difficult. You are very wise to listen to your parents."

Mr. and Mrs. Tanner looked very pleased. But it was Mrs. Tanner who had more to say to her daughter.

"In the meantime," she counseled her, "you can go on treating Rick as a pal—a platonic friend. You can enjoy each other's company at the party tonight, and tomorrow, after you return to your university, you can begin to break away from him. When Noah returns next month, you will see things more clearly. "

To her mother's words, Olivia listened with docile attention.

"Yes," she answered her. "I'm sure that I will."

Even now, as she was looking back at that November morning so many years later, she saw in Olivia's face what Mrs. Tanner did not see. There was uncertainty. There was deviousness. There was fear of the anger that she would ignite within Rick if she crossed him.

PART ONE

CHAPTER FOUR

Charlotte

Wednesday Afternoon, 4 October 1967

Looking Back to November & December 1950

But only a threat of violence disturbed that weekend. There were no melodramatic scenes at the dinner party. In that glamorous setting, within the ballroom of the Tanners' sixteen-room penthouse on Sutton Place, corporate moguls from London, Berlin, Melbourne, South Africa, and New York danced with their wives while a discreet blonde and a tall, dark-haired crooner sang ballads by George Gershwin, Jerome Kern, and Cole Porter. To placate her father, Olivia danced with several young men who were the scions of great wealth and prestigious families. On this evening, she looked especially beautiful in a wine-red velvet evening dress, made even more elegant because of its crew neckline, its long sleeves and silver belt, and her graceful carriage. Her bright smile and her poise concealed the tension that only she—Charlotte Scott, her duplicitous friend—had noticed.

Here, at her desk within her home office in Greenwich, Connecticut, she saw herself as she was seventeen years ago, moving with casual ease away from the dance floor toward the terrace that looked out upon the sleek panorama of Manhattan. Minutes earlier, she had noticed Rick, with a glass of scotch in hand and a cigarette dangling from the corner of his mouth, walking onto the terrace. On that long-ago evening, she felt glad to be alive. She was young, vivacious, and radiant. She sensed that she looked especially pretty. She was wearing a royal blue floral, sleeveless evening dress with a demure V-neck. Mrs. Tanner had complimented her upon its being "exquisitely right" for her. The gown *was* right for her. It enhanced her raven-haired poise and her self-possession. The pleasure of wearing it dispelled her plot-weaving calculations. She was thoroughly enjoying the evening, dancing with several handsome men and exchanging lighthearted words with all of them.

Then she caught sight of Rick making his way to the terrace, and she remembered the plot that they were devising.

As soon as the musicians finished their set, she took leave of her dance partner and made her way to the terrace. Waiters were moving with deft subtleties as they attended the needs of those guests who had kept their places at the four banquet tables. A younger group of waiters began greeting the couples that were leaving the dance floor and returning to their seats at the tables. She caught sight of a dashing banker from London accompanying Olivia to the places reserved for them near her father, who was seated at the head of the first table. Mr. Tanner beamed his approval when he saw his daughter with a partner other than Rick Blanchard. Olivia was smiling demurely, probably at a witty remark that the banker had whispered in her ear. Yet, while she simulated an interest in his words, her eyes were scanning the ballroom in search of Rick Blanchard. Even from this fleeting sight of her, she was certain that Olivia was unhappy. Rick was not sitting next to her. She was missing his always-thrilling presence. She was yearning for the exciting promise of his sensuality.

So she imagined as she moved past the dance floor and past the banquet tables. With smooth gait and authentic poise, she reached the threshold of the terrace. Pausing there for a moment, she allowed her gaze to rest upon Rick's brooding handsomeness. He looked as though he were waiting for someone. Whether he was waiting for Olivia or for her, she could not rightly discern. Nor did his demeanor reveal anything more than his self-assurance and his willfulness.

"Good to see you," he said, as he offered her a cigarette. With his rugged charm, he brought the flame of the gold lighter that Olivia had given him to the cigarette and watched her as she took a drag on it.

At first, she observed him quietly and observed as well the vaporous rings of smoke that wafted away from her cigarette. She stood close to him as they observed in the faraway distance below them the splendid lights of New York City and in the corridors of space above them the crescent moon and the cluster of stars illumining the dark sky. Only then, after peering upon the city lights and the moon and the stars, did she choose the careful words that might persuade him to tell her what was on his mind.

"You have something to tell me."

"Yes."

"You've let Mr. Tanner win this round."

"You know me well."

"Tell me about it."

Rick offered her a sly smile.

"You won't be surprised," he said. "But I think that you will be pleased."

Now, with understated ease and with muted bitterness, he told her about his meeting with Mr. Tanner.

Calculating yet self-controlled, Rick was playing the Tanners like the cool hustler that he was. He was holding on a taut leash the fury that he felt only a few hours before the party, when Mr. Tanner told him in the privacy of his study that there would be trouble if he moved too fast in his relationship with Olivia. With respectful demeanor and stoic disposition, he allowed Mr. Tanner to make his father's speech. The words, as blunt as they were cautionary, satisfied Robert Tanner's hardened nature and his awareness of the power that he wielded on Wall Street and in so many other locales, including his home.

At first, Rick politely resisted Mr. Tanner's arrogant words. Rick had his eye on that top spot as a Wall Street insider. He did not permit himself to forget that Robert Tanner could be his power link. Besides, he wanted Tanner to believe that he genuinely loved his daughter. Confronted by this willful father, he chose careful and heartfelt words that might give pause even to a disagreeable and overbearing man.

"I can't give your daughter up," he began. "I love her. I don't exist alone any more. She is an essential part of me. I can't imagine life without her."

"That's romantic talk," Mr. Tanner said. "Don't let it trap you or her."

"Olivia loves me as much as I love her."

"You are young hot bloods. You're confusing lust with love. Think about your future. Think about hers."

Rick lowered his voice now and intensified his deferential manner.

"We want to make our lives together, sir."

"You mustn't do that. She will have a better life without you. Her mother and I want her to marry Noah Blake. He's a boy from her own class."

Rick contrived a frown. He looked crestfallen.

"So that's how it is."

Mr. Tanner quickly told him more.

"Before you barged in, they were practically engaged."

Rick continued to explain the way it was with Olivia and him.

"She loves me now."

"She has never stopped loving Noah. I know my daughter well. She's using you to punish Noah for going off to London without her."

"She's forgotten Noah. I made her forget. She wants to make her life with me now."

Mr. Tanner threw out another of his arrogant questions.

"Do you think that she will feel that way when Noah returns next month?"

Rick pretended to be taken aback. He fell silent.

"Well, do you?"

"I'm not sure. I'd like to think so."

Noticing his hesitation, Mr. Tanner became even more insistent.

"Let her go. Without her, you will still be a success. You'll have your Ivy League connections to push you into the big time. You will also have my backing, if you step aside so that Olivia can make her way with Noah Blake."

Understated though assertive now, within the parameters of ingrained masculinity, Rick made his way forward with a conciliatory promise.

"I want to do what is right for Olivia. I'll step aside if she tells me that she doesn't really love me."

Mr. Tanner was very pleased.

"You are doing the right thing, my boy," he said. "You won't regret it."

Rick's acquiescence as well as his willingness to do the right thing on behalf of Olivia impressed Mr. Tanner. He went away from this private conference convinced that Rick Blanchard wasn't such a bad sort, after all. He'd keep an eye on him as he made his way up the ladder. He'd be true to his word. He'd help him to ascend faster.

So Rick explained to her, his secret confidante ("my wonderfully devious Charlotte," he'd once called her), as he recounted that meeting with Mr. Tanner.

"That bastard gives himself too much credit," Rick said. "He thinks that he can push me aside with a few blunt words and a vague promise that he'll open the right doors for me once I earn some university credentials."

"That promise isn't enough for you, is it?"

"Not when I can have his daughter, too."

"She still wants Noah."

"Not when she's in bed with me."

"What about the times when she's not in bed with you?"

"She knows that I'm keeping my eyes on her. Every minute. Even when I'm not standing beside her. She's afraid to make the wrong move."

"Are you sure of that?"

As though she meant to resolve this uncertainty, Olivia was suddenly there, on the threshold of the terrace. She appeared anxious and fragile, yet her beauty glowed with new intensity. She was somewhat flushed and even breathless after hurrying from the dance floor in search of Rick. For an instant, she observed them with searching eyes. For the first time, it crossed her mind that Rick and she—her trusted friend, loyal Charlotte Scott—were more than pals.

Her friendly smile quickly reassured Olivia. So, she imagined, did her next remark.

"I've been having a wonderful time," she pushed herself to say. "But after dancing for an hour, I needed some fresh air."

"I know how you feel," Olivia said.

Saying so, Olivia also smiled, as if she wanted to remind herself of their solidarity. At any rate, she brushed aside the thought of any intimacy between Rick and a trusted friend who had always been so helpful to her. Instead, she directed her attention to Rick alone.

"I've been missing you," she said, as she approached him. "I've felt trapped by all these fellows that insist upon dancing with me."

Once again, she invoked her infantile helplessness to disguise the pleasure that she had experienced while dancing with so many different partners. She wanted Rick's approval. She did not want to rouse his anger. There was a fear of him that gave her pause even as it excited her.

He recognized her little girl's petitioning. It pleased him, because it was anchored to her fear of him. Now he chose understated words that aimed to put her at ease.

"You seemed to be having a good time," he said. "I thought that you were enjoying the party."

Olivia was more certain of where their words were guiding them. She spoke more confidently, and she chose new words that she believed were genuine.

"The party is where you are. There is no other party."

Rick was impressed that she was trying so hard to be on the level with him.

"What will your father think?"

She moved closer to him and, with a delicate movement of her hand, caressed his face. She made her voice softer, as if to suggest the intimate bond between them.

"I don't care what he thinks. It's what you think that is important."

Rick summoned a grin that, for a fleet instant, made him look boyish. He held her in a steady gaze. Proprietary yet restrained, he took hold of her shoulders and drew her even closer to him. He kissed her lightly on her forehead and made it appear a natural gesture. He had already staked his claim, and he was reminding her of it.

"Good to hear that, baby. You and I are going to have a fine life together."

As though his apparent gentleness were a sign of an accord that they were now renewing, Olivia beamed at this promise of their sharing a bright future.

"Oh, we will, Rick. We will."

"Tonight, though, make your father happy. I don't mind your dancing with the other guys. I know that, even when I'm not on the dance floor with you, you're thinking about me."

"Always, Rick. I am always thinking about you."

"Make your father happy," he told her once more. "Dance with the other guys. When we're back on campus, you and I have days and days of being together. And plenty of nights."

"You're not angry with me? For letting Father have his way."

"No, baby. I'm not angry."

Here, in the silence of her home office seventeen years afterward, she recalled how subtly she had moved into the shadows cast by a marble column on that moonlight night, there on the terrace of the Tanner penthouse. As though she were one of the Fates who was influencing the destiny of those persons she was observing, she waited quietly while Olivia petitioned Rick for his understanding and while Rick, as clearheaded and unprincipled as ever, bound her with chains to his will.

When they had confirmed the pact that held them together, she—Charlotte Scott, Olivia's trusted friend— came forward to coax her back to the ballroom.

"Let's go back to the dance," she said to Olivia. "The night is still young. There are several gentlemen waiting to dance with us."

Olivia wasn't taking any chances. She asked for Rick's consent.

"You're sure that it's all right?"

In this dangerous game that they were playing, Rick held all the best cards. It was easy for him to appear casual and affable, even while Robert Tanner's callous treatment of him lived, vivid and stinging, within his memory.

"I'm sure," he said, appeasing Olivia's need for his approval. "Enjoy the night. But don't let me see you kissing any guy."

"You are the only one I want to kiss," she said.

She moved closer to him and, with a delicate gesture that enhanced her femininity, she brushed her lips against his lips.

Rick pressed his lips more firmly upon her lips. Then, he slowly withdrew from the kiss and studied her face. Only after he noticed the glow in her eyes and the tremor of excitement that was touching her slim body did he guide her to the threshold of the terrace where, as Olivia's sisterly friend, she was now waiting.

"I'll be coming back to the dance, too," he told Olivia. "I'll enjoy watching you."

She wondered whether Olivia detected the undercurrent of menace in that parting remark. If so, she gave no sign of her unease.

As she and Olivia made their way into the ballroom, she looked back at Rick. He was taking a drag on his cigarette.

He offered her a sly smile. His slyness was a language that she understood. He was even more convinced that, if they kept making the right moves, they were going to win all that they wanted. The plan that she had devised was working—in spite of Mr. Tanner's interference and because of Olivia's fear and need of Rick.

The party was in full swing. She and Olivia recaptured the spirit of it and shared their ebullience with many new dance partners. When they were not dancing, they exchanged lighthearted and even witty remarks with some of the prestigious guests that the Tanners had carefully invited. Even before the party had ended, Mrs. Tanner found a place next to her at the table and whispered how pleased she was about her influence upon Olivia.

"You have been a positive role model for her, my dear," she said. "You have helped Robert and me to save her for Noah Blake."

Here, at her desk so many years later, she recalled how politic she had acted on that problematic evening, pretending with conviction to be Olivia's best friend.

"I want her to be happy," she'd told Mrs. Tanner once again, "as much as you and Mr. Tanner want it."

"Of course you do. You are an absolute treasure."

Mrs. Tanner, ensnared by inveterate artifice and by her other contrivances, believed too firmly in "admirable Charlotte Blake's" good will toward her daughter and in Olivia's placating docility. Mr. Tanner, equally tangled by his arrogance and his egotism, also misread the influence of his arbitrary powers and the motive behind his daughter's show of obedience. The Tanners underestimated, as well, Rick's street-wise capacity to subvert their expectations. She knew Olivia and Rick better than they did. Rick was the true renegade. He was going to play the game his way. He was going to win all that he wanted.

Two days later, she returned to the Brown University campus with Olivia and Rick. Except for one unexpected incident, as swift as it was brutal, nothing extraordinary happened in the weeks that quickly followed. Each of them focused on their studies and welcomed the brief Thanksgiving visit to their families.

Before they took their holiday leave of each other, Olivia and Rick joined Steven Bennington and her at an exclusive social club that was located on College Hill, within walking distance of their campus. Because it was raining lightly, Steven drove them to the club in his Mercedes- Benz. They were permitted to dine at the club because both Olivia's and Steven's parents, as well as her own, were members. With its beautiful antiques, burnished mahogany, rich fabrics, and dignified ambiance, as well as original canvases by Mary Cassatt, Winslow Homer, and Thomas Hart Benton, the club offered them a setting that was elegant as well as dignified. Unaware that Rick was in their party, Mrs. Tanner—from her home on Sutton Place—had reserved a table in one of the second-floor dining rooms, where their preferred placement enhanced the pleasures of the evening. Only in retrospect did she perceive that the four of them had chosen so staid a setting for their dinner because the refined atmosphere, the upright conduct of guests young and older at neighboring tables, and the disciplined cordiality of the servers might hold their senses still.

At the very start of the evening, even before they reached the club in Steven's Mercedes-Benz, there were signs that Rick and Olivia had been quarreling. Seated in the rear passenger seats, Rick flared out his impatience with Olivia.

"We've gone over this so many times," he said, spewing out the words that were yoked to anger and menace. "This time, listen hard, baby. I don't want to say it again. I'm not joining you in New York."

The moment that the four of them arrived at the club, Olivia drew her into the powder room while Rick and Steven sat at the bar, drinking scotch. Once she and Olivia stepped inside the powder room, with no one else there to hear them, Olivia began complaining about Rick's tyranny over her.

"I'm weary of him," she said. "He wants everything his way. If I don't agree with him, he threatens to leave me. Once or twice, he's slapped me around. Hard. I really don't know why I stay with him."

On this sun-misted afternoon so many years later, she could hear the soft words that she'd used to pacify self-centered Olivia who, without exploring her ambivalence, was learning to love and to hate Rick, though not in equal measure. It was of the utmost importance that Olivia and Rick stayed together. She did not want Olivia to thwart the plan that would help her, unscrupulous Charlotte, to win the love of Noah.

So, with words meant to appease her pampered friend's dismay and resentment, she reaffirmed her own makeshift belief in the extraordinary nature of Olivia's love of Rick.

"You love Rick," she had said, seated as she was before the mirror in the powder room at the start of that volatile evening at the club. "That's why you stay with him."

Olivia, while applying new gloss to her lips, pondered her remark. At first, she said nothing. Then, as she began combing her hair, she did something quite rare. She expressed her true feelings.

"Maybe I'm afraid of him," she answered her. "Maybe that's why I stay with him."

She coaxed her further. She wanted her to admit her perverse need of Rick.

"Maybe that's a part of your relationship with him that you like. Maybe you like being slapped around."

Olivia frowned. The truth stung at her, a little. She was no stranger to her perversities, no matter how cleverly she often concealed them from her parents and her friends and sometimes from herself.

"Maybe," she said. "Maybe I do like it."

Leaving the powder room, they joined Rick and Steven at the bar. Both men were talking about hockey and enjoying their scotch. With his suave manner and knack for pushing the evening forward, Steven ordered cocktails for Olivia and her. Then he drew all of them into a conversation about their Thanksgiving plans. Steven intended to spend the holiday at his family's compound in Acapulco. She mentioned that she was joining her parents and her brothers in Palm Beach. Olivia was returning to her parents' home on Sutton Place. She wanted Rick to join her, even though her father had made it clear that she must end her friendship with Rick. But Rick had made other plans. He was heading home for a family reunion in Manchester, New Hampshire. He did not want to cross swords with Mr. Tanner for so small a reward as a seat at Tanner's dinner table. When the time came for him to declare his defiance of Robert Tanner, the stakes would be much higher.

So she imagined, understanding the danger that was in Rick and the treachery.

At the dinner table, Olivia pretended to be carefree and even effervescent. Olivia and she merely picked at their dinner, though Olivia had drunk several rounds of scotch. As it was their habit, the men ate and drank heartily. She'd kept in mind all these years afterward exactly what they had eaten on that evening. She had admired the menu and had often drawn upon it for the many dinners that she hosted later, while she was married: red and green cabbage salad with apples, filet mignons with artichokes and béarnaise sauce, Pont Neuf potatoes, and almond-filled Basque cake. Two middle-aged waiters, adept and precise, served their every need. In the proximate distance, near a panoramic window that looked out upon the late autumn glow of the streetlights within the rain-swept university campus and upon, as well, the immaculate brownstones, an accomplished pianist played Rachmaninoff's "Vocalise" and love ballads of that period, including "Laura," "My Foolish Heart," "Tenderly," and "To Each His Own." On almost any other evening, the romantic lilt of the scene would have dispelled doubts and anxieties and disappointments. But on this evening not even the exquisite music or the presence of the guests at neighboring tables could deflect Olivia's willfulness or suppress Rick's rising anger.

Olivia wouldn't let up. The scotch had revved up her courage. She kept harping on the same subject. Rick was her boyfriend. Boyfriends spent their holidays with their girlfriends. She had every right to expect that he would share the holiday with her in New York.

"I'm not exactly a wallflower," she said. "Plenty of guys would like to be there in New York with me."

Rick swallowed his fourth scotch and quickly rebuffed her.

"Not anymore, they don't," he said. "Those guys know that I can be very rough. They know that I'll be dealing with them if they try to team up with you."

"You don't own me," Olivia said, her tremulous voice on the cusp of anger and panic. "I'll choose any guy that I want. I don't need your permission."

Rick's brooding demeanor, brusque reply, and heavy drinking transformed the cool-headed and charming persona he had studiously cultivated. His steely gaze and barely suppressed grimace were chained to the fury that, with hair-trigger propensities, was poised to overtake him.

"Shut up," he said, still low-key and guttural. "Stop being a spoiled bitch."

Steven changed the subject. He spoke of planning to buy a Maserati at the end of the school year. He and Rick began talking about The Indianapolis 500 and a terrific driver named Johnnie Parsons.

Olivia wasn't interested in The Indianapolis 500. She took pleasure in goading Rick further, in spite of her fear of him. She wanted to talk about her Thanksgiving holiday.

"Maybe it's better that you don't come to New York with me," she said. "My mother has written that Noah Blake may be there. She persuaded Noah's mother to send Noah a cable, urging him to change his plans and head home for Thanksgiving."

Rick's entire body grew taut. Stillness, ominous and menacing, was taking hold of him.

Heedless of the consequences, Olivia went on goading him.

"Until Mother mentioned him, I hadn't realized how much I've been missing Noah."

As soon as she uttered those words, Rick grabbed hold of her and, pinioning her to his brute force, began slapping her over and over.

"Don't ever mention him again," he snarled. "Don't even think about him."

Olivia began screaming. It was an adolescent girl's scream, helpless and whimpering. Caught inside that scream was an insolent warning.

"I'll tell my father! I'll tell him everything!"

Rick slapped her again, this time so hard that she fell out of her chair. A half-filled wine glass spilled across the carpet and shattered, leaving a stain that looked like blood. The clasp of Olivia's necklace broke, the delicate symmetry of its sunflower design still intact as the necklace also fell upon the carpet.

The two waiters—tall, silver-haired, and solicitous—hurried toward their table only to be pushed back by the commotion. The pianist—accomplished, youthful, and good-looking—went on playing the romantic melodies of George Gershwin, Jerome Kern, and Lorenz Hart. Three senior couples at the table nearest them peered at the confusion with startled and apprehensive countenances.

All this while, Steven had risen from his chair and was struggling to restrain Rick. As swift as he was powerful, he passed his hand under Rick's arm and locked it on his neck.

With his other hand, he held down Rick's wrist while he pulled him away from Olivia. For a moment, Rick struggled against his opponent. But, when he saw wailing Olivia hurrying away to the powder room, he relaxed his body. Her hair and clothes were disheveled. Her face was bruised, and her lips were bleeding. He noticed, perhaps for the first time, that his friend Steven was the man who had drawn him away from Olivia.

"Calm down," she remembered whispering to Rick, even now seventeen years later. "You've got too much to lose if you make the wrong move."

"I had to stop you," Steven explained. "You were really roughing her up."

""I know what I'm doing," he said. "I want her to remember that I don't like being played with."

"She knows that," Steven said. "Tonight, she made a mistake. She went too far."

"After tonight, she'd better not make mistakes."

She—Olivia's apparently loyal friend—had secretly enjoyed watching Rick beat her rival for Noah's love. She had made no attempt to stop the assault. Olivia deserved the beating. For her, it served as a reality check. Neither the world, nor Rick Blanchard existed to accommodate all her demands.

With that thought in mind, she hurried to the powder room to help Olivia repair her face and her cocktail dress. Olivia was sitting before the large mirror that compassed the entire wall. Bertha Jenkins, the powder room attendant who was a middle-aged woman with a good-natured disposition and motherly concern, was standing beside her. She had already helped her comb her hair and readjust her diamond necklace.

"She'll be all right," Bertha said. "She's just shaken up a bit."

Intuitive as well as experienced, she quickly left the room. She understood that they wanted to talk privately.

No sooner had she left than Olivia blurted out her confession.

"It was my fault," she sobbed. "I said mean things to make Rick angry."

"I'm certain that Rick feels as sorry as you do."

"I don't know why I said all those terrible things. I really love him."

Understated and devious as well, she carefully nudged Olivia once again to do and say the things that would draw her closer to Rick and far way from Noah.

"Of course, you love him. But Rick may stop believing that you do, if you keep on mentioning Noah."

"I won't mention Noah ever again," she said. "That's a promise."

"That's a good promise. Now dry your tears. You want to look your best for Rick."

Olivia brightened. The prospect of using her beauty to keep Rick at her side appealed to her. It made plausible the certainty that Rick would always want to be her bed partner.

While they were finding their way back to the dining room, she noticed that Olivia was moving with her usual feminine grace and with inherent poise. But, once they arrived at their table, she began trembling almost imperceptibly. Steven and Rick were talking quietly about football. Steven had been able to calm Rick at the same time that he ordered him to stop giving Olivia a hard time.

Apparently, Olivia liked being roughed up. In spite of her tremulous air, her bruises didn't prevent her from taking her place next to Rick and planting kisses upon his lips and neck and right ear, all the while asking for his forgiveness.

"I'm so sorry," she said, as her eyes misted with tears again and her voice invoked a soft sobbing. "You have to forgive me. I love you too much not to be forgiven."

For a moment, Rick carefully observed her. He liked the tearful eyes and the sobbing voice. They seemed deferential and nearly genuine. He accepted the kisses, though they did not persuade him that Olivia's sorrow would be long lasting. Nor did her kisses dispel his ambivalent manner and the equivocating words that suggested his compunction would be as superficial as her own.

"I'm sorry, too, baby," he said. "I'm just as sorry as you are."

Olivia and Steven did not notice the ambivalence. But she did—she, Charlotte Scott, whom Olivia had accepted as a friend to be trusted.

She was not surprised that Rick and Olivia could so smoothly patch things between them. They had done so before. They might do so again. That wayward evening convinced her that Rick was not finished with his violence against Olivia.

When they returned once again to the campus, they moved successfully through their examinations and the end-of-the-semester seriousness.

All this while, their unspoken awareness that, come mid-December, Noah would be returning from London never left them. But even in this period, when their fates hovered near them without yet disclosing themselves, she did not doubt Rick's capacity for making a friend of wild chance.

She was not caught by surprise when he made his move before Noah returned. On Wednesday, the twentieth of December in 1950, Rick ran off with Olivia and married her in a quiet ceremony in Northern California.

PART ONE

CHAPTER FIVE

Charlotte

Wednesday Afternoon, 4 October 1967

Looking Back to 1951 and 1952

When, in that January of 1951, Olivia and Rick returned to the Brown University campus as a married couple, they moved into a luxury apartment only a street away from Noah's townhouse. They appeared to be very happy. They reveled in the weekend parties that celebrated their marriage. They seemed ideally mated, too, during the February weekend when they went skiing with their closest friends in Stowe, Vermont. They looked compatible and fulfilled at the end of March, when they were studying for their mid-term exams in the silence of the crowded main room of the largest library on campus. In April, during Spring Festival Week, they were the university's most romantic married couple as they danced away the night in the glamorous ballroom of a Newport mansion.

During this period, Rick's hockey team won the league championship, and he went on to win a couple of medals for the swimming team. Olivia showed real talent in her performance with The Modern Dance Group and in the leading role of the university's production of *Laura,* Vera Caspary's play about love, obsession, and murder.

"Lake Tahoe was our lucky charm," Olivia had told her shortly after she returned from her honeymoon with Rick. "It changed everything for the better. It made Rick absolutely gentle most of the time, and it made Daddy and Mother come round."

"What did Lake Tahoe have to do with your parents?"

Her face beamed. She was eager to explain all of it in detail.

Now, nearly seventeen years later, all of it was coming so clearly back to her, as she sat before her desk with the unopened letter from Noah. She saw, vivid and nearly palpable, the excited face of Olivia Tanner. The face was a living presence. The tan that Lake Tahoe had given her still gleamed in the first days after her January return to the campus. The tan made her appear healthy and wholesome. Lake Tahoe and possibly her marriage had relaxed her tension and enhanced her buoyancy.

In that faraway moment, Olivia imparted the vague remnants of her innocence and the vitality of newly discovered happiness. She wanted to tell her all about her happiness because she—trustworthy Charlotte Scott—was a friend to be cherished.

"My parents flew into California the day after Rick and I were married. They thought they could persuade me to get my marriage annulled. But I wouldn't listen to them. Daddy was in a rage, and Mother was beside herself."

"What changed their minds? What made them come around?"

"Many things. Not just one thing. They saw how happy Rick and I were together. They noticed that Rick was proficient on so many levels, whether he was skiing on Pacific waters, piloting a Piper PA-20 Pacer from a private airfield, or discussing the latest Wall Street maneuvers. Daddy also saw that Rick is not afraid of him. He's a tough guy. He can play rough, if he has to."

"You love Rick because he plays rough."

"Yes," Olivia said, echoing a confession she had made weeks earlier. "I do. Most of the time."

"So your father has changed his mind about Rick."

"Daddy is very impressed. He had a long talk with him when we were at Lake Tahoe. He likes what he calls Rick's 'streetwise confidence.' He thinks that he will do well on Wall Street."

"What does your mother think?"

"Mother thinks that Rick is very smart. She sees him now as a man on his way to the top."

"It sounds too good to be true. Are you sure that's the way they feel?"

"I'm very sure."

"I thought that your parents wanted you to marry someone else."

"You're thinking of Noah Blake."

"Yes."

"Well, I'll admit that Daddy was disappointed that I didn't marry Noah. But I reminded him that the Tanners and the Blakes will still have their corporate merger."

"Then everyone is happy. You and Rick. Your parents and Noah's, too. All's well that ends well."

Olivia pondered these words while allowing a momentary stillness to hover near her. Then, with a tighter breathing and in a voice that sounded matter-of-fact and insistent, she clarified the situation.

"Noah's not happy," she said. "How could he be happy? He wanted to marry me."

She hadn't let go of Noah. She wanted Rick, and Noah as well.

A few days later, forty miles away from the campus and in a secret meeting with Rick at her parents' summer home in Newport, she—Olivia's duplicitous friend—told Rick what she thought. She knew that she and Rick would be alone. After the summer, the housekeeper and the groundskeeper came to the house twice a week, on Tuesdays and Thursdays.

That Sunday, at midnight, she told Rick about Olivia's conflicted desires. It was an hour or so after she and Rick had made love in the oversized bed with the scented silk sheets and the comfortable array of pillows that eased their senses even as they roused their sensuality.

"Noah's still in her blood. She still loves him, no matter what she tells you."

"Maybe she does," Rick said. "But it doesn't matter. She knows me well enough not to make the wrong moves."

That weekend, Olivia was visiting her parents in New York. Rick had not accompanied her, because—he told her—he was studying for his chemical engineering exam. He lied with such conviction that Olivia easily believed him.

They had not spoken about Olivia during the drive to Newport or at the private club where they dined on that Friday evening. Nor had they mentioned her the next day, when they rode beautiful Arab Bay stallions on a horse trail in nearby Middletown. On Sunday morning, they had reveled, carefree and complicit, in tandem skydiving from a Cessna 182, floating and freefalling along the sun-glittering coastline of Newport. Later that day, they tested Rick's new Jaguar XK120 (a gift from Olivia) along a speedway in Bristol, and they fired Colt 38 Specials, Beretta M1951s, and Remington 870s at an indoor shooting range in Portsmouth.

With weapon in hand and accurate aim, she felt empowered. Yet she needed no weapon to manipulate the plan that she had devised against Noah and Olivia. Sometimes, murders are committed without pistols or poisons. Through the plot that she had woven, she was murdering the lives that Olivia and Noah would have shared. She was murdering the persons they would have become if they had stayed together. For each of them, dying had become a nearly endless process—the eking out of days and months and years without the rightful partner that The Fates had planned for them. She was usurping the powers of The Fates. She was disarranging their plans. She was imposing her fallible will against those formidable powers.

There, on the shooting range, she felt her ghost hovering by her. She had a premonition, ominous and unexpected, that she was bringing some terrible punishment upon herself because of her devious ways.

Quickly she brushed the thought away. Strong-willed and purposeful, she watched Rick firing the Remington 870. Her thoughts turned to him. In so many ways, they were like one another. They were wily, arrogant, and hard-hearted. They belonged together.

Being with Rick during this weekend prodded her nostalgia. Their bond felt authentic. Their mutual attraction seemed natural and inevitable. Yet, for reasons that she could not completely fathom, she yearned for Noah. Her wanting him was a perversity of her will.

During the three days that she and Rick shared in Newport, she had avoided speaking of Noah and Olivia.

"This weekend is for you and me," he told her at the start of their drive to Newport. "Let's forget everything else. Let's leave everyone behind that we know."

He needed to break free of his university schedule. He needed to put some space between Olivia and him.

She understood Rick well. She imagined that, even when Olivia was on her best behavior, he harbored his contempt of her infantile needs. Yet, in spite of his coldhearted disposition and his cynical refusal to give his heart to any of the many women he had known, he was falling in love with Olivia. Even with her faults, he loved her. In his eyes, those faults made her seem vulnerable and needy. He had not yet come to terms with his new feelings. He was not yet ready to admit that, casual and unrestrained, Olivia had stolen his heart.

Nor would she speak of his feelings for Olivia. Instead, she told him about Olivia's feelings for Noah.

"Olivia still loves him," she said. "She's not willing to let him go."

Quiet yet insistent, Rick rejected her remark.

"But she has let him go," he said. "She married me."

She wanted him to see what Olivia was hiding from him.

"If she knew that I want Noah for myself, she might forget that she's married."

Her words did not disturb Rick.

"She won't forget," he said. "I'll make sure of that."

Then, after a moment's reflection, he spoke the words that dispelled the hesitation that had taken hold of her.

"Anyway, it's time for you to make your move. You won't win Noah if you keep your feelings a secret. You'd better move fast, before some other girl files her claim."

She did move fast. Two weeks later, she gave a lavish party for Rick and Olivia at the private club near the Brown University campus where they had dined with her and Steven a few months earlier. The seven rooms on the second floor of the club provided a glamorous setting for the celebration. Two hundred eighteen guests were there to cheer on the newlyweds as they began their exciting adventure together. Many of the guests were Rick's hockey, swimming, and fraternity friends and Olivia's theater and sorority friends. Some guests had flown in from Boston, New York, and Philadelphia. Her father did not mind picking up the tab. Worldly and pragmatic, Gregory Scott regarded Olivia's father as a useful power link and a ruthless businessman whose success equaled his own.

Looking back seventeen years later, she saw that she had been very clever. Though the party celebrated Rick and Olivia, she had arranged its luxurious amenities not for them alone or even first of all. It was true, of course, that she had contrived an evening in which Olivia and Rick would be the center of attention. At the start of the evening, with an upright minister presiding, they had renewed their wedding vows. An elegant decorum infused the atmosphere. A string quartet played Johann Pachelbel's "Canon in D." A respectful hush came upon the place. Everyone was properly awed by the ceremony and by the romantic glow of the couple. In her cream-colored dress and diamond necklace, Olivia was radiant. Rick looked confident and authentic in his navy suit. They looked right together.

Nor did the rightness of that evening include only Rick and Olivia. Everything about that evening was right. All of it had played itself out exactly as she had planned. With the assistance of the club's excellent staff and its prize-winning chef, as well as the team of decorators who had transformed the seven rooms into a flowing space with an art-deco setting, she had provided not only a wedding and a banquet, but also an illusion of an upscale night club of the twenties, replete with a handsome dark-haired crooner; his blonde, sensual partner; and a band of popular musicians. The nightclub atmosphere quickly displaced the churchly ambience that had served as a prologue to the evening. The youthfulness of the guests brought a carefree and buoyant flair to the party. A few of the men drank more than they should have. A fight brought out at the bar when two athletes harboring a grudge gave vent to their animosity. Women amused themselves with new dancing partners. A few of them returned to off-campus apartments with unanticipated lovers. Everyone had a good time, including the guests of honor who looked as though they might be willing, at least for that night, to believe in the fairy-tale emblems of the celebration.

No parents or other relatives intruded upon the scene. The Tanners and the Blanchards were planning a more formal wedding in New York at the end of May to accommodate all the relatives and friends who had missed Rick and Olivia's runaway ceremony at Lake Tahoe.

"You are a wonderful friend," Olivia told her as she and Rick, making their way through the flowing openness of the nightclub setting, stopped briefly at every table to exchange casual remarks and quick-witted insights with the friends who had come to wish them good luck. When they reached her table, they conversed lightheartedly with Steven, who was her escort, and with the three other couples who were seated there. Olivia's enthusiasm for the surprise and the sumptuousness of the evening was both palpable and affecting. She offered special praise, because it was she, "loyal and sensible Charlotte Scott," who had brought Rick Blanchard into her life.

Olivia wanted to believe all that she said to her. Yet her effusive praise seemed false. The fear in her eyes subverted the lightheartedness of her words. She wanted to believe that she was happy with Rick. She wanted to convince herself that her happiness no longer depended on Noah.

Steven knew the score. He knew how unhappy Olivia really was. Street-wise and matter-of-fact, he had recently mentioned, as a passing reference to them, that their marriage was conflicted and even fraudulent. He told her that and more during one of their New York weekends.

"Rick plays rough with her," he said. "On a night when he'd had a few too many drinks at his private club, Rick complained to me about their marriage. Olivia always wants things her way. When he doesn't give in to her whims, she begins taunting him with her memories of Noah. That's when he slaps her around. He broke her ribs a few weeks ago. But she kept her mouth shut. She didn't tell her father. And she didn't dare tell the police."

Steven's words intrigued her. She—the woman that Olivia regarded as her best friend—was more intensely aware now of the confusion that her plot had wrought upon Olivia and Rick.

"There's a part of her that loves Rick," she said.

"Maybe there is," Steven answered her. "Maybe she likes when he plays rough. There's a perverse love in the danger of that. But that kind of love isn't enough."

Steven paused while he reflected upon the troubled relationship between Rick and Olivia. Then, certain that his perception of them was correct, he said more.

"Even though he gives her a hard time, Rick may really love Olivia. But he won't admit even to himself that he loves her. How can he, when he won't give himself a chance to understand what he is feeling?"

Steven told her how it was with them only two weeks before the party that meant to celebrate Olivia's marriage to Rick.

Now, here at the wedding party, she was witnessing Olivia's maudlin display of gratitude that she did not feel and her pathetic intimation that all was well with her marriage. She, the faithful friend, was not taken aback. She brought conviction to her own false part in the scene. Their pretense was of no importance. What was important was that she had pushed Olivia away from Noah.

"You are not merely wonderful," Olivia told her. "You are most wonderful. Mother is right. You are a treasure."

"Don't say another word," she remembered answering her. "I'll start believing that I'm a saint."

"You have a knack for nudging people in the right direction," Rick said.

He had a glint in his eyes. He was enjoying the show. He had helped to initiate it.

"You've done all this for us," Olivia added, just before she and Rick moved on to another table. "I'll never forget it."

She smiled at Rick and Olivia, because she was elated. But it was not they who influenced her happiness on that evening. True, she took perverse satisfaction in having devised a wedding celebration that insisted the bride and groom were going to be happy for the rest of their lives. Heart-felt and plausible, her grand party gesture concealed her dissimulation and her plotting. She did not believe in their marriage. She thought it improbable that Rick, impelled by cunning and deception, and Olivia, ensnared by selfishness and eventually grown weary of the falsity of their bond, could ever find lasting happiness together. But they were together now and for the time being. Olivia was caught in a trap from which she would not easily extricate herself. Married to Rick, she was no longer her rival for the love of Noah. In a year or two, in spite of or because of the perversity of their love, Olivia might free herself of Rick, especially if Robert Tanner was willing to pay him off. A year gave her plenty of time to override Noah's regrets about losing Olivia. In that year, she would make Noah forget Olivia. She would get the man that she wanted. She would gain all of his love.

It was Noah for whom she gave the party first of all, though he and all the other guests were unaware of her purpose. It was he whom she had invited to the wedding celebration without telling Olivia or Rick. She did not know him well. But she felt certain that Noah would come to the celebration. She knew his kind. He was as adept at disguise and duplicity as she was. She was not surprised when he made a belated appearance at the party. He had intended to miss the marriage ceremony and much of the banquet. He arrived wearing a black suit, a cobalt-blue shirt, and a red paisley tie. Sandra Lancaster, a seductive, titian-haired girl in an emerald green evening dress, was his date for the evening. She was a student at Vassar and from an affluent family. Noah wanted no other kind. They teamed up with each other when they were between more serious romantic alliances. He kept Sandra with him while some of his many friends drew him to the bar and, later, when he greeted Olivia and Rick at their table. She and Steven had joined the newlyweds at their table, right after they returned from their visit to all the guests who had come there to celebrate them.

She noticed once again Noah's extraordinary handsomeness and his devil-may-care confidence as he and his occasional girlfriend greeted everyone at the table.

"You've surprised all of us," Noah said, turning his attention to Rick and Olivia. "You've tied the knot."

His manner was brisk, and his grin made him appear affable and jaunty.

"It's a very pleasant knot," Olivia said, perhaps too quickly.

If Rick was aware of her sudden nervousness, he gave no sign. Instead, he offered Noah, who was his hockey teammate and tough-hearted rival in so many pursuits, a too-casual remark that meant to bruise his already-damaged ego. Noah was the guy that Olivia had spurned. He was the runner-up in this game that she had been playing with him. He had never been interested in tying a marital knot with any of his women. But, she imagined, Noah did not like Rick's having tied the knot with Olivia in a secretive episode. They had eloped. They had not given him a chance to dissuade Olivia from the folly of marrying and to draw her back to his bed without infringing upon his freedom or her own. If the runaway marriage had left a scar that he was concealing, Rick's blunt rejoinder to Noah's remark about marriage knots left a new wound.

"You ought to find a girl who'll show you how to tie one," Rick said.

For an instant, Noah fell silent. He grimaced. He clenched his fists. It looked as though he was going to punch Rick. But, as quickly as the wild anger had flashed across his face, he caught hold of himself. The grimace became a broad grin.

"Maybe I'll do just that," he said, smoothly parrying Rick's verbal jab.

He paused before uttering a kicker.

"In about twenty years."

Everyone laughed.

"You are a renegade," she remembered telling him. "You make your own rules."

It was in that moment that Noah gave her his full attention, possibly for the first time. He held her in his steady gaze. His brown eyes penetrated her surfaces. They drew her into sensual privacies that he alone was sharing with her—right then, in that moment when everything between them was beginning. Her calling him a renegade pleased him.

"I do make my own rules," he said, "when I need to."

He may have noticed that she was partnered with Steven, there at the festive table. But that would mean nothing to him. Clearly, she had roused his interest. She would be seeing more of him.

After chatting amiably for a few minutes with the ten people there, Noah and his girlfriend hurried away to another circle of friends.

Olivia watched his leave-taking with special interest, enclosed as she was within the privacies of her stillness.

She remembered that, right after that, Olivia watched her. For the rest of that evening, whenever they were in each other's company or when she could observe her from across the room, Olivia studied her elated face. She may have been wondering whether her friend, the upright and loyal Charlotte Scott, was especially happy that evening because she was there at the party with Steven or because Noah Blake had become aware of her in an altogether new and romantic way.

Rick noticed his wife's stillness. He hurried to rescue her from the nearly imperceptible tension that was taking hold of her spirit and touching her brow. He did not care that she harbored a secret love for Noah. Her neurotic attachments did not surprise him. He had married a selfish and devious schoolgirl. But he planned to outwit her. He would get everything he wanted from their marriage. Because of her father and his own capacities, he was going to become very wealthy. Believing so, he put a dash of romance into the scenario that he was playing with her. He was not merely playing the role that was expected of him. He was testing his feelings for her. He was trying to discover whether, in the deepest recesses of his heart, he was beginning to love her.

"Come dance with me," he said to her. "Tonight belongs to us especially. Let's enjoy it."

Olivia eagerly accepted his invitation. She wanted to get away from the table. She wanted to escape her sullen thoughts.

"Of course we'll dance," she said. "We'll dance the night away."

Everybody danced. Everybody changed partners.

Seated at her desk nearly seventeen years later, she remembered only one partner from the dozen men who had danced with her. She remembered Noah. She remembered the thrill of his asking her to dance with him and the even more intense thrill of his taking her in his arms and not merely leading, but collaborating with her as they swayed and twirled and dipped to the rhythms of a waltz, a foxtrot, and a samba. Once more, his eyes held her in their gaze. He was casting a spell. He was testing his influence upon her. So she imagined.

"You dance very well," he said. "We're good together."

"We are, indeed," she said.

He might have told her more. But Steven cut in.

"I want my girl back," he said, patting Noah on his shoulder. "I don't mind when she dances with other guys. But the limit is three dances, even for my hockey buddies."

"She's all yours," Noah said. "Treat her well. She's special."

On that evening, he had bowed to her with genuine appreciation. Then, saluting Steven as though they were military comrades, he took his leave of them. He moved with calm assurance around the edge of the dance floor and joined a group of men and women who were delighted to see him.

Later, she saw Sandra Lancaster dancing with Steven and with other eligible men. Her glamorous façade, subtly erotic and fashionably modern, concealed her cynical subversion of sentimental bonds and romantic codes. Toward the end of the evening, she was not surprised that, when many of the guests were returning to their university quarters or catching an air flight home, Sandra left with a recently divorced business executive who had flown in from New York.

Noah, with a drink in his hand, was sitting alone at the bar. She remembered the poise and elegance of her movements as she joined him there. The bartender brought her sherry and served Noah another round of scotch. The band was still playing for the six or seven couples that still wanted to dance. The dark-haired crooner was offering a heart-felt rendition of the perennially favorite ballad, "Love Letters."

The bartender left Noah and her and hurried to the opposite end of the bar to serve drinks to another couple.

Sitting next to each other, she and Noah appeared compatible and intimate. A casual observer might have taken them to be lovers of long acquaintance.

She seized the opportunity that this meeting was offering her.

"You're lonely," she said.

She was opening her gold case and offering him a cigarette.

Once more, his sensual eyes were studying her, as though he were mentally peeling away all the layers of artifice that were hiding the truth of her from him.

"Maybe," he said, answering her remark about his being lonely.

He accepted the cigarette. Then, without saying another word, he brought out a gold lighter and lit her cigarette and his.

"I'll help you get rid of your loneliness," she said. "I'm good at that."

"I thought you were Steven's girl."

"Only when I want to be."

His eyes studied her even more intensely. Then, certain of where they were headed, he lifted his glass to seal the bond they were devising.

"Let's drink to your not being Steven's girl."

So began their love affair.

She waited two weeks before she moved into his apartment. That gave her time to level with Steven.

"We've had a good time together," she told him one Sunday morning after he had made vigorous love to her and while they were sharing breakfast on the terrace of her parents' Newport summer home. "But I want to move on."

Steven stopped eating his omelet. At first, he became very still. He stared at her, as though he were trying to decipher the meaning of her words or, possibly, to allow his cynicism to deflect the surprise of her remark.

"Who is it this time?" he asked. "Who is the new guy who wants to share a few adventures with you?"

"Noah."

He scoffed.

"Don't imagine that he'll fall in love with you. He's not the type. He'll play his game with you and then leave."

"It's not a game. I really love him. I can make him love me."

"You are talking like a schoolgirl. You are lying to yourself. You are imagining that, because of you, a self-centered man who has never been loyal to any woman is going to change."

"He's ready to change. Olivia walked away from him and left scars that won't easily heal. My timing is perfect."

"He still loves Olivia. He's not finished with her yet."

"I'll make him forget her."

"Seeing is believing."

"You *will* see. I'll prove to you and everyone else that I'm the right woman for Noah."

"I wouldn't bet on it, if I were you, baby. I think you'll be coming back."

She didn't go back to Steven—at least, not right away. For nearly two years, she and Noah lived together. It was not only the sex that held them together. It was the excitement of being in love. It was the thrill of being stirred in new ways by their sensuality. So she kept telling herself, while she accepted as a pledge of his loyalty and his love all the happiness that he too casually brought to her. During those years, they kayaked in Finland. They skied in the Swiss Alps. They sailed in a regatta in Newport, Rhode Island, and they fished for marlin in Key West, Florida. They attended the bullfights in Mexico, and they hunted for tigers in East Africa. There were nightclub evenings and ballroom occasions. There were luxurious episodes in New York, California, The Bahamas, and Europe. There were all the lovely episodes that they shared on the Brown University campus. There were the quiet walks in country settings. There were so many nuances and gestures, so many glances and caresses. There were all the wonderful things that two people share when they are in love.

But they were not enough to persuade Noah that he loved her. Not even when she murmured intimate and tender words to him did Noah change the rules that he had devised for their living together. Theirs was not to be a conventional romance. While it lasted, they would revel in their freedom and in their youth. They would make their world spin faster and faster. But never would they become prisoners of one another. Never would they encroach upon each other's sovereignty.

She knew the rules well. But one time the sheer happiness of being with Noah compelled her to express openly the tremendous love that she felt for him.

"I love you so much," she said. "Nobody could love you as much as I do."

He resisted the pull of her love and the complicated emotions that were at the heart of that love.

"No strings," he told her. "Remember?"

"I remember," she answered. "I love you without the strings."

"That suits me fine. That's the way I want things."

"Always?"

"Always no strings," he said, as he left her bed, naked and satisfied.

His casual flippancy defined at once his cynical view of things and his callous disregard of her feelings. Yet, on that February morning, so many years ago, she perceived these flaws not as the signs of an intransigent character. She saw them, instead, as evidence of his masculine swagger and his matter-of-fact assurance. She told herself now that most men were like Noah, whether they concealed their arrogance inside steely self-control or revealed their overbearing nature through blunt remarks and aggressive behavior. But in her eyes then, when she was only twenty-one, Noah could do no wrong. He was the lover for whom she had been yearning. He was the charismatic man that might rescue her from the wildness that sometimes betrayed her and from the loneliness that left its sting without warning.

She and Noah had enjoyed a weekend of tree-lined, snowfield skiing and free-spirited partying with university friends while they were staying at his parents' chalet in Shawnee Peak, Maine. Now, after a night of vigorous sex, they had awakened to the sun streaming through the panoramic bedroom window and to the snow-capped mountains that were shrouded by floating clouds and that, to her imaginative eyes, appeared in the faraway distance as the remnants of a discarded world. She and Noah had been sleeping together for a year.

Though she kept her room in one of the Pembroke dorms to appease the vigilant propriety attending her, she spent much of her free time in the immaculately appointed townhouse that Noah's parents had given him. On those weekends when she was allowed to spend her nights away from her dorm, and sometimes on Wednesday afternoons, she and Noah often made passionate love. She had grown used to awakening on Saturday and Sunday mornings to the muted exhilaration of having won Noah's love. At least, she told herself that his sensual hold upon her signified his love for her as well as her love for him. Only later did she understand that, with his vigorous thrusts and protracted climax, he was more interested in pleasuring himself than in accompanying her to mutual ecstasy. For him, copulation was a greedy, unsentimental act of well-honed physicality.

On that February morning in 1952, there in the Blakes' chalet in Maine, she had awakened with the happy belief that Noah would eventually love her as much as she loved him. The ardor of his lovemaking thrilled her. In spite of her experience with men, she was not aware of the selfishness of his love. She had not loved those other men. Noah was an altogether new experience. Even in the early days and nights of their being together, her love for him had become an obsession. Potent and experienced, he took possession of more than her body. He took hold of her spirit. He controlled her mind.

In April of that year, she discovered that Noah was betraying her. He had rekindled his love affair with Olivia.

It was all coming back to her now, here in her home office more than fifteen years later. Her bitter confrontation with Olivia, the unforgiving response of Noah's father when he learned of her pregnancy, her violent reprisal against Noah and Olivia—all these unhappy episodes rose up as if to accuse her. She had kept them at bay for so long. She had held them prisoners in the secret recesses of her memory. Now, when she had not anticipated their insurrection, they had escaped. They were hovering about her, with their wretched scenes and their bleak consequences. The arrival of Noah's letter, still unopened, had brought them to life again.

She turned away from the letter. For a few more minutes, she would hold back its message. But she could not hold back her recollection of the unhappy episodes that were suddenly overtaking her. Nor could she elude the memory of that morning when she placed a snub-nosed revolver in her purse and drove to Saranac Lake to avenge herself against Noah and Olivia.

PART ONE

CHAPTER SIX

Charlotte

Wednesday Afternoon, 4 October 1967

Looking Back to 1952

Noah's betrayal of her ignited tense scenes before the morning that she drove to Saranac Lake with a Colt Cobra revolver in her purse.

First, there was her discovery of Noah's betrayal. On Sunday, the sixth of April in 1952, she had returned earlier than expected from a weekend visit to her parents in New York. Dark clouds had been gathering all through the day. She had wondered whether her flight might be delayed. But no fog overtook the corridors of space through which her plane would be traveling. Nor had the winds roused their powers to thwart the flight. But no sooner had the plane landed safely at an airport in Warwick, Rhode Island, than rain and fog came sweeping through the area. By the time that she arrived at the apartment that she and Noah had been sharing on a street of pristine homes not far from the Brown University campus, heavy rain and turbulent winds had made her ride in an airport taxi a precarious experience. Happily, the rosy-cheeked driver, a middle-aged Irishman by the name of Seamus O'Malley, had not been deterred by the heaves and swirls of the storm. She rewarded him with a handsome tip.

She was relieved when she entered the brownstone in which Noah's townhouse occupied the entire third floor. As she entered the private elevator that brought her to the apartment, she felt safe and protected, having returned to the home that she had shared with Noah for two years on weekends and during Wednesday afternoons. Because it was nearly midnight, she imagined that Noah was already asleep. On the previous Friday, she had left him in his study, poring over physics and calculus textbooks as he prepared for exams that he would be taking on Monday and Tuesday. As meticulous in his study habits as he was daring and even reckless in his social life, Noah would make certain that he had a good night's sleep before taking his physics exam on Monday.

She entered the apartment quietly so that she would not awaken Noah. Yet it was more likely that not she, but the storm would awaken him. The rumbling of thunder, the heavy rain beating against the panoramic window, and the eerie flashes of lightning had already disturbed the quiet of the living room. Still, she saw the room, with its rich furnishings and carefully selected amenities, as a solacing refuge. Noah was not in the room, but he was in the apartment. Even though he was not right here, standing near her, she felt his dynamic presence. Within the hour, after she had bathed and powdered and covered her perfumed body with an azure blue negligee, she would slip into Noah's bed. She would not stir him awake. But, as he had done in the past, he might turn in his sleep and become aware of her presence. Perhaps the touch of her scented body next to his nakedness would rouse him out of his sleep. He would start by kissing her. He would notice her brown, consenting eyes and know that she had been waiting for him. He would come fully awake and make passionate love with her.

On entering the apartment on that storm-tossed night, she imagined that all these things might happen.

She did bathe, powder, and perfume her body. She covered herself with the azure blue negligee that had won Noah's praise. She sipped some brandy to allay the April chill that had suddenly taken hold of her, as though her ghost were hovering near her. The howling wind, the lashing rain, and the booming thunder intensified her need to be with Noah. Now she hurried to the master bedroom and paused before the closed door. Its being closed convinced her that Noah had sought the privacy of sleep after spending a weekend studying for his exams.

But when she opened the door, she saw an altogether different scenario from the one that she had been imagining. The soft lights of the lamps on the night tables that flanked the large bed revealed Noah to her eyes first of all. He was lying on his back, asleep. His naked body caught some of the lamplight and glowed with an otherworldly, rugged handsomeness. Leaning against a galaxy of pillows, he looked contented. There was no trace of the brooding dismay that had sometimes touched his face when he was with her. He looked like a man who, for this night at least, had reclaimed the happiness he had lost.

Olivia was lying next to him. She, too, was naked and her smooth-skinned, delicate beauty glowed as if she also were otherworldly. She was sleeping as peacefully as Noah was. A smile creased her lips, and her right hand caressed Noah's arm.

For a moment, as if she were held prisoner by what she saw, she froze at the threshold of the room. The surprise of seeing Noah in bed with Olivia set her senses reeling. The room swooped and swirled away from her. The walls and ceiling seemed to fold into one another, tilt, and scatter. In almost the same instant, the capacious room hurried back to reassemble itself and then listed, careened, and keeled over, throwing away with a spinning velocity the vividly textured paintings, night tables and lighted lamps, and the oversized bed with cobalt blue Egyptian cotton sheets, bear-skin blanket, and a galaxy of colorful pillows.

So she believed, as she leaned against the door and struggled to find her proper balance. She closed her eyes and, like a schoolgirl who has confronted for the first time the harsh subversion of her romantic notions, she waited for the vision that had flashed before her seeing to disappear.

But, as soon as she opened them, she saw that her eyes had not betrayed her. Noah and Olivia were lying in bed, their bodies sensually connected by Olivia's caress of Noah's arm and by the mutual touch of their legs. In her haste to be gone, she turned from her view of them and, with her back to the light, groped uneasily for the doorknob. She wanted to enter the private corridor and retreat, only fifty feet away, to the guest bedroom. But she stumbled, and her hand brushed against the switch that turned on the central lights. At the same time, the key fell out of the door lock and tumbled across the hardwood floor. Over and over it rolled, its metallic sound rising up to declare itself even while the wind and rain kept swirling their powers outside the panoramic window.

The echoing tinkle of the fallen key and the flare of light shooting out of the ceiling's crystal bulb pendant awakened Noah and Olivia. Startled and disbelieving even in their languor, they rose from their pillows and with searching eyes surveyed the room. The key had ceased its tinkling and had come to rest near the plush Egyptian rug that covered the area around the bed. But the central light shone with modulated warmth and coaxed the two lovers out of their languor. At first, she could not bear to look at them again. Instead, she willed herself to concentrate on the crystal bulb pendant, with its hand-carved patterns that replicated those found on whiskey glasses and decanters. Determined to maintain her self-control, she focused her gaze upon the gold silken fabric cord from which the lighting fixture was suspended. Noah's mother had traveled to Italy to confer with the famous glassblower who had designed and created the pendant. She stiffened at the thought of Noah's mother, whom she regarded as her adversary. The thought grounded her to the complicated situation into which chance had plunged her. It took only a moment for her to recover herself and to face without flinching too-amorous Olivia and equally faithless Noah.

Olivia was the first to speak, as she hurried out of the bed and covered her nakedness with a short pink kimono robe. With her tousled blonde hair, her straight and slender legs, and her shapely hourglass figure, she looked very young and very seductive. A frown marred her beauty, and her tremulous voice yoked her willfulness to an infantile protest.

"I'm not sorry," she said. "I'm not sorry that I love Noah. I loved him long before you did. I've never stopped loving him."

For one uncertain moment, she thought that she would rush across the room and slap Olivia's face until she drew blood from it. But her fear of the consequences held her back. If she made a violent scene, she would destroy whatever chance she had to maintain her affair with Noah.

Instead, she chose understated and insinuating words that might dissuade Olivia from her folly.

"What about Rick?" she asked. "You said you loved him. You married him."

Her words gave Olivia pause. But they did not eclipse her selfish motives. She was not willing to abandon the pact that she had made with Noah.

"Maybe I loved Rick—a little—when I married him," she said. "But I've never loved him the way I love Noah."

"So you're going to walk away from your marriage. Just like that."

"Plenty of girls have done it," she said. "Now it's my turn."

She hurried to the bathroom to shower and to cleanse her body with expensive lotions.

During this exchange of words, Noah had leaned into the comfortable array of pillows and observed Olivia and her with cynical detachment. Now, when he was alone with her, he brushed aside his betrayal of the bond that he had made with her.

"These things happen," he said, as he rose from his pillows and took a cigarette from the gold case on the night table near him. Only after he brought a gold lighter to his cigarette and took a drag on it did he cover his nakedness. There was no modesty in the gesture or any concern that in this wayward hour his nakedness might offend her. He did not care what she thought. He cared only for himself and for the pleasure that he had taken from Olivia. On that long-ago night, though, she was willing to forgive him for his careless disregard of the love that she had been offering him. Apprehensive that she might lose him forever, she matched his carelessness with the familiar words that defined his relationship with her.

"No strings," she said. "You don't owe me an explanation."

"I'm glad that you remembered," he said. "I don't like shouting scenes, and I have no pity for women who cry."

"You'll get no tears from me. I prefer to live on the realistic level, even when I'm having a love affair. I can accept a lover, warts and all, as long as he levels with me."

"Then you and I understand each other perfectly."

"But I wonder whether you are living on the realistic level," she said. "You are playing with fire when you sleep with Rick Blanchard's wife."

"I can take care of myself."

"Don't underestimate Rick. He'll kill any man who tries to steal his wife."

"Not if I kill him first."

"Forget Olivia. Stay out of trouble."

"Grow up, Charlotte. Being morally concerned doesn't become you. It turns you into a phony. Admit it. You're as promiscuous as any of us."

"Of course I am. I've been around. I like to play. But I have my standards. I don't sleep with married men."

"Too bad for you. I've found married women to be especially good in the sack. I show them what they've been missing from their dull husbands."

"You're only making trouble for yourself."

"Olivia needs me. Rick doesn't do the trick for her."

"Don't fool yourself. Don't believe what she tells you about Rick. She loves him. She won't give him up. But she loves you, too. She wants to keep Rick as her married partner. She wants you on the side."

"That suits me fine. She and I have gone a few new rounds together. But they don't mean anything."

"Try telling her that."

"I won't tell her anything. She doesn't listen to anyone except herself. She's a crazy romantic. She has a schoolgirl mentality. She actually believes in love."

"What do you believe?"

"I believe that whatever happens to two people having sex is nothing more than a biological act. Anything between them apart from that is either an easygoing friendship or a casual indifference."

"You play by your own rules."

"So do you. That's why you and I can still have a good time together."

"Not while you're sleeping with Olivia."

"That's mostly over. But I won't be telling you when I sleep with her. If you're smart, you will look the other way."

"You are a real bastard."

"I never said that I was a saint. I take pleasure wherever I find it."

He left the bed quickly and covered himself with a burgundy robe. With a cigarette perched in the corner of his mouth, he looked like a street tough. The hint of a sneer suggested a callous nature and a ruthless disposition. He took one last drag on his cigarette, snuffed its remains in an ashtray, and headed for the guest bedroom that was located in the east wing of the townhouse. There, she imagined, he would use the shower in the adjoining bathroom to wash away Olivia's scent and his own carnal odor.

Without offering her any other words or acknowledging that her being there was of any importance, he left her standing alone at the foot of the bed. Dressed in her azure blue negligee, she must have appeared to his eyes to be an unexpected visitor that planned to stay. But he did not want her there—at least, not until Olivia returned to her apartment a few streets away. She remembered that Rick was spending the weekend in New Hampshire with his parents. When he arrived at their townhouse late in the morning, Olivia would be there to greet him with tender kisses and the murmurings of her adulation before they hurried to their afternoon classes.

For the first time, she hated herself for consenting to Noah's humiliation of her. She hated him now almost as much as she loved him. Hers was no ordinary love. Noah was her lifeline. He was her obsession. He was an addiction from which she was not willing to break free. Tonight, though, she sensed a new danger in her loving him. The danger, with its sensual complications, thrilled her. It also made her apprehensive. Noah had made no pledge of loyalty to her. In fact, he had intimated that after their university graduation he was going his own way. Nearly two years ago, the thought that he might leave her did not alarm her. She believed that she would make Noah fall in love with her. Even now, in spite of this renewal of his affair with Olivia, she told herself that he really loved *her*, not Olivia. Only now and only to himself was he willing to admit that he had fallen in love with her. He was testing his feelings. He was making certainty even more certain. A few nights with Olivia might convince him that he no longer loved Olivia.

But what if he discovered that he still loved Olivia? What if he stole her away from Rick and made a splendid life with her in Chicago, San Francisco, or London, or in any other city where the Blake and Tanner Corporations were flourishing? The thought made her pause. She wondered what she would do then. She wondered whether she would eventually kill Noah and herself.

As bitter as she was uneasy, she waited for Olivia to emerge from her bathing, fully awake now, carefully perfumed, and revealing no evidence of her intercourse with Noah. While she waited, she stood at the rain-spattered window and observed the new flashes of lightning, the wind-sieged branches of trees, and the quickened streams flowing across the wide, empty street. A pale moon was peering from behind a dark cloud, and thunder was still booming over the swirl and sweep of the rain. In spite of the torrential rains and the punishing winds, the brownstones that lined the affluent street stood formidable and resilient. She needed that kind of strength. She needed to rediscover the tough-minded capacities that had always enabled her to confront without flinching the raw bruises and scalding betrayals of life. By capitulating to the self-centered terms that Noah had invoked for their relationship, she had forfeited those capacities. By deferring to his will, she had lost her own. She had turned weak-willed and petitioning. At the start of their relationship, she told herself that was her gift to him. This surrender of her unbridled freedom and her self-possessed individuality was, she believed, an appropriate exchange for the love of the man whose presence thrilled her beyond measure. But now, almost two years later, she saw that after she had placed her once-iron will in his keeping, Noah had made of it a chain that he used to bind her to his arbitrary inclinations.

To dispel these bitter thoughts, she stared at the storm-roiled street with a more intense concentration. She wanted to hold the scene in her memory so that she could bring its flares of turbulence to a watercolor canvas.

This happier thought prodded her to leave the bedroom. She hurried into the living room and headed for the bar in the east corner of the large, richly appointed room that overlooked a terrace and, beyond that, another dimly lighted street that appeared to be moving, at least for an instant, because of the rivulets of rain that were running along the street and off the curbs.

She poured herself a snifter of brandy, her second that night. She left the bar and took a seat on the richly upholstered sofa in the living room. She drank this brandy more swiftly than she had the first. The liquor warmed her and brought a semblance of pleasure that momentarily pushed away the disheartening effects of the past hour. The brandy revived her belief that she could change Noah for the better and win his love. But no sooner had this makeshift conviction, with its fantasy subtexts, persuaded her that happiness was within her reach than Olivia came into the room. An undercurrent of tension did not eclipse her glamour or diminish her blonde beauty. She wore a navy-and-white stripe top, white jeans, and navy ankle boots. On her arm, she carried a beige double-breasted trench coat that navy buttons made even more stylish. The look was absolutely right for her. It enhanced her feminine appeal even as it subdued the calculated artifice that sometimes attended her.

Olivia was also carrying a beige overnight duffel bag. It had loop handles and adjustable shoulder straps, and its zippers and clasps were colored in gold. This duffel bag completed the elegant image that Olivia meant to convey. As fraught with tension as she was, she would not betray the careful presentation of herself to anyone observing her.

She guessed that Olivia had dressed quickly because she wanted to get away from Noah's apartment. Noah was going to drive her back to the penthouse she shared with Rick a few streets away. As she observed her, she wondered whether this "best friend," this spoiled heiress named Olivia Tanner, was experiencing even a particle of remorse because of her adulterous fling with Noah. Did she feel, even for a moment, some anguish or shame that she had also violated the trust of the young woman whom her mother had more than once referred to as "upright and reliable Charlotte Scott"? She did not think so. Though she disliked her, she had to admit that, in some ways, Olivia and she were sisters under the skin. They were selfish, conniving, and untrustworthy.

But, unlike Olivia, she did not lie to herself. Inveterate schemer that she was, she had stolen Noah away from Olivia. She would go on lying and cheating to keep him.

Now, as soon as she entered the room, Olivia was the first to speak. The rebellious courage that she had faked only a half hour earlier had left her. The danger of her situation was closing in upon her. She had betrayed Rick, and she might have to face the ugly consequences. Her new quick words, imparted with a soft and nervous breathlessness, were yoked to little girl helplessness and misty-eyed petitioning.

"Don't tell Rick," she implored her. "Don't let him know about Noah and me."

There was a harder edge to her voice as she answered Olivia. No longer did she care to pretend that she was her friend. By sleeping with Noah, Olivia had declared that she was her adversary. Now she chose words to increase her fear.

"Rick will find out," she said, "even if I don't tell him."

Olivia moved closer now. Her lips were trembling, and her eyes were filling with tears. The prospect of having to face Rick's anger clearly frightened her.

"You'll make things worse for all of us if you tell him."

She felt no pity for this Tanner debutante. It pleased her to rouse this pampered creature's fear.

"Stay away from Noah, or I will tell Rick."

Olivia grew very still. No longer did her lips tremble, and her eyes, though misty, did not shed any more tears. Instead, she pressed her lips together. She was summoning a remnant of her earlier spirited protest. This time her words sounded credible. It was one of those rare occasions when she allowed herself to tell the truth, as far as she understood it.

"I can't stay away from Noah," she said. "I love him, and he loves me. We were meant to be together."

"It's a little late for that. Noah may go to bed with you once in a while. But you are no longer on the list of women he may want to marry."

"I don't believe that."

"Stay away from him."

She returned to the bar, poured herself another brandy, and lit another cigarette. This time she drank the brandy more slowly while she stood by the window and once again peered at the storm-laden street. Though Olivia was still in the room, she no longer acknowledged her presence. Only when she heard Noah's voice did she turn to see that Olivia had taken a seat on the sofa and had withdrawn to her own private musing.

Noah looked refreshed and complacent. He was wearing a collarless blue shirt, gray trousers, black tailored trench coat, and black ankle rain boots.

"Let's go," he told Olivia. "I'll get you home safe and happy in a few minutes."

He grinned at her with casual affection. She, in turn, rose from the sofa and planted a light kiss upon his lips. The sight of him had instantly dissolved her tension, at least on the surface.

"I'm ready," she said. "This is one time that I won't keep you waiting."

The kiss inspired him to help her with her raincoat. After tying the belt in the front without buckling it, she was ready to leave.

Noah grabbed her duffel bag, took hold of her arm, and made his way toward the door. As they passed, Olivia did not look at her. But Noah offered her the same devil-may-care grin that he had flashed at Olivia a minute earlier.

"I'll be back," he said. "You can't get rid of me so fast."

"I'll be waiting," was all that she replied.

Now, fifteen years later, looking back upon that scene, she felt contempt for herself. With no regard for her feelings, Noah had humiliated her. She had not only accepted the humiliation. She had also waited nervously for him to return, so that she could plant her kiss upon his mouth. When he came back to the apartment twenty minutes later, she rushed to the door to greet him. She helped him remove his wet trench coat and, with eyes that yearned for his caress, she gazed upon his handsomeness. In his collarless blue shirt, navy pullover, and gray trousers, he had a preppie look that modulated his cynicism and his arrogance. It was at that moment, while she was closely observing him, that she planted the kiss upon his mouth. He did not resist it and, in fact, returned the kiss with a strong press of his lips against hers.

"I don't care how many women you sleep with," she said after he broke away from the kiss, "as long as I'm one of them."

He met her remark with a husky laugh.

"You are a good sport, baby," he said. "You're fun to be with because you know that we are only playing a game."

They moved to the bar, where she poured each of them a snifter of brandy. They toasted one another, and—after moving to the sofa, where she curled up to him, grateful and even blissful because of his acceptance—they spoke of the many things that pleased them. In a week or so, they planned to kayak in Vermont with two other university couples. During their spring break, they would be in France for the Grand Prix races. They also planned a New York visit that would include a brief hobnobbing with their parents and some enjoyable evenings of nightclubbing and theatergoing.

It was past two when they went to bed. Still potent and vigorous after his adulterous tryst with Olivia, Noah made passionate love with her. When she awoke the next morning and hurried forward to her busy day of classes, she felt buoyant and hopeful. Once again, she believed that she would win Noah, after all. But the buoyancy and the hope did not stop her from telling Rick that on more than one occasion his wife had been sleeping with Noah.

On the following afternoon, she was not surprised to learn that Olivia was in the hospital. Two girl friends who were allowed to visit her there returned to the campus to talk about her fall from a favorite stallion when she and her husband were playfully racing each other on a horse farm about ten miles from the Brown University campus. The fall had left her with a concussion; a black eye and a bruised, swollen face; and two broken fingers, around which she now wore splints. The friends spoke of how lucky Olivia was that her husband had been with her and had summoned medical attention in a timely manner.

She did not believe one word of the story. She knew Rick Blanchard too well to accept the riding accident as the cause of Olivia's injuries. Rick had given her the beating that she deserved. Nor did she visit Olivia in the hospital, though she would have liked to confront her and remind her that her present injuries were only the beginning of the pain that awaited her if she continued to sleep with Noah.

She was not even surprised when Rick challenged Noah to a boxing match in the school gym. If they had fought in any other place, they would have risked expulsion. Because they belonged to the university boxing team, their coach arranged a match between them that took place three weeks later and that their classmates witnessed. The coach was not aware that they were fighting because Noah had slept with Rick's wife. He and the dean who had approved of the match believed that the two young men, who were superb athletes, simply wanted to put their boxing skills to the test now that the season for competing with boxers from other schools had ended. She did not witness the match. Her abiding affection for Rick and her obsessive love for Noah persuaded her to stay away. But she heard later that evening that the men had waged a brutal fight. They had acquitted themselves supremely well, even though each of them had suffered injuries to the temple, eyes, ears, and jaw.

Rick suffered a dislocated shoulder, and Noah endured the pain of a concussion. The fight ended in a draw. Both men earned accolades from the crowd of students and professors who were there to observe their prowess. The popularity of both men increased. Many men and women on the campus compared them to the Greek warriors who had often tested their mettle by boxing with their friends. Other university persons who had attended the match regarded Noah and Rick as Renaissance men, because they excelled in various sports and in their academic studies.

The boxing match did not resolve the two men's hatred of one another. Instead, a new enmity grew between them, unforgiving and irrevocable.

Olivia, recently released from the hospital, did not attend the match for fear of rousing Rick's anger anew. Nor did she tell the police about his beating of her. But she did tell her father. She wanted him to help her get her marriage annulled.

When he heard the news of the beating, her father was enraged.

"Don't you worry," he told his daughter. "I'll speak to Rick. I'll fix his wagon. He won't beat you again."

"He's slapped me around a few times before," she explained, tearful and supplicating. "He hurt me then. But this time he went too far. I had to spend a week in the hospital."

Her father's empathy had its limits. His fatherly protectiveness kept him on her side. But his hardheartedness enabled him to understand Rick's point of view.

"You are married to the guy. What did you expect him to do when you jumped into bed with another man?"

"I couldn't help myself," Olivia murmured. "I love Noah. I've always loved him. And he loves me. He wants to marry me."

The news about Noah's wanting to marry his daughter roused Mr. Tanner's interest. For many years, he had wanted his daughter to marry Kendall Blake's son. Her marriage to Rick Blanchard had subverted that plan. It had also disappointed Kendall, who regarded the marriage between Noah and Olivia as the strongest confirmation of the bond between the Blake and Tanner families and a testament to the successful merger of their corporations. Now, with Rick out of the picture, that marriage might well take place.

"Are you sure that Noah wants to marry you?"

"Yes," Olivia said, while lying to him as well as to herself.

Her father was pleased.

"I'll have that talk with Rick as soon as possible. I'll pay him off. Rick's a smart young man. He'll take the money and run with it."

To this remark Olivia said nothing. She wanted to be freed of Rick, at least as her partner in marriage. But she did not care to hear that any man would be willing to leave her if he could be paid for it.

Within a week, Mr. Tanner had bought Rick out of his marriage to Olivia. He settled three million dollars on him and lined him up for a top spot with a Fortune 10 company after he was graduated from The Wharton School in Philadelphia.

All these things she learned from Rick during one of their private meetings at her parents' summer home in Newport. Though she was still living with Noah, she continued to enjoy an occasional weekend with Rick. On this particular weekend, they enjoyed some of the activities that had often quickened their intimate time together. They had flown to Newport in Rick's new Cessna. They had sailed, wind-stirred and free-spirited, over the sun-misted waters of Narragansett Bay. They had dined with some of Rick's Harvard friends in Boston. Then, after they returned to Newport, Rick had made vigorous love to her. On this weekend, there was an electric connection between them. They were both needy. They gave their bodies to each other, eager to solace and to be solaced. Now, looking back on that long-ago weekend, she saw it with new understanding. For her, the intimacy between Rick and her was not only an expression of her casual love of Rick. It was also an act of vengeance against Noah.

On the Monday morning that followed, she served up a breakfast of orange juice, waffles, blueberries, and coffee. It was then that Rick told her about his imminent divorce and about the money that Mr. Tanner was giving him so that Olivia might break free of their marriage.

"It's a big pay-off," he said. "And it comes with a promise of a great job in three years, after I've finished Wharton."

She had not counted on Rick's divorcing Olivia. She had thought that Olivia's fear of him, as well as her erotic bond with him, would have kept her in the marriage. She did not want Olivia to be free. She did not want her to pursue Noah. On this morning, while they were having breakfast, she told Rick how she felt.

"You ought to move on," he said. "Forget Noah. That guy could never fall in love with any woman. He's a narcissist. He'll sleep with plenty of women, but he won't marry any of them. They're not good enough for him."

"What about Olivia? Will Noah marry her?"

"Not if he has any say in the matter. Of course, his father and old man Tanner may make him offers he can't refuse."

"Meaning…?"

"Mr. Blake may threaten to disinherit Noah, if he doesn't marry Olivia. Both Blake and Tanner will give Noah plenty of money if he cooperates with them."

"He'll never do that," she protested. "He wants to stay with me. He said that this new fling with Olivia was temporary."

"He's no better than I am. I'm leaving Olivia because Tanner is paying me off and steering me to a path that will make me a very wealthy man. Tanner and Blake will pay off Noah to marry Olivia. He'll do their bidding. He has too much to lose otherwise."

"If what you say is true," she said, "there's going to be trouble. I'm not giving up Noah without a fight."

PART ONE

CHAPTER SEVEN

Charlotte

Wednesday Afternoon, 4 October 1967

Looking Back to 1952

At the beginning of that April in 1952, Charlotte made trouble by devising another plot that involved Noah. She got herself pregnant. She told herself that a child that their love had created would make a difference to their relationship. Noah would want to marry her. He would not abandon the child that carried his blood. The news of the child would surely dispel his self-centeredness. The new life that was growing inside her would inspire Noah's transformation. The being who was just now being formed and who was going to be a son or daughter of Noah Blake would put him in mind of the personal code of honor that had influenced him all through his adolescence. The child would be her greatest gift to him. Noah would cherish that gift. He would marry her, because it was the right thing to do.

So she told herself, unwilling then to admit that Noah was a ruthless man, casually leaving in his wake the wreckage of friendships that he had betrayed and love affairs that he had spurned.

Not even when Noah made clear his antipathy toward the child that was forming its identity within her body did she really believe that he was heartless. She understood his unease, and she could overlook it. The fact of the child's existence had alarmed him. He had not anticipated becoming a father so soon. He was not yet twenty-two. His natural instinct told him to break free of the responsibility.

"Get rid of it," he said, steely and adamant, when in mid-May she told him that she was carrying his baby.

In the days that followed, confronted as he was by her petitioning, he kept telling her to get rid of the baby. He also told her that their makeshift romance was over. From the start, he reminded her, they had agreed that they would go their separate ways after graduation.

"You'll have to make your way on your own," he told her on that bitter afternoon when, only a few days after graduation, he was packing his belongings and leaving the Brown University campus for good. "I won't be around for you to lean on."

"I've never asked much of you," she answered him. "I've made my way on my own before. I thought you wanted me to lean on you. I've played the game the way you wanted."

She remembered that her voice was nearly tremulous. She was pleading for his acceptance. Cautious yet urgent, she wanted him to comprehend the full weight of her dilemma. But his angry response, chained to self-control and contempt, made absolutely clear his pitiless abandonment of her.

"You're a cheat," he said. "You set a trap. You got yourself pregnant because you wanted me to stay around forever."

"Our baby *will* make a difference. You'll see."

"You're on your own," he said once again. "You and I are finished."

From this distance of fifteen years and for the second time within this hour remembering all of it, she went on pleading with Noah. Once again she heard his two college friends hurrying up the stairs to his apartment. They were eager to help him complete his packing so that they could begin the drive to Saranac Lake and to the exciting summer awaiting them. Whether these friends sensed the tension between Noah and her, she did not know. They were rugged young men who closed themselves off from any show of emotion. She took their cue and, while summoning a discreet cheerfulness, assisted them as well as Noah with the packing.

When the four of them had delivered Noah's belongings to his Bentley, his two friends sat in the car while she and Noah returned to the apartment to say their goodbyes.

He took hold of her shoulders and planted a kiss upon her forehead. He looked into her eyes and, for an instant, allowed himself a carefree grin. Then he brushed her lips with a kiss that carried no passion or even a trace of pity.

"Remember the good times," he said. "If you can't do that, then forget me. Forget us."

"I'll never forget you," she said. "How could I? I'll have your baby."

"Don't have it. Get rid of it."

Before she could answer him, he hurried away.

She ran after him, pleading with him as she followed him down the stairs.

"Wait! Don't leave like this. Listen to me. Please listen. If that's what you want, I will get rid of it. We can begin again in London."

When they had reached the bottom of the stairs, Noah threw out new, rancorous words. He did not turn to her. Nor did he pause as he hurried past the doorway and down the red brick stairs that brought him to the sidewalk and to his waiting car.

"We can never begin again. Our days together are all used up."

She quickly followed him as he took his place behind the wheel and started the engine. His two friends, one in the front passenger seat and the other in the rear of the car, kept their heads down, not caring to witness her shame or to reveal their conflicted emotions. Even now, so many years afterward, she could hear her voice screaming out her protest.

"You can't just walk out of my life now. It's not fair! It's not fair!"

The Bentley drove swiftly away, and she—all the while screaming her anguish—ran after it.

"I'll never let you go! Never! Never!"

Here in her home office fifteen years later, reassembling the human actions that drove that wretched scene, she wondered whether she had recalled it with the accuracy that anchors its awareness to truth. Was Noah as villainous as her memory of him insisted? Or was he merely an all-too-human male, freewheeling and self-centered, whose young fires were burning brightly and lighting his way into the wider world? His rejection of her and of the child they had conceived did cast a dark shadow upon him. Yet, after the passage of so many years, his repudiation of the trap that she had set for him seemed inevitable. She had gambled with the life of an unborn baby, and she had lost. He had hurried away from her, guarding his freedom and launching the first of many adventures in which she would play no part.

She did not forgive him then. She could not forgive him now. All through these fifteen years and against her conscious will, her hatred of him had lingered, adamant and furious.

She noticed his letter once again, there on the burnished mahogany of her desk. She had a sudden impulse to rip it up without reading it. Whatever news Noah was sending her could only disarrange the serenity that she had, with rigorous discipline and hard-won patience, brought into her life.

Why, after all these years, should he write to her? Was he asking for her forgiveness? Had some sudden cataclysm in his life—some life-altering experience—prodded this soul-searching? After all this time, why did he need to ease his conscience? No, she could not imagine that he was suffering recriminations for what he had done to her or that he was asking for her forgiveness. Self-willed reformation was beyond the Noah Blake that she remembered.

Besides, she was the one who had fired the Colt Cobra revolver. It was she who had tried to kill him.

Her hands grasped the letter as though she were about to tear it apart. But the memory of those unhappy days that preceded the shooting overtook her will. She did not tear the letter into small pieces and toss its undisclosed fragments into the wastepaper basket at the foot of her desk. Instead, she pushed the letter aside and, with the fierce animosity that she had kept at bay for all these careful years, recalled the two fateful meetings that precipitated her shooting of Noah and Olivia.

In the second week of June, she drove to the Blakes' palatial home in Greenwich, Connecticut. It was one of their summer residences. Mr. and Mrs. Blake spent most of their summertime here. They allowed their sons and their university friends to take over the Saranac Lake residence, with the proviso that they follow all the rules of propriety. A cadre of proficient servants, including a groundskeeper, two gardeners, a housekeeper, and a chef, maintained the property with meticulous care.

(Many years later, she too would own a grand home in Greenwich, though not so very close to the home of the Blakes. By that time, she was an immensely successful novelist who avoided all contact with the Blakes.)

The Blakes' home in Greenwich was a waterfront property on Long Island Sound that anchored its solidity to Gothic and Romanesque elements. Stone dominated the exterior of the building: fieldstone rubble walls and chimneys, limestone piers, and steeply pitched slate roofs. From inside the entrance hall, three steps led down to a long room, measuring about seventy feet in length, that encompassed the family room, the living room, and the library, each with its own fireplace. A floor-to-ceiling wall of mahogany-framed-leaded-glass windows and French doors offered spectacular views of Long Island Sound and the radiance of afternoon sunlight. Enormous beams of antique white oak and reclaimed-chestnut floors enhanced the elegance of the room.

She was no stranger to splendor. The four homes that her parents owned, in Manhattan, Newport, Santa Barbara, and London, contained an equivalent splendor that was both luxurious and tasteful. Her love and knowledge of architectural structures and interior designs enabled her to scan and to appreciate the vocabulary of the rooms as she passed quickly by them and followed the tall, elderly butler up the stairs that brought her to a second-floor sitting room and face-to-face with Ruth Blake, Noah's mother. Her attention to the décor that played off the wood, stone, and glass of both exterior and interior subdued at least a little the tension that had threatened to overtake her as she made her way to the meeting with Mrs. Blake.

She had met Ruth Blake on many occasions—some of them at the grand soirées that the Blakes, the Benningtons, and her own family hosted two or three times a year. At these dinner parties, she had sometimes conversed with her about art, theater and films, and charity projects. She often caught a glimpse of her with married couples who were her contemporaries and with her husband at New York supper clubs and concert halls. More than a few times, she had crossed paths with her at ski lodges in Lausanne, Switzerland, and in Stowe, Vermont. She and Mrs. Blake had also shared enjoyable conversations at afternoon teas in the Blakes' Manhattan penthouse and at her parents' apartment on Sutton Place. In those years, she was blossoming as a proficient young woman. She had made a success at the sumptuous ball that declared her a beautiful debutante. She had excelled as a university student. She had proved herself an adept swimmer, a superb horse rider, and an agile tennis player. Mrs. Blake had always expressed a genuine respect for her accomplishments and an appreciation of the self-possession that enabled her to negotiate and maintain her freedom with the young men who were courting her favor.

On all those occasions, she had never met Noah. He was away at school or out of the country. Without the burden of a tangled relationship with him, her meetings with Ruth Blake were always pleasant and usually exhilarating. Invariably, Mrs. Blake would close their conversations with words that she offered as good counsel and as a warning.

"Protect your freedom, my dear," she would say. "Don't give it away. Don't sell yourself short."

Her parting words became something of a trademark, a verbal emblem defining who she was and suggesting an unspoken part of her history.

From her carefree girlfriends, whose parents knew the Blakes well, and from her taciturn mother, she had learned about Ruth Blake's unhappy life with Kendall Blake. Before her marriage, Ruth had enjoyed life-loving experiences with her parents, Terence and Barbara Grainger. In those years, she and her brother and two sisters, who were a few years older, had traveled the globe with their parents. South Africa, India, Europe, Australia, China, and the United States had made their itinerary vivid and even astonishing. A sense of adventure and of the unexpected had inspirited their relationship. Her father was an eminent art dealer who brought his expertise as an art historian and his business acumen to the discovery and acquisition of some of the greatest canvases. His purchase and sale of these canvases and his wise investments on the stock market made him a wealthy man. Ruth Blake's mother, often referred to in their private circle as a bluestocking, was also more than ordinary. She was a gifted author and illustrator of children's books.

Both parents were a positive influence upon Ruth's awareness of her own gifts and upon the various transformations of her individuality. Like them, she was drawn to the world of art. From her early teens and on into her twenties, she established herself as a talented painter. In the nineteen-thirties, ravaged as the world remained after its World War One traumas, her hard-edged canvases expressed a world torn apart by the greed and betrayal of wayward leaders and by the hatred and prejudice that human beings often directed against men and women whose skin color and personal beliefs were not like their own. Her parents and her friends saw her early work as an American extension of Cubism. Her art was at times close to that of Léger, because of her use of color: bright and clear, solid and flat. She also worked through the styles of Picasso, Miró, and Kandinsky. She developed a personal Surrealism that verged on Abstract Expressionism. Dramatic forms coagulated and merged, as fluid as the rich paint creating them.

Art critics in New York, Paris, and London noticed her work. Galleries invited her to exhibit her paintings. *Time*

Magazine ran a cover story about her. Then, suddenly, at the age of twenty-eight, she disappeared from the scene. She had married Kendall Blake, who compelled her in the sixth year of their marriage to abandon her painting. He, as well as his parents and their circle, did not approve of her maintaining so public a profile as that of an artist whose avant-garde canvases often stirred controversy and sometimes offended politically conservative spectators. Kendall threatened to divorce her and to take full custody of their four sons. Without any melodrama attending her decision, she capitulated to her husband's threats. She cut away part of her soul. She murdered her spirit and did not count the cost. Her closest friends guessed that she no longer loved her husband. But she stayed with him, fearful of losing a respectable place in society and the well-ordered life that enabled her to hold her senses still. At least some of the time and despite her ambivalent relations with her husband and their four sons, she found solace in her role as a devoted wife and mother. She made peace with the private destitution that had overtaken her life. She busied herself with her country club friends, with charity projects, and with the work of emerging painters, poets, and writers whom she supported with generous grants and fellowships. Occasionally, she took refuge from her disappointed life by drinking ninety-proof vodka, scotch, or bourbon.

Whenever, as the promising debutante Charlotte Scott, she happened to meet her, Ruth Blake never spoke of these things. Always, though, she would remind her to protect her individuality.

"Don't give up your freedom to anyone," she would say. "Guard it. Cherish it."

"I will," she always answered her. "I won't let anyone steal me from myself."

Mrs. Blake's soft blue eyes would carefully study her. No new words explained her melancholic glance. But then, just before they bade each other farewell, she would alter her countenance and summon a smile. She did not care to mar their friendly meeting with any words that might reveal the heartache and disappointment of her marriage to Kendall Blake.

The warmth of these meetings had almost always displaced the stories that her friends and her mother had told her about Ruth Blake. The meetings were, she came to believe, special occasions that Mrs. Blake—Noah's mother— had come to cherish.

But her meeting with Mrs. Blake on this June afternoon in 1952 was an altogether different matter. They would not be discussing art or theater or charity projects. They would be talking about her pregnancy and about Noah's refusal to save her reputation by marrying her.

She had phoned Mrs. Blake two days earlier to arrange the visit. As gracious as ever, Mrs. Blake sounded eager to see her.

Even at the start of their meeting, she saw that Mrs. Blake had been drinking her favorite Long Island Iced Tea, which contained vodka, tequila, rum, gin, and triple sec. She guessed that this extraordinary woman, for whom she felt genuine affection, had been drinking for a few hours. The misty gaze and the slight tremor of her hands belied the inherent discipline of her straight-backed posture and her quick-witted remarks. Nevertheless, she showed no other sign of having drunk too much. She was, in fact, immaculately groomed. Her silver hair, her oval face, and a jaw that was narrower than her cheekbones gave her a patrician appearance. Her light skin was flawless, even though vague lines beneath and at the corners of her blue eyes diminished some of her radiance. On that afternoon, she was wearing a powder-blue linen dress and white spectator pumps with blue patent accents stitched on to the shoes and lined with bronze metal rivets. Diamond stud earrings complemented and enhanced the formal look of her diamond wedding ring.

She herself was wearing a white silk blouse, mauve pink high-waist sailor pants, and beige sandals. Her raven-black hair glowed, caressed as it was by soft sunlight streaming into the wide expanse of the room. Only after she greeted Mrs. Blake did she remove her dark glasses. She would not use the glasses to conceal her feelings from this admirable woman. She intended to tell her all of the truth, without flinching and without portraying herself as a victim.

She began right away, right after the butler had brought her some lemonade and after she had sipped it to ease her lips, which suddenly felt parched, and to calm her tension, which might otherwise make her voice raspy.

"It's about Noah," she began.

"I thought it might be," Mrs. Blake said. "I'd heard, though not from Noah, who never discusses his private life with me, that you and Noah have been living together."

"We have," she answered her. "And now I'm carrying his baby."

Hearing these words, Ruth Blake at first said nothing. Only a slight crease upon her brow suggested her concern and her solicitude. Then, as though she were brushing away the stillness that had momentarily hovered about her, she asked three probing questions.

"Have you told Noah?"

"Yes."

"How does he feel about the baby?"

"He doesn't want me to have it."

"How can I help?"

"I thought that you and Mr. Blake might talk to him. You might make him see that I'm the right girl for him. I love him. I could make him very happy because of that love. I want to devote my life to him."

Her words brought a benevolent smile to Mrs. Blake's lips.

"You sound very romantic, my dear, and very idealistic. You are setting yourself up to be hurt, because Noah is neither romantic nor idealistic."

"I believe that my love will make a difference. It will change him."

Mrs. Blake took another long swallow of her cocktail. Then, she fell silent while she went on observing her with a pensive glance that was both maternal and sorrow-laden. Only later did she imagine that Mrs. Blake needed that stillness and her studious regard of the young woman who sat opposite her before she was ready to summon the words meant to help her. Only in retrospect did she understand that, on this summer afternoon, Ruth Blake's drinking had set her free from the rules that her marriage to Kendall Blake had imposed upon her.

"You're lucky. You can get rid of the pregnancy. There's still time for you to escape the prison of being married to a Blake."

"I want the baby. It belongs to Noah, too. The baby will keep Noah in my life."

"You're being foolish. Noah will only wreck your life. He'll never make any woman happy."

"I'll be happy just being with him."

"Think, girl. Think! Don't squander your chances of making a good life for yourself. Forget Noah. He's selfish, callous, and domineering. He's on his way to becoming as rotten as his father. Even if my husband compelled Noah to marry you, there would be no happiness in the marriage. The Blakes would see to that. They'd crush your individuality. They'd suppress your natural instincts and your creative impulses. They'd brainwash you. They'd make you believe that you were not a suitable wife and mother if you challenged the rules that make you an acceptable member of our class."

"I love him. I can't give him up."

"Let him go. For your own good, let him go."

"I can't. I can't."

"He's going to marry Olivia Tanner."

"He never will. He told me so."

"His father will see that he does marry her. Kendall regards the marriage as a profitable arrangement—a business coup that strengthens the merger of the Blake and Tanner Corporations."

"Olivia will only bring Noah trouble."

"Don't be fooled by her. In spite of her show of individuality and her fits of rebellion, Olivia is made from the same cloth as I am, and as her mother and all the other matrons who have compromised their freedom. She'll follow all the rules."

She was disappointed by Mrs. Blake's blunt appraisal of the troubled situation involving Olivia, Noah, and herself. She felt hurt and even angry.

"I came here because I believed that you would help me."

"I thought I was, by telling you the truth."

She softened her voice now. She needed Ruth Blake's motherly affection. She needed this good woman to speak the words that would give her hope.

"If you knew how it's been between Noah and me, you wouldn't say those things."

Intuitive and solicitous, Ruth Blake recognized her need. She was going to say the words that might grant her some hope. But she was also going to qualify those words, binding them firmly to her honest appraisal.

"I'll speak to my husband about you and Noah, if that's what you want. But it won't do any good."

"Not even though I'm going to have Noah's baby?"

"Not even."

"I believe in Noah. I believe that he is better than you say. He'll come round. He'll do the right thing by me."

"I wish he would, if that's what you want, my dear. But I don't think he'll come round. Count yourself lucky."

Mrs. Blake rose from her chair now. Their meeting was over. There was nothing more to say. The hardheartedness that this unhappy woman held within herself, secret and protective, was compelling her to close herself off from problems that she was unable to resolve. She did not like feeling helpless before the dilemma of a young woman whom she had always regarded with motherly affection. Every day must have been a struggle for her. In her home, she was a lone woman whose fate had cast her in a company of willful and overbearing men who happened to be her husband and their four sons.

Now, disheartened by her meeting with Ruth Blake, she turned to her own parents.

A few days after her meeting with Mrs. Blake, she chose a quiet time to tell her parents that she was pregnant and that Noah was the father. They were sitting within the porch of the family's Newport summer home. It was two o'clock on a Monday night, shortly after her parents had said their goodbyes to the twenty-six guests who had attended one of the grand parties that they, Gregory and Eleanor Scott, had hosted with their customary exuberance.

On that evening, she made certain that she pleased her parents. Surrounded by sophisticated and influential guests, she had done all the right things. She had spoken all the appropriate words. That weekend, she sailed with them in the regatta of boats that journeyed smoothly over blue-green, sun-misted waters. She swam with them in the heated pool within the east wing of their three-story house. She dined with them in the glamorous banquet tents that rose from manicured lawns and that looked out upon the wind-stirred, ocean waters. She danced with the CEO of the Brazilian corporation that was negotiating a partnership with her father's company. Later, demure and quick-witted at the banquet table where she was seated with him and his wife, she conversed with both of them in fluent Portuguese about subjects as diverse as the novels of Jorge Amado, the poems of Adalcinda Camarão, Brazilian football, Brazil's water polo team, Andalusian horses, and Britain's Gloster Meteor—the first jet aircraft of the Brazilian Air Force.

She danced with other impressive guests, including ambassadors from Sweden and Germany, a classical violinist from Australia, and executives from CBS, U.S. Steel, and Kaiser Aluminum. She was careful to include their wives in the conversation, drawing upon her knowledge of gardening, architecture, American and French cuisine, and the current style of clothes that appealed to fashionable American women and that often appeared in the films of Gene Tierney, Claudette Colbert, and Joan Fontaine. All these guests with whom she had conversed found her intelligent and appealing. They also thought well of her parents, who had helped their daughter to become a cultivated and self-possessed young woman. So they said, as they dispensed their praise with delicate formality and with the pleasure that derives from meeting a young person who reflected their own values.

She might have enjoyed the unintended irony of their remarks. She was, after all, well aware of how far she had traveled from their conservative expectations. But, all through the weekend and into the early Monday hours when the guests were leaving, there lingered in her mind the worry of telling her parents that she was pregnant. Solaced by the success of their party, her parents were seated within the enclosed, wrap-around porch that looked out upon the wind-stirred waters of the bay and upon the glow of the moon that illumined those waters and caught sight of a yacht making its way to Nantucket, perhaps, or to Hyannis. The stone fireplace that anchored the porch brought a warmer glow to the late hour and to an untypical chill in the summer air. If the success of their party solaced her parents, the sight of the porch and all its amenities eased her tension, at least momentarily. On this night, she viewed familiar objects with clarified perception and found comfort in their homespun ambiance and their stylish subtexts. Never before had she noticed so clearly or appreciated so completely the twig chandelier, the wicker chairs with their paisley cushions, the teak cocktail and dining tables, the long, white curtain, and the blue-and-white throw pillows and outdoor rug. The porch and all of its pristine conveniences provided an ideal setting for mollifying her father's anger and her mother's dismay when she told them her news.

Before she spoke the words that would alter her parents' understanding of the fallible young woman that she had become, she joined them in a post-midnight toast meant to celebrate their success as the hosts of a glamorous and exciting party. She and her mother were sipping Veuve Clicquot from Champagne stem glasses. Her father was enjoying scotch on the rocks served in a gold-banded tumbler made from finely cut crystal. In this late hour, after they had banqueted with their friends and after they had danced and laughed with them and allowed themselves to be caught up inside the colorful whirligig of their party, they were experiencing a rare contentment. Everything had gone well. With affable ease, they had maintained all the rules of decorum. They had pleased steadfast friends and delighted new acquaintances. For this special evening, they had kept the dark aspects of the world at bay. Their party had invoked an all-encompassing happiness.

She felt a pang of guilt as she pushed herself to speak the words that would dispel that happiness and dissolve in an instant her parents' attention to the wind-glanced waters of the bay, the moon glow caressing those waters, and the pristine yacht hurrying toward new, nocturnal adventures. She noticed the serenity of her mother, seated as she was in a wicker chair and sipping her Champagne. In the after-years that followed that evening, she had frequently studied the color photos that professional photographers had captured during the party. At forty-six, her mother was the epitome of a very attractive society matron. The subtle traceries of age that attended her could not yet diminish her inherent radiance. Her fair, Scandinavian complexion and her tall, slim figure enhanced her natural beauty. Tonight, she wore a tea-length lace evening dress that had won much praise because of its absolute rightness for her. Its three-quarter-length sleeves revealed the elegance of her lower arms and her diamond-clad wrists. The light plum, summery hues of the dress served well her gray-flecked, titian hair that was pulled neatly back to form a coil at the nape of her neck.

On that evening, her father's strong, chiseled features often beamed with his matter-of-fact assurance and his capacity for enjoying the moment. World-weariness had not yet overtaken him. Nor, at the age of forty-eight, had his protective cynicism prevented him from seizing every challenge and relishing even the most formidable battles that took place in prestigious boardrooms and in the conference rooms of government officials. His tall, brawny physique enhanced his vigor, which shrewdly yoked his grit to a well-harnessed arrogance. For this festive summer gathering, he was wearing an off-white dinner jacket and black flat-front dress slacks. His casual, freewheeling posture subdued the formal look of the jacket and its accessories that included a shawl collar, a single off-white button closure, a white shirt and black bow tie, four buttons on each cuff—all in white mother of pearl, and black patent leather shoes. His prematurely white hair gave him a credible dignity on this special night when he was in the company of friends, but also on all the days and nights when he was under fire from duplicitous adversaries. On evenings like the one he experienced at this lavish summer party that he and her mother hosted in Newport on that second weekend of June in 1952, his tough-minded understanding of the world gave no quarter to thoughts of adversaries. Instead, he expressed a keen appreciation of the rock-solid friends with whom he shared Wall Street stories and the cherished recollections of adventurous vacations in South Africa, Australia, and South America.

Now, impatient to send out a distress signal to her parents and guilt-ridden because she was dispelling their contentment, she hurried to tell them her news.

"Something important has changed for me," she began. "I think you will want to know what it's all about."

Her father and her mother looked away from the moon-glanced waters of the bay and gave her their full attention. Her furrowed brow and the tension in her voice were all they needed to comprehend her unhappiness.

Her mother was the first to answer her.

"You surprise me," she said. "All evening, you were the belle of the ball. I've never seen you so delighted by any of our other summer parties."

"I was determined to be happy tonight," she answered her. "I wouldn't allow the Fates to slap me around. I held my head high and laughed at them."

Intuitive, her mother sensed at once the gravity of her unhappiness. She urged her to tell more.

"Why did you need to do that? Why did you need to laugh at the Fates?"

"I'm going to have Noah Blake's baby, and he doesn't want any part of me."

A hush took hold of her parents. They glanced at one another as they struggled to conceal their dismay. She knew her parents well. They were not shocked by her news. Nor were they priming themselves for a melodramatic scene. In the stillness of this moment, they were calculating their bearings. They were charting the course they would follow and the counsel they would offer her.

She, too, held herself still. Patient yet strong-willed, she waited to hear all that they would say to her and to imagine all that they would leave unsaid.

Her father was the first to speak.

"You are not the first woman to get yourself into this sort of mess," he told her. "The important thing is that you don't allow it to ruin your life."

Her father was offering her even-tempered words. From him, she expected no less. Not for him was a tyrannical and judgmental persona. Most of the fathers in their circle might rage at or even disown an errant offspring. But Gregory Blake's paternal loyalty was stronger than theirs.

"I'm trying not to," she began answering him before her voice quavered and before she had to pause momentarily to distance herself from the self-pity that she loathed. "I'm trying not to ruin my life."

"I'm glad to hear that," her father said. "I admire you most when you show your tough edge. Besides, you wouldn't be very convincing as a helpless female. You've made your way as an independent woman for a few years now. You know the score. The world doesn't treat a helpless woman very well. As a matter of fact, the world doesn't treat a strong woman well, either. But, whether or not it disguises its feelings, the world accords her a grudging respect."

"I'm prepared to fight my own battles," she said. "I don't intend to lean on you and Mother. I'd just like you to be on my side."

"Of course we are on your side," her mother said. "You've committed no crime. You've simply had the bad luck to fall in love with a man who doesn't love you—at least, not enough to marry you."

"Noah Blake has used you," her father said. "You've been a convenient source of pleasure for him. You've been a means to that end and nothing more. He's a bastard, and you are well rid of him."

"I still love him."

Her mother came into it again.

"How, in Heaven's name, can you? The man has got you pregnant, and he's discarded you. He's not worthy of your love."

Anguish overtook her once again. In murmuring tones, as though she were alone in the room and speaking to herself, the grievous words rushed out of her.

"I know. I know. But I can't help myself. I don't know how I am going to live without him."

Her mother tried to console her.

"You'll find a way. We'll help you to find it."

Her father asked a probing question.

"What do you plan to do about the baby?"

"I haven't decided."

"You could get rid of it," he said. "There's still time. Everything could be done in Switzerland. No one need know."

"I would know. I would always know. All my life I would have to admit that I'd killed a child that belonged to Noah as much as to me. I would have killed the son or daughter of the only man that I will ever love."

"You'll fall in love again," her mother said. "You'll see. Give yourself time."

Always the pragmatic realist, her father resisted his wife's sentimental prophecy. Instead, he gave her a much darker forecast of the life awaiting her.

"If you keep the baby, you're going to have a rough time of it. Our circle may protect you. They may even conceal your so-called shame from everyone outside our group. But they will look upon you differently. You've broken the rules. You've allowed yourself to be indiscreet."

"I'll get by. I'll know how to handle them."

"Yes. I believe you will. But have you thought about what happens to the baby? What name will you give her or him?"

"I don't know."

"It will be a rare man who is willing to marry you if he finds out that you are an unwed mother."

"I may not want to marry."

"That won't do the baby any good. The baby will need a father who is willing to give him his name."

"I'll give the baby Noah's name. The child will be a Blake."

"You may face legal problems."

"So will Noah, if I choose to involve lawyers."

Her father reflected upon her words. He wanted to be on her side. He wanted to help her devise a workable solution for her problem. He wanted the solution to be hers, rather than his own. After all, she would have to live with whatever decision she chose to make about the baby and about her future. As though he were examining a spreadsheet that offered a variety of solutions, he set forth a different scenario that he'd quickly drawn from his street-wise calculations and from a matrix of strategies and remedies.

"If you keep the baby, I could have my team of lawyers speak to Kendall Blake. He'll want to keep his name and Noah's out of the newspapers and out of the courts. I don't think it will be difficult to prove that Noah is the father of the child you are carrying. A blood test will do that. Your university friends will testify that you have been living with Noah and that he has been your lover for two years. Kendall and I and our lawyers might arrange a city hall marriage. Noah can walk away from it after he's signed the necessary papers. You'll be legitimate then and so will your baby."

"I don't want to do that to Noah. If I don't bring the lawyers into it, maybe he'll come back to me."

Now her mother came into it again.

"Don't fool yourself," she said. "Don't be trapped by wishful thinking."

Her father was even more abrasive. He was not interested in letting Noah off the hook. Her refusal to compel Noah to marry her pushed her as well as her parents onto a far more dubious path. Neither he nor the board members of his corporation would be pleased. His next words were blunt and accusatory. He was disappointed in her. He'd waited for her to make the right decision about her dilemma. He'd expected her to be smart enough to avoid the harsh consequences of having placed her trust in a selfish and uncaring man. She wasn't thinking straight. She was involving all of them in the free fall of her reputation. With no further hesitation, he told her as much.

"Without a marriage license, you're setting yourself up for a scandal," he said. "Your mother and I will be involved. You'll tarnish our name."

The truth of his words made her pause. She could not find the words that might gainsay his remark.

Her mother noticed her hesitation. She quickly set forth the plan that she'd hoped her daughter would have chosen without any urging from her mother or father.

"You don't have to get married," she said. "You don't have to keep the baby. You can turn this thing around. You can make something good from your situation. You can have the baby in Switzerland, perhaps, and you can give it up to a couple who can't have a child of their own."

For a moment, she considered the character of her parents. There was a hard-heartedness hidden beneath their usually even-tempered and agreeable manner. The world was a rough place. To protect their interests and the wellbeing of their loved ones, they drew upon that hard-heartedness without compunction or vacillation. They expected her to draw upon the same hard-heartedness that she had often used as a strategy for outwitting her adversaries and eluding the recoil of her misdeeds.

She respected the shrewdness of their calculations. But she resisted their plan.

"I'm keeping the baby," she told them. "The baby will be my lifeline to Noah. After I have the baby, he'll see things differently. He'll come back to me."

Her father reminded her of the way things stood.

"I heard that Noah's going to marry Olivia Tanner."

Angry, she hastened to refute his remark.

"That's not true. Noah will never marry her. He told me so."

Her father persisted.

"His parents want that marriage to take place. Nobody says 'No' to Kendall Blake. Not even his son."

"It's not true, I tell you. It's not true. It will never be true."

Her father's face softened. He studied her with a melancholy that he could not conceal.

"I hope you're right," he said. "This is one time that I don't mind being proved wrong."

PART ONE

CHAPTER EIGHT

Charlotte

Wednesday Afternoon, 4 October 1967

Looking Back to Tuesday Afternoon, 17 June 1952

And to Wednesday, 2 July 1952,

The Afternoon and Evening of the Shooting,

And Some of the Years That Followed

But her father was right. A few days after she had spoken with her parents, she heard news of Noah and Olivia. Jennifer Crawford and Nancy Lange, who had been her classmates and sorority sisters at Brown University, mentioned—as casual remarks during a Newport luncheon she shared with them at her parents' beach home—that Noah was going to marry Olivia. Her parents were spending a few days in Vermont with her favorite aunt. Except for the housekeeper, the cook, two groundskeepers, and two or three other household assistants, she and her friends were alone on the property.

The day was raw and overcast. Smoky clouds hovered in the sky with intimations of rain. For that reason, she and her friends were dining inside the house. Jameson, who was her parents' middle-aged, meticulous butler, and Giselle, who was a young, efficient maid recently arrived from the Provençal region of France, were serving the lunch on the glass-enclosed patio that overlooked the teal-blue waters of the lake. From their places at the lunch table, they could observe the pristine-white yawls and multi-colored sailboats that were hurrying across the breeze-tossed waters. They saw in the faraway distance as well the cloud-shadowed green hills and the jagged limestone rocks that rose out of the lake as though they were the fragments of a discarded world. Because Jameson and Giselle were often circling the table as they served the meal with their usual expertise and with the deft subtleties that kept their presence unobtrusive, she and her friends regarded the setting as private. They conversed freely about the subjects that mattered most to them on that Tuesday afternoon in June 1952. What mattered most to her two friends was their telling her as gently as they could that a tremendous change was about to take place in Noah's life. They wanted her to know about this change before less friendly acquaintances caught her off-guard and told her the news while they studied her dismay and her anguish.

Jennifer and Nancy took turns as they told her of the change and while they gently urged her to activate the self-possession and the resilience that had always, before Noah, reflected her strong-minded capacities. They had to repeat their words because she would not at first accept them. The news that they brought her would not have surprised her, if she had been willing to admit the failure of her relationship with Noah. But she could not admit that failure. Nor could she fully comprehend the inevitable finish of her affair with Noah.

She remembered all over again, as though the scene were only now unfolding, the significance of the words that Jennifer and Nancy were telling her.

The Blakes and the Tanners were planning a lavish engagement party to be held at Saranac Lake on the Fourth of July. On that day, Noah and Olivia would reveal the date in early autumn when their marriage would take place in New York.

"It can't be true," she protested when Jennifer and Nancy told her the news. "Noah will never marry Olivia. How could he ever trust her after she walked out on him to marry Rick Blanchard? Your news is merely a rumor—idle gossip that will fade away the moment that Noah heads out to London for graduate studies."

"It is true," Jennifer insisted. Her dark red hair and her sun-tanned features enhanced her well-bred appearance. She made her remark with the courtesy and the decorum that her privileged background required her to maintain. "It is not idle gossip."

Nancy, a good-natured blonde who also belonged to their class and who always upheld the rules of civility, reinforced the truth of Jennifer's assertion. Although she was as polite and as even-tempered as Jennifer, Nancy's manner was more straightforward and more matter-of-fact.

"Olivia's mother is spreading the news. She and her husband are delighted that Noah has asked Olivia to marry him."

After all these years, she recalled the empathetic way in which her two friends were studying her reaction to their news. They were good friends. They sensed her pain. They wanted to help her, if they could. They brought her this unhappy news before any gloating adversaries might hurry to tell her of Noah's impending marriage. They wanted her to be on guard. They wanted her to hold her head high, as if whatever was happening in Noah's life no longer mattered to her. They knew that, in spite of her break-up with Noah, she still loved him.

"Forget Noah," Jennifer advised her with a softer voice that meant to comfort her. "Move on to someone who is absolutely right for you."

"How can I do that?" she asked her, bereft and broken-hearted and untypically tearful. "How do I fall out of love with the only man that I can ever love?"

"Stop making Noah into someone he never was," Jennifer answered her. "He's not Mister Perfect. He's not a god. He's a fallible human being who has given you a hard time. He's not worth your tears."

Then, because they wanted to cheer her up, Jennifer and Nancy changed the subject. They began talking of the winter vacations that would bring them and their current boyfriends to St. Moritz for skiing, ice-skating, and tobogganing. They also spoke about the New York shows that they had recently seen, including the new Rodgers and Hammerstein musical *The King and I* with Yul Brynner and Gertrude Lawrence, and Samuel Taylor's sophisticated comedy *Sabrina Fair* with Margaret Sullavan and Joseph Cotten. They diverted her attention, as well, to thoughts of the coming winter's new fashions and to the stunning creations of the new French couturier Hubert de Givenchy, including a chic shirtdress and an elegant Oxford-gray wool suit with a cinch-waist, a double-breasted scoop-necked jacket, and a slim, calf-length vented skirt. They talked as well of the New York-based fashion designer Oleg Cassini, with his creation of simple, geometric dresses in sumptuous fabrics and tailored suits with oversized buttons and boxy jackets.

She never forgot the kindness they extended to her on that day. Even now she was surprised by the success of her friendship with them all through their university years and through all the years afterward. They were so different from her. They were relatively staid women. They were safe. They had always been in awe of her because of her adventurous ways. Only in retrospect could she now regret that their sisterly conversation on that cloud-shadowed afternoon in 1952 could not entirely dispel her dark thoughts. A voice within herself kept telling her that, if

Noah chose not to marry her, she would make certain that he married no other woman.

During the next two weeks, she often telephoned Noah at his parents' home at Saranac Lake. Nancy and Jennifer had confirmed what she already knew. Noah was vacationing there until he began his graduate studies at Cambridge Law School in London. Whenever she telephoned him, though, the Blakes' senior butler told her that Noah was sailing or water-skiing or that he was out of town. Each time she called, she told the butler her name and gave him her telephone number so that Noah would call her back. But Noah never returned her calls. His failure to call her was anchored, she imagined, to his adamant refusal to bring her back into his life. Though he knew about the baby that she was carrying, he had turned away from her. All through these last two weeks in June, she brought to her memory of their two years together a new and rancorous perspective. The hatred that she now sometimes felt for him had been growing within the most secret recesses of her heart. Her love for him, as impulsive as it was erotic and obsessive, had turned ambivalent and self-destructive. After two years of enduring Noah's casual affection, melded as it was with his apparent indifference, her love of Noah had complicated its powers. That love had made silent partners of bitterness and malice. Only now was she willing to admit that enmity and malice were the militant sentries watching over her. Hidden within her heart, they were waiting to act on her behalf. She had only to give her consent and they would unleash their fury against the man who had betrayed and then spurned her.

Yet, despite her realistic appraisal of Noah's speckled character and her conflicted feelings about him, she still loved him. She wanted to believe that, if she petitioned him once more, he would see things differently. Although he had rejected similar appeals only a few weeks earlier, his need to resist his father's threat of disinheritance if he did not marry Olivia Tanner might compel him to run away with her, romantic Charlotte Scott, whose seductive charms always thrilled him and who treated him as if he were a god. His rebellious spirit might then send a message to his father that he, the usually reliable son, was not to be taken for granted or pushed around. This was the scenario, contrived from wishful thinking rather than from realistic appraisal, that pushed her forward. Surely, if she could speak with Noah face to face, she would convince him that the baby he had helped her to create was going to bring tremendous happiness into their lives. With these thoughts in mind, she made a plan as extemporaneous as it was decisive. She was determined to have that face-to-face meeting with Noah. The timing could not be better. In days past, the Saranac Lake parties had never failed to brighten Noah's spirits. During the forthcoming holiday celebrations, he might look upon her with new, affirmative eyes. Nancy and Jennifer had mentioned that Noah would be there, enjoying a freewheeling summer day with his friends. They themselves would also be there, with their boyfriends.

On Wednesday, the second of July, she hurried away from Newport to set her plan in motion. Everything about the plan was clear to her now. At five o'clock that morning, she left her parents' home while they and the household staff were sleeping and began the six-hour drive to Saranac Lake. The gleaming sun that was peering over the horizon quickened her senses. She accepted it, as well as the temporary turquoise of the sky and the perfectly white clouds, as good omens. She was driving her new Mercedes-Benz, pristine with its silver-grey exterior, its saffron-beige interior leather, and its interior bamboo trim. If anyone had asked her why she had placed a Colt Cobra revolver in her purse, she would have answered with the artfulness that smoothly consents to its duplicity. She needed protection from the highway thieves who lately had hijacked more than a few cars that lone women were driving. After they robbed them, they raped them. Sometimes, they killed them. She was aware that these highway thieves usually attacked their victims at night. But driving alone in these uncertain times even in daylight was dangerous. She would be foolish not to carry a revolver.

So she told herself on that fateful Wednesday morning in July when she hurried toward Saranac Lake and toward Noah Blake, who still believed that happiness for him would be a life-long inheritance.

She arrived at the east wing of the Blakes' summer estate shortly before noon. Lars, the Danish second butler who today was serving as a young, rugged sentry that kept away the uninvited, and his brother Kurt, who was functioning as an efficient valet, recognized her at once. They stood tall and militant at the sturdy cedar door of the shingle-and-stone main house. They did not ask her to show them the monogrammed invitation that the Blakes had sent to all their guests, though not to her. They accepted her being there as both appropriate and natural. She was wearing a checked shirt knotted at the waist and made even more stylish with its collar and sleeves turned up. White shorts hugged her slim form and white ballet flats completed the summery look. It was the right look for a July celebration. With their carefully modulated glances, Lars and Kurt approved of her appearance. She belonged here, at the Blakes' party weekend. They did not know that she was carrying the Colt Cobra revolver inside her white purse. At the rim of her conscious awareness, there lived vivid and plausible the belief that she might need the revolver to protect herself against thieves. Only later, after the terrible hour that she was now entering was finished, did she admit to herself the reason for carrying the revolver. She had not let go of the idea that, if Noah refused to stand by her, she would kill him and, right afterwards, kill herself.

"Good day, Miss Scott," Lars said as he greeted her with a precisely calibrated decorum. His courteous smile and respectful manner pleased her. In that hour, so ordinary a gesture as a servant's dutiful solicitude eased her tension.

"Good day to you, too," she answered him, "and to your brother."

"We hope that you enjoy your visit," Kurt said by way of greeting her as she handed him the keys to her Mercedes.

"I intend to do just that."

In an instant, he had started the engine and was heading toward the twenty-car garage in the north wing of the house.

Mrs. Conway, the head housekeeper, whose matronly figure matched her motherly appreciation of Noah's friends, offered her a warm "hello" that told her that Noah and his friends were outdoors.

"You'll find them everywhere you look, but not in the same area," the good woman remarked, jovial yet soft-spoken. "It's summer, and they want to make every bit of it their own."

She knew this house well. During the two preceding summers, she and Noah had spent many happy days here.

Mrs. Conway quickly guided her to the wrap-around, glass-enclosed patio in the south wing of the house. There, she saw at once the blue-gray sheen of the lake and, in the hazy distance, three or four sailboats and yawls briskly moving across the quickened waters. Nearer than that, all along the full span of the patio in which she and Mrs. Conway stood and across the expansive greenery of the lawn that stretched its manicured beauty to the white sands of the private beach, she caught sight of six or seven couples in yellow, blue, or white swimsuits who were diving into the lake or emerging from its sun-blanched waters.

She thanked Mrs. Conway for accompanying her to the patio and then hurried down the steps that brought her to the edge of the cobalt green lawn and to her new awareness of the large party tents with cathedral window sidewalls that five workmen were assembling for the Fourth of July celebration that was only two days away. She saw that they had constructed six of the tents and had furnished them with red, white, and blue tent liners, pole drapes, and floral hangings. In each of these assembled tents, two of the workmen were placing six white cedar tables and chairs that would accommodate twenty-four guests. Mrs. Anderson, creative and meticulous, and three of the Blakes' proficient maids were decorating each table with floral centerpieces and carefully laying place settings of monogrammed china with red, white, and blue trim.

Everything that she observed within the first minutes of her arrival here at the Blakes' summer home subverted her expectations. The sight of the busy workmen and of the equally adept maids took her by surprise. She had not expected them to be here. Nor had she anticipated the twenty-two guests who had already arrived for the holiday weekend, caught as they were inside the exhilaration of swimming or sailing or merely sunning on the sands of the private beach. The absence of Nancy and Jennifer was an even more pressing concern. She was counting on their greeting her with their discreet flare and with their friendly recognition of her as their well-regarded peer who belonged to the same privileged class. Their decorous greeting would have made her presence here at the Blakes' holiday weekend seem plausible and perhaps inevitable. The guests who were aware of her intense love affair with Noah would have taken their cue from Jennifer and Nancy. Those guests, young explorers of their own sensuality, might have given a clever spin to the breakup between her and Noah. They would probably have perceived both Noah and her as life-loving individuals who, having parted, were moving on to new people, different places, and more intricate adventuring. But Nancy and Jennifer were not there to greet her or to give their friends the proper cues for interpreting her otherwise unanticipated appearance at a holiday celebration that included her former lover and his current girlfriend. Nancy and Jennifer and their boyfriends were having "a grand time on the lake," Mrs. Conway told her when she inquired about them a few minutes later. They were competing in an extemporaneous sailboat race with three other couples.

Nor were Mr. and Mrs. Blake present. They had not yet arrived from their Greenwich residence. Nora Anderson, Mrs. Blake's personal secretary, an accomplished and gracious brunette in her early thirties and the upright widow of a heroic World War Two Air Force pilot, was overseeing the preparations for the weekend festivities. That Mrs. Blake was not here, at the Saranac Lake summer place, increased her uneasiness. The empathy that Mrs. Blake had shown her a few days earlier counted for a great deal. Despite her ambivalent relationship with her son, Mrs. Blake's approval might influence Noah to see her with new eyes. She was, after all, an heiress to the Scott fortune. Two years earlier, she had made a favorable impression as a New York debutante. More recently, she had demonstrated her talent as a writer of serious fiction. Magazine editors referred to her as a new prodigy with a special gift for conveying the disquiet of repressed characters and the grave consequences of even small betrayals. Already, two of her stories had appeared in *The New Yorker* and *The Paris Review*.

Her success as a writer had impressed Noah, though he tried not to show it.

"You're okay," he said during an evening when they were alone in his apartment and there was nobody around to hear him. "You write a good story. I'm impressed. I never imagined that I've been sleeping with a bluestocking."

She had laughed when she heard his words. His praise had exhilarated her. On that evening, he had laughed, too, caught up as much as she was by their lightheartedness and by the sheer joy of being so completely alive in that moment.

There had been so many days when they had been happy together, whether they were swimming in the heated pool here at his parents' summer home on Saranac Lake or skiing and tobogganing in St. Moritz or co-piloting his Piper PA-20 Pacer from Newport, Rhode Island, to Philadelphia, or dancing in a Manhattan supper club. All these favorable occasions were swiftly coming back to her as she stood on the edge of the tawny sands of the beach in search of Noah and uncertain of the place where she might find him.

After a few minutes of surveying the busy scene, she convinced herself that Noah was not among the excited summer people sailing and skiing on Saranac Lake. Nor was he among the rugged young men who had chosen to swim in the lake with their lovely partners rather than in the heated pool that was located in the south wing of the main house. Now she persuaded herself that Noah had chosen the comforts of the heated pool and the amenities of the pool house, with its mahogany-framed French doors, floral curtains and slipper chairs, candelabra-like chandelier, and easy access to the bluestone loggia that faced the teal waters of the pool.

She hurried to the pool area in the south wing of the house. There, she saw Noah at once, his long, brawny physique at rest on a lawn chair and his handsome face expressing a casual joy at observing in the distance six or seven couples that were either swimming playfully in the pool or sitting around the pool in chaise lounges, chatting and drinking draft beer, scotch, and Champagne. So she believed, even though aviator sunglasses concealed the language of Noah's steady gaze. The smooth tan of his skin enhanced the look of his hunter green swim briefs and the excitement of his inherent sensuality. Exactly at that moment, the pentagon-based tumbler of scotch in his right hand was catching and reflecting the sunlight and including him in its glow. Free of care or seeming so, he sat in the chair and smiled at the young couple cavorting in the corner of the pool nearest him.

He was alone. Neither Olivia nor Sandra Lancaster nor any of his temporary girlfriends were with him. She remembered so clearly, even from this distance of fifteen years, that her heart began to beat faster and that she was once again convinced he was waiting for her to appear.

She walked toward him with an assurance that reflected her renovated certainty that he was waiting for her. But she was careful not to startle him or to disarrange the solace that the party atmosphere had conferred upon him. No one else, except the fun-loving couple in the pool, was there, in that sun-glistening corner. Yet the happy couple playing tag in the pool seemed a nebulous presence—two human beings who were merely shadows within some faraway corner of her glance. To her excited eyes, Noah and she were the only persons there.

Despite her excitement, she kept herself at a discreet distance from the place where Noah was sitting. When she began speaking to him, she made her words sound both gentle and affable.

"You look like a man who has found the path to happiness," she said. "Maybe you'll show me how to get there. I want to be happy, too."

If Noah was astonished to see her standing a few feet away from him, he gave no evidence of surprise. He was not in the least disconcerted. His steady gaze and understated reply held him to well-honed detachment and casual dismissal of her sentimental appeal to his better nature.

"I'm not the man to show you anything," he said. "You're strictly on your own."

"You underestimate yourself. You can do so much for me and for our baby."

"Do we have to go through this again? Don't you know when you've been left behind?"

"I told you how it is with us. You will never leave me behind. I won't let you."

"You don't have any say in the matter. We're finished."

Suddenly, Olivia was there, glaring at her with unfriendly eyes in the same moment that her caustic voice summoned an angry question.

"What's she doing here?"

Noah answered her quickly.

"Begging for my favor."

Olivia pushed forward.

"You don't belong here, Charlotte. Stay out of our way."

She answered her with a low-keyed yet incisive statement.

"You're the one who's in my way, and I'm going to push you aside."

Olivia fired back a volley of bitter remarks and blunt accusations.

"Noah loves *me.* He always has. He always will. Stop making a fool of yourself. You were never the woman he wanted. You're not good enough for him. In your heart, you know that. You've come here to make a scene. You want to make trouble. You want to steal our happiness. But you'll never do it. We won't let you."

"Don't be so sure of that. I may surprise you."

Now Noah came into it.

"Shove off," he said. "You're not wanted here."

Olivia drew nearer him, her body clinging to his rugged physique.

"Let's go for a swim," she said, while finding once more the voice that was both mellow and seductive.

Noah placed his arm across her waist and began to lead her away. Only after he and Olivia had gone forward twenty paces did he turn to deliver an ultimatum.

"If you're still here after our swim, I'll call the security guards to show you the way out."

She stood her ground and threw out her own blunt remark.

"I warned you before. I'm warning you now. I won't let you leave me."

Noah sneered at her.

"You don't have any say in the matter."

She felt her rage churning inside her. But she did not shout or scream. She kept her voice low and insistent.

"I won't let you push me aside."

Once again, Noah sneered.

"You're history. Get used to it."

Having said so, he and Olivia turned away from her, hurried forward a few more paces, and dived into the pool. It was a perfect dive. Noah's taut muscularity and Olivia's seductive figure made them a well-matched couple. Once again, the thought that they did, indeed, belong together goaded her anger. Fury overtook her. Her senses reeled. The room, with the teal sheen of its pool, its merry swimmers, its colorful chairs and tables, and its portable bar suddenly pitched away from her. It swayed apart from ordinary seeing. It tilted and soared and hurled itself away. So, to her disarranged sense, it seemed.

In the next instant, she took the Colt Cobra revolver from her purse and ran closer to the pool. She fired a wild shot that drew the attention of Noah and Olivia, as well as all the other couples in the pool. She did not mean to warn them. So fierce was her rage and so intent was she on killing the two people who had betrayed her that her finger pressed the trigger too quickly.

In that moment, she saw only Noah and Olivia, who paused in their swimming and looked back at her, startled and suddenly apprehensive.

Without giving them time to dive beneath the water or to shout their protest, she shot them again and again.

She fired two bullets into Noah's body. The first bullet grazed his left temple. The second ripped through his chest and threw him away from Olivia. From the impact of the second bullet, blood surged out of his back and spilled into the blue-greenness of the water. For a moment, he struggled to stay afloat. Then, losing consciousness, he sank beneath the surface.

The room was all the while spinning when she saw Noah disappearing beneath the water and as she fired a bullet into Olivia, who was screaming now in fear. It was, once again, a wild shot, because the horror of what she was doing kept flashing in and out of her comprehension. The bullet pushed its way through Olivia's right arm and sprayed the whiteness of her swimsuit with the deep redness of blood.

She fired another shot and another and another. The bullets struck Olivia's left temple, her right shoulder, and her spleen.

Olivia's screaming stopped. Her body fell limp from trauma. She groaned with pain and, like Noah, sank beneath the bloodstained surface of the pool.

From far away, inside the deepest recesses of her awareness, she heard herself mumbling, as if her words were directed to a ghostly spirit upon whom she had cast a fatal spell.

"I warned you, but you wouldn't listen."

Compelled even now by the fury that had driven her to the brink of madness, she stood by the poolside and pointed the barrel of the Colt Cobra revolver next to her heart. She placed her hand on the trigger and was ready to fire the bullet. But something made her pause. Was it her fear of the unknown darkness into which she would hurl herself? Was it her remorse because she would be taking not only her life, but also the life of the baby she was carrying? Was it her unwillingness to fall dead into the same pool where the bodies of her two adversaries were sinking? Whatever it was, the time in which she paused allowed her to think more clearly. She would kill herself, though not with pistol or dagger or poison. She would drown herself in the wind-tossed waters of the lake where roiling waves would pull her body down into the fathomless deep.

So her shattered mind imagined.

With this new resolve spurring her on, she tossed the pistol into the pool and ran out of the room. In her hurrying passage, she was vaguely aware of the young men who were diving beneath the waters of the pool to retrieve the bodies of Noah and Olivia. Other swimmers, husky fellows and their demure girlfriends, still stunned or frightened by the shootings, stared warily at her as she ran out of the room and made her way to the west side of the property and onto the sands of the beach.

Now, fifteen years afterwards, she wondered whether her memory of that terrible hour had held, accurate and knowing, all that had really unfolded there in the Blakes' pristine pool house. Or was hers a false recollection, an incomplete narrative stream of images that still confused her so many years later?

What she remembered with certainty was that the room kept swirling away from her comprehension. The men who were trying to rescue or at least recover the bodies of Noah and Olivia lurched and sloped and dived inside the haze of her seeing. The young ladies who were swimming, helpless and weeping, out of the blood-tarnished pool, and the two or three braver women who were joining the men in their diving and search efforts belonged to the velocities of a kaleidoscope of images, gone wild and nightmarish. The chairs and cocktail tables and portable bar reeled once again, momentarily recovered themselves, and then swung away from her accurate seeing. The room catapulted and hurled itself away. As she ran from its chaos, she believed that it was following and overtaking her. She cried out her protest. There was no fear in the cry. There was only rage.

"Get away from me! Get away!"

Then, as she hurried toward the beach in the west end of the property, the room vanished. Or had it exploded? She was not certain. Nor did her uncertainty about what was happening deter her from running past the four couples playing volleyball along the tawny sands of the beach and past the young man and two women swimming in the sun-blanched waters of the lake. All of them were her friends. Some of them waved to her. The ones who were used to her adventurous spirit accepted as appropriate and even inevitable her superb dive into the lake and her vigorous strokes that were pushing her toward the deeper, wind-roiled waves.

She swam until she was exhausted, drained of all energy and depleted of the will to live. The weight of her clothes had made her passage difficult. Yet she had succeeded in swimming against their resistance. She had welcomed the heaviness of the clothes. They would force her to tire more quickly. They would hasten the moment when she became too tired to go on. In that instant, she would plunge into the dark, fathomless bottom of the lake. Water would fill her lungs and burst them apart. The same punishing waters would erase her consciousness and batter her lifeless body as she dropped down and down into the jaws of a murky death.

So she anticipated as she swam with punishing swiftness. Resolute and accepting, she now recovered her more accurate seeing. What she saw as she swam across the darkening powers of the water were the white purity and silky sheen of cirrus clouds crossing the gold disk that was the sun. Beneath those clouds, six or seven black-backed, screeching gulls were flying south. Toward the east, green hills rose into a forest and meandered into a community of summer homes. Nearer than that, huge limestone rocks rose up out of the lake as though they were the remains of a discarded world. Nearer still, a cobalt blue catamaran, about forty feet long, was traveling fast and leaving in its wake a spume-fed swirl of waves. Nearest of all, the steadfast powers of the wind-glanced lake were claiming her as their own.

Weary at last, she stopped swimming. The waters battered her more swiftly and began drawing her down into an unremitting darkness, her body already bruised, discolored, and swollen from her rough passage. Her lungs began filling with water. Her head throbbed, as though it were imploding. Before she lost consciousness, she felt her entire body shaking with painful convulsions. The darkness of the lake became even darker. She could not see. She could not hear. But something or someone was grabbing her. Weakened though she was, she struggled to free herself from whatever or whoever was pinioning her, tightly holding her arms so that she could not escape. Whatever creature held her in its grasp was spewing light from its head. But the light merely deepened her blindness. Had she died? Who was this creature that fastened its body to her own? Was it Death? Had she escaped from one prison only to fall into a darker prison for all eternity? She struggled to think clearly. Her torturous passage across the lake had washed away the realistic underpinnings of her perception. Those same waters had washed away her thoughts. She could no longer think. The shock of this assailant that she could not see and against whom she could no longer struggle kicked her out of consciousness.

On that Wednesday afternoon, she did not die—at least, not visibly. The death of one's soul is, after all, a secret process that is known only to one's self. She did not die, because Lars, the Blakes' second butler and sometime security guard, had saved her for the life-in-death to which she had condemned herself. It was he who had held her fast in a rescuing hold underwater. It was his scuba mask with a headlight attached to its straps that had gleamed a blinding light upon her moments before the shock of his being there and the weight of the surging water and the water filling her lungs had thrown her out of consciousness.

She awoke in a Long Island hospital. Her parents were standing near her bed, their faces held to muted anxiety, melancholic affection, and genuine regret.

"We thought that we'd lost you," her mother said, whispering the words as her way of gently drawing her back to familiar things.

A silver-haired nurse in an immaculate white uniform was standing with her parents, carefully observing her.

"Lucky for you that Lars is a champion swimmer, even underwater," her father said.

"Lucky?" she asked. "Am I lucky?"

"Absolutely," the nurse, whose name was Miss Beauregard, said.

"Something bad happened, didn't it?"

"Don't think about it," her mother said. "What's done can't be undone."

The memory of the shooting was coming back to her. The violent scene was unfolding, vivid and palpable, before her. She saw herself at the edge of the Blakes' swimming pool, firing bullets from her Colt Cobra revolver into Noah and Olivia.

She sprang away from the galaxy of pillows into which she had been leaning. The horror of what she had done cut through her revived awareness. She heard an anguished cry, like that of a wounded animal in a dark forest, rising out of herself and out of the taut stillness that harnessed her senses. No longer completely sedated, she saw once again Noah's startled expression as she shot him and the outrage that lived on the cusp of his resistance when he fell beneath the water of the pool. She saw as clearly Olivia's fear and heard her moaning protest as the bullets entered her body.

"I killed them! I killed them!" she screamed.

All the while that she was screaming her confession, she tried to get out of the bed. But her body, still enervated by strong medication, held her back. Her parents, disheartened by her trouble-haunted lament and by her utter disarrangement, were telling her words that she could not decipher. She heard only her ghastly shrieking and felt the prick of the needle that Miss Beauregard was pushing into her arm.

PART ONE
CHAPTER NINE
Charlotte
Wednesday Afternoon, 4 October 1967
Looking Back to the Autumn of 1952
And Some of the Years That Followed

Now, fifteen years afterward, she could not recollect with any accuracy the hospital days and nights that immediately followed. Only months later, after her parents had arranged for her to be transferred to a clinic in Lausanne, Switzerland, did she learn about the aftermath that her shooting had precipitated. Only then, when Jacob Reutenauer, an eminent psychiatrist with thick, white hair and cragged features, had guided her to a clarifying awareness of what had happened and why she had willed herself to act so violently, did she discover the particular details of her breakdown and the consequences of her criminal behavior.

Nobody died. Though they were seriously wounded, Noah and Olivia survived. They looked buoyant and life affirming in their wedding photos that were circulated in the leading newspapers and magazines the following October.

Her parents, as well as the Blakes and the Tanners, kept the scandal of the shooting out of those same newspapers and magazines. They paid off the police and a few lawyers, and they rewarded Lars, the security guard, for saving her from drowning. They also rewarded his brother Kurt, who was smart enough to keep his mouth shut about everything that happened at Saranac Lake on that July afternoon.

The forty guests who were there that day, enjoying the pre-holiday merriment, stayed quiet, too. They did not have to be paid for their silence. They knew the rules of their privileged class. It was the same class to which she belonged. True, the shootings made her a renegade. But she was still one like them. Indeed, her family was thriving more brilliantly than ever during the current surge in the stock market.

Through all of the traumatic months after the shootings and during the uneasy months of her pregnancy, she continued to confer with Dr. Reutenauer. He was working hard to save her. For several weeks, Dr. Reutenauer dismissed her lies without harshly judging her and with a matter-of-fact openness that she gradually came to respect. She began to trust him. She started to tell him the truth. Now, as she imparted the conflicted narrative that was her life, she did not hesitate to reveal the deviousness of her nature and the ingrained cynicism that had often ignited her plots against both friends and adversaries. Because of his probing questions, his fatherly manner, and his even-tempered guidance, Dr. Reutenauer helped her to confront her anger and her fears.

"Why is Noah Blake so essential to your well-being?" he once asked her. "What are the qualities you see in him that make his loving you absolutely life-saving?"

Those were the questions that Dr. Reutenauer called out to her at the end of one of the sessions when even the truth as she perceived it could not clarify her obsession for Noah. A few days later, when she resumed this conversation with her psychiatrist, she answered his questions.

"I'm drawn to Noah because he knows how to contrive an illusion of perfection," she said. "And he is perfect in so many ways. He's the perfect athlete, the perfect student, and the perfect physical specimen. He also has a gift for withholding himself from even his close male friends and from the women who are attracted to him."

"You say that his perfection is an illusion. Yet you fell in love with him. What made you fall in love with him?"

"I saw him as a challenge. I wanted to find out how close he was to being perfect."

"Do you think you found out?"

"Maybe. Maybe I know him better than he thinks I do."

"What makes you believe that?"

"He's like me. He's imperfect. He's self-centered. He's devious."

"You say you love him. But you were willing to kill him because he had turned away from you. You were willing to end your own life."

"I shot him because he had already killed me, without a pistol or poison or a dagger. The Charlotte Scott that lived with him for two years and that loved him unconditionally is dead. Whoever I become now will have to be a different person. The Charlotte whom I thought I once knew, the one who died, is a stranger to me, in spite of our long acquaintance. The new Charlotte will have to learn how to live without Noah."

"Do you think that you can learn how to live without him? Can you learn to be new?"

"I'm not sure. What I am sure of is this: The Charlotte Scott that died for Noah Blake chose him because she thought that they completed each other. Both of them were no good. Although *that* Charlotte died for him, Noah is still alive. He'll always be no good."

"Maybe. Maybe not. Life has a habit of taking us by surprise and changing us."

"Noah may change, but he will never change for the better. He'll only learn to be more rotten."

"You say that he's dead, as far as you're concerned. Yet you are willing to have his baby."

"The baby will be mine. Whether I give birth to a boy or a girl, the baby will never meet Noah or learn anything about him. Noah will never be mentioned."

"I admire your spirit. But I hope that you can learn to forgive Noah. You will never be rid of him unless you forgive him. Not even the new Charlotte will escape him."

"I'll try," she said. I'll try to forgive him. That's a promise."

Many other sessions followed with good Dr. Reutenauer. Even after all these years, she valued every one of the conferences with her psychiatrist. Those sessions sometimes explored her relationship with her parents and her two brothers. She came to understand that, although she admired and even loved many aspects of her mother's character, she could not choose her as a mentor or even as an occasional role model. She disdained her mother's too-cautious life style and her complete acquiescence to the artificial codes and hypocritical rules of their male-dominated society. Nor could she regard her father and her two brothers as her mentors. She appreciated their support of a woman's right to choose her own destiny, whether she found that destiny in a challenging career or as a dutiful wife and mother. But, whenever they perceived that her behavior was too radical or too adventurous, they frowned and took steps to constrain her independent nature. Her relations with them, on the surface temperate and accommodating, disguised the small and larger rebellions that she contrived against their will.

From her father and her brothers and from the three men who were her lovers before Noah, she learned the importance of maintaining a wily and adamant possession of her independence. Determined to be light of spirit and to be vigilant and discerning in the weaving of her plots, she regarded her relations with men, whether those relations were familial, platonic, or erotic, as an enjoyable game because she knew when to maintain her secrets and when to dispense or withhold her favors. All men were a challenge. They were cryptic individuals whose chauvinistic codes she had learned to decipher.

She, too, was cryptic. But only Noah Blake had deciphered her intricacies. Only he had discovered her secrets. She was vulnerable because she gave her heart so completely to him. She no longer wanted to be her solitary self. She wanted to be bonded with him. She wanted to disappear inside him. He was her compensation for the father and the brothers who had accepted her only conditionally. He was the lover who had shot his seed inside her and, with her collaboration, procreated a baby. Their child would be a living emblem of their bond. The child would be a vital proof that Noah and she had loved each other.

So she came to understand because of her sessions with Dr. Reutenauer, knowing because he had advised her that her review of her past would never be complete or altogether accurate. Like men and women, the past was also cryptic, a formidable montage of events imparting ambiguous impressions and requiring careful analyses.

She had wondered then whether in years to come she would view with a more profound comprehension her relationship with Noah. She was aware that, despite her professed hatred of Noah Blake, she was consenting to give birth to their baby because that baby would serve as a substitute for the absent Noah. Yet, paradoxically, she was determined to forget Noah. She wanted to kill all memory of him. The child would belong to her and to no one else.

So she told the good doctor who was counseling her. But his honest, fatherly demeanor told her that he was not convinced that she would ever dispel her memory of Noah.

"Let's see what happens," he said. "Let's see what kind of life you make for yourself and for your child."

Amanda Cooper, the good-natured nurse and midwife who was staying with her during her confinement, also urged her not to allow her complicated feelings for Noah to put her off her proper course. Mrs. Cooper was a godsend. Her meticulous care of her and her wise counsel had complemented the soul-searching sessions with Dr. Reutenauer during the hard months of her confinement. Mrs. Cooper shared Dr. Reutenauer's skepticism about her ability to forget Noah. At ease with her matronly appearance, Ms. Cooper was a learned and cosmopolitan woman. Born in Southampton, about a hundred miles from London, and educated in Germany, France, and England, she spoke fluent French, German, and Italian as well as her native tongue. Her husband was a professor of contemporary literature and a well-regarded poet. Currently away from Cambridge University, he was teaching in an exchange program at the University of Lausanne. The Coopers' son and their daughter, who were Cambridge graduates now in their thirties, were enjoying successful careers as a neurosurgeon and a playwright, respectively.

By way of her keen-minded intuition and her experience of life, Mrs. Cooper understood how much Noah's rejection had destroyed her peace and how far she had journeyed away from her better nature because of him. Yet it was not going to be easy to forget him. Noah was leaving behind a child who was a genetic image of the father who had abandoned him—a living individual who might in time replicate Noah's features and his singular presence. She must not permit her hatred of Noah to thwart her future or to undermine her belief that she could discover new happiness.

"Hold your head up high," Mrs. Cooper said. "You have a long road to travel. It's too early to tell what or whom you'll find along the way or where that road will lead you."

In November, a few weeks after she was released from the Swiss clinic and while she was staying at her parents' chalet in Lausanne, Steven Bennington paid her a surprise visit. They shared dinner in an upscale supper club not far from the chalet. By then, she was in the seventh month of her pregnancy. Yet her face never looked lovelier. She wore a navy blue, loose-fitting maternity dress, knee length and fashionable, with rose shoulder details, short ruffled sleeves, and a boat neck. Givenchy had designed it in a cotton and nylon fabric, and her mother had bought it to remind her that she could be glamorous even when she was carrying a baby. Diamond earrings and necklace, low-heeled shoes, and a full-length ermine coat enhanced her youthful sophistication. Her raven-black hair, pulled back to form a neat coil at the nape of her neck, completed an appearance that was not only elegant, but also charismatic.

So Mrs. Cooper told her, pleased that she was learning to be happy again.

She and Steven were seated in the main dining room of the supper club that gave them a panoramic view of the festive evening unfolding around them. Walls decorated with vivid canvases in the style of Toulouse-Lautrec, chairs cushioned with brocade designs, and chandeliers glowing with delicate crystal intensified the opulent ambiance. Women, young and older, wore fashionable evening dresses in colors as various as chartreuse, fuchsia, dark green, burgundy, red, and gold. All of the men looked impressive in black or navy suits. Waiters moved about the capacious room with easy assurance, and on a stage in the southwest corner a seven-piece band imparted mellifluous notes and jazzy riffs. There, a beautiful Nigerian girl in her early twenties, accompanied by a superb trumpeter and an accomplished pianist, sang a ballad about finding her true love on Green Dolphin Street. Later, a French baritone brought poignant immediacy to a love-haunted narrative that told of his finding and eventually losing the *Mam'selle* who was the love of his life.

On that life-changing occasion, she allowed herself, eventually, to drink two glasses of Champagne, and Steven enjoyed three rounds of scotch. Yet they remained clear-headed and eager to hear each other's remarks. Though their meal was delicious, they ate sparingly, so excited were they by the unexpected news that Steven was bringing to her. Nevertheless, she remembered all the details of the meal: *gratinéed* onion soup, trout with almonds, English-styled boiled potatoes, and fruit salad with a red sauce made from raspberries and strawberries.

Their oblique awareness of the food notwithstanding, she could recall even more clearly the words that gave to the evening a special gravity and gave to her a thrilling surprise. The words were Steven's, and their matter-of-factness belied the genuine feeling behind them.

"I want to marry you," Steven told her while she was sipping her Champagne. He had not yet touched his scotch.

Her pulse fluttered. Her heart beat faster. For a minute or so, she did not speak. The cynicism that had taught her to resist sentimentality and to distrust eleventh-hour rescuers swiftly worked its powers. The unexpectedness of Steven's remark dissuaded her from saying the words that would give her baby a substitute father's name. The value of those words did not elude her awareness. Those same words would dispel the conservative dismay, muted though it was, of her friends and her family. Her words would also keep at bay all the enemies who would eventually enter her life and, pointing to the illegitimacy of her child, would brand her a pariah.

For his part, Steven accepted the stillness that had too swiftly come there as an invisible presence to observe their every move. There was no tension in him. There was only a quiet resolve that was navigating him with perfect self-control into this new chapter that he was initiating.

When she found her voice, she willed herself to remain understated and to question his motive.

"Why?" she asked. "Why do you want to marry me?"

"There are many reasons. Some of them are too complicated for casual explanation. At any rate, you and I have had some good times together. Maybe we can have good times again. Let's see what happens."

"Of course I'd like you to marry me. But I want to be honest with you. I'll lay it on the line. I don't love you in the way that you deserve. I don't love you with the intensity that I once loved Noah."

"Maybe that's a good thing. I'm not interested in being a woman's obsession."

"I'll admit that you are surprising me. I never thought of you as the marrying kind."

"Neither did I. But right now you need a husband. Since I'm available, I thought that we'd have a go at it. Besides, our baby needs a father."

"Our baby?"

"It will be, once we're married."

She felt like crying. Instead, she pressed her lips together as tightly as she could. She held back her tears. She did not want to draw any more of his pity than the subtle portion that he was offering her. That he felt more than pity was in his favor. Otherwise, her pride and her self-possession would have pushed him away from her. Yet there was one more question that she needed to ask him.

"Do you love me, Steven?"

He quickly answered her, never compromising his manly confidence and his street-wise poise.

"Love you?" he asked, echoing her question. "Sure I love you. Enough to marry you. I'd like to find out whether I might learn to love you more. That's the kick of it. There's the adventure."

She appreciated his tough-mindedness and the perverse nature of his offer. She felt certain that ingrained perversity ignited his proposal. Steven liked activating the unexpected. He enjoyed surprising his friends and initiating the ricochet of his actions.

"It may not work out," she reminded him.

"Maybe it will. Anyway, I want to help you."

"You like rescuing women."

"Sure I do. Doesn't every man?"

"Let's have an adventure, then. Let's find out where and how far it will take us."

The room was humming with the murmur or chatter of voices, the tinkle of glasses, the sweep of arriving guests, and the smooth passage of waiters. The band was still playing its jazzy riffs, and the lovely Nigerian was singing another song about lost loves and makeshift joys.

She remembered it was precisely at this moment that Steven and she lifted their glasses and toasted each other. They held the glasses together for a long moment, recognizing that in a special way their marriage began with this pledge. Steven's eyes gleamed with a devil-may-care willfulness. He was enjoying the moment. He was gambling with the happiness that the Fates had thus far dispensed to him. He was complicating his future with a woman carrying another man's baby. The father of that baby had broken her heart, and the pieces were strewn around her and around him, Steven Bennington, a man who—with wildness in him like her own—took pleasure in subverting the rigid codes of their social group. He was daring himself to love her and daring her, as well, to return his love.

At the end of that month, Steven and she were married in a quiet ceremony within a chapel in Lausanne. In the middle of January, she gave birth to a son that she named Adam. Two years later, in April 1955, after they settled in

Connecticut, she gave birth to Steven's son. They named him Ryan.

For all these years afterwards, Steven and she appeared to be happy.

Today, though, she found no need to dwell upon their marriage. She thought, instead, about Noah, the man who had betrayed her love and walked away. With an unanticipated message, he had come suddenly back into her life.

Now, fifteen long years after she shot Noah and left him with grievous wounds that she hoped would kill him, she took hold of the letter that he had sent her. Before she opened the lightweight envelope, she guessed that the letter was not long. Even so, her curiosity was sufficiently roused to keep her from tearing the envelope and its contents and tossing them into the basket that stood by her desk. She wondered why, after all these years and after the violent episode that had finally separated them, Noah was writing to her.

Was he asking for her forgiveness? Was he trying to assuage his troubled conscience? Did he actually believe that a belated apology could make amends for his pitiless treatment of her? Was he one of those men who, having ignited his youth with self-centered and dangerous exploits and ruthless disregard of enemies as well as friends, had experienced as he moved through his thirties both a new self-awareness and a deep-seated remorse that was goading him to seek forgiveness?

She could not believe that he was capable of so profound a transformation.

Without hesitating a moment longer, and at the same time noticing the smooth and confident penmanship, she opened the letter.

She noticed first of all that the letterhead contained the address of his law firm in Manhattan. Noah was being careful. As a married man, he refrained from using the more personal stationery that included his private residence and carried the suggestion of a more intimate correspondence. She respected his choice. He was not pretending to be her friend or a confidant offering her his prudent counsel. He was the lover who had used and betrayed her. He was the arrogant man who had become her enemy for all the years that were left to her. Perhaps, after all, he understood the unremitting powers of her hatred. Possibly, his ingrained cynicism and the recoil of all the wrong that he had done to her and to others gave him knowledge of that hatred. Contempt of others and abrasive dismissal of their anguish were familiar resources. They were his stock in trade. They empowered him. They burned out his soul to its socket.

So, she told herself, while waves of bitterness rushed over her and caught her by surprise. The hatred that she had suppressed for every hour and day of these fifteen years rose up as if to toss and heave her asunder. Left momentarily breathless, she struggled to regain her ballast. The waves of bitter hatred rushed upon her. She felt herself swooning. Her heart was racing. The waves kept rushing upon her. She had the horrifying sensation that she was drowning once more so many years after she had tried to drown herself beneath the deep waters of Saranac Lake. Yet this was an altogether different sensation. Never had her heart beaten so painfully. Never had her pulse raced so dangerously. That she was safely seated in her chair eased her fear that she might collapse and fall upon the carpeted floor. She closed her eyes and willed herself to be very still. Ten minutes passed, and her panic-struck heart regained its proper rhythms. Slowly, she took hold of the thermos of spring water that she always kept on the right side of her desk, not far from her typewriter. She poured some of the water into a Dixie cup and carefully drank it.

Then, heedless of the consequences of pushing herself too quickly into the scenario that Noah was devising for her, she began to read his letter.

Good day to you, Charlotte.

After all the years that have passed without our seeing one another, I come to you as a stranger. You do not really know me. Nor do I know you. The friendship that we shared during our university years, tentative and confusing as those years were, offered unreliable clues about the persons that we would gradually become. Each year has shaped and revealed new layers of our individuality. Each one of those years has tested us in different ways. The years, which in retrospect have passed so swiftly, have altered our identities. We are not now the persons that we were for one another when we first met seventeen years ago or when we parted in 1952.

For this reason, I have hesitated to write to you. The words that I am sending to you belong to a man that you have never really met. Yet I am compelled to write the words. Something important has happened to my life. Something has been lost that can never be recovered. I need to meet with you to explain what I have lost and to tell you why you are the one person who can change my life for the better. During these last months, because of all that has happened, I have felt like a drowning man. Only you can throw me the lifeline that I need.

I'm counting on your willingness to forgive me for the ways that I wronged you when I was a young, selfish fool. I believe in your goodness. I believe that, in spite of our grievous last days together, you will want to help Olivia and me to find some peace and to restore the happiness we have lost.

I plan to travel into Connecticut next Tuesday afternoon. I shall be very grateful if you will agree to our meeting in the privacy of your home or in a secluded corner of a restaurant. Please ask Steven to be there, too, if his presence will make you more comfortable.

I'm counting on you, Charlotte. I'm counting on your generous spirit and your forgiving heart.
All the best,
Noah

At the surprise of his words, she grew very still. It was possible, she told herself, that life had tempered and even beaten down the arrogance that had stained Noah's character more than fifteen years earlier. His radical transformation, if it actually existed, may have been entwined with disappointment and even failure. Whatever happened to him during these long years of being absent from her life must have invoked and perhaps compelled this tremendous change that had overtaken him. He had written this letter not only as a testimony of that change, but also as a petition for her clemency and her forgiveness.

So she told herself, even as traceries of doubt were urging her to resist Noah's plea and to suppress the memory of having once loved him so completely. Yes, it was possible that life had knocked him around. It was also possible that the battles that he had waged against rancorous adversaries in the world of business and on the home front with devious relatives and friends had worn him down. All these things were possible. But she did not believe any of them, at least not as they might apply to a man like Noah. Yet something—some sea change, some sudden upheaval, some disturbance or tribulation or misadventure—had prodded him to reach out to her.

What that disturbance was and why he was calling out to her goaded her need to know more about the plight that was now confronting Noah. There was in her, as well, a desire to witness first-hand Noah's dejection and the shadows of defeat, punishment, and sorrow that were hovering about his every move. The misfortune that he was now suffering must be, she imagined, so grievous that its anguish and pain were overriding the hesitation that might otherwise have kept him from meeting with her. She was, after all, the woman who had tried to kill him because he had spurned her love. He believed that she had changed for the better, because Time had changed him. Of those transformations—his as well as hers—he must have convinced himself before he felt compelled to petition her help.

She did not feel transformed. The bitterness that she had concealed through all these uneasy years was her constant companion. Whether that bitterness was tethered to the confused residue of love that she still felt for him and that she did not always suppress, she could not say. But she had learned from her mistakes. She would not try to kill Noah with a revolver. This time, she would try to kill him with a plot that required neither pistol nor dagger nor poison. She needed only to discover the cause of his malady. Then she would move against him.

Her eyes caught sight of the business card that had slipped to the left inside corner of the envelope. The card, with its classic black lettering and its thin, black border grounded on an ivory background, carried Noah's name, business address, and telephone number. Beneath that information, he had written these words: *Please write or call. Tell me the day and time when we can meet.*

Her mind raced with thoughts of what might happen when they did meet. No longer hesitating, she took from the top right drawer of her desk an elegant ivory, fold-over note card with its gold border and its floral imagery of six pink, yellow, and red roses on the front of the card. Above the floral images her name was monogrammed in black letters: *Charlotte Scott Bennington*. Then, before she could negate the impulse that drove her, she quickly penned the note for which Noah was waiting.

> *Noah,*
>
> *Your letter has intrigued my interest. I am wondering why you imagine that I can help you and Olivia. Let us meet in L'Espère, a French restaurant on Ferryboat Road in Greenwich, at noon on Wednesday afternoon, the fourteenth of October. Steven will be out of town on*

business for his firm. But I shall be happy to meet with
you. In fact, I am looking forward to our meeting.
Charlotte

She was pleased that Steven was away in London, attending a symposium about international trade laws. His presence would have complicated her meeting with Noah. Realist that he was, Steven would have favorably regarded the meeting with Noah. He would have viewed it as an opportunity to settle old scores and to bring to their revised friendship with Noah and Olivia hard-won maturity as well as loyalty and truth. "Life gives us very few second chances," he sometimes remarked. He might have been alluding to a business competitor who was trying to recover from the crimes he had committed on Wall Street. Or he might have been referring to a friend whose drug addiction had cost him his once-thriving career, the trust of his friends, and the love of his first and second wives. She could not gainsay the rightness of Steven's remark. But she was not interested in recovering her friendship with Noah and Olivia. It was Fate that was giving her a second chance. If she maintained her wiliness and adopted a circumspect manner, she might find a way to avenge herself once more against Noah and Olivia, who had robbed her of her inner peace and condemned her to a life of makeshift happiness cobbled from Blind Chance and from the rigorous and always stoical laws of self-discipline.

She was also pleased that Adam and Ryan were away at the prestigious boarding schools where they excelled as gifted students and versatile athletes. She had no intention of telling Noah anything at all about them. She planned to take special care not to mention Adam, who was the son that Noah had refused to recognize as his own.

With special care, she placed her letter inside an ivory-colored envelope and wrote Noah's address in the center of the front side. Her own address was printed with black letters and numerals on the envelope's flap. This ordinary task took on an altogether different significance. It was part of a series of irrevocable actions. Once she placed a stamp on the envelope and then sealed and mailed it, she would not be able to call back her decision to correspond with Noah. She was aware that her letter was initiating new uncertainty as well as the possibility of new conflict. But she would not allow her momentary reticence to keep her from entering the unknown territory before her. She was prepared to outwit whatever adversaries were hastening toward her. She was capable of weaving her own plots against the persons who had already marred her happiness. She would allow Noah to speak his mind. She would listen to his self-deluded story about the penitent individual that he had become. She might even begin to believe that his was a valid reformation. But she would never forgive him. Never. Never.

PART ONE

CHAPTER TEN

Charlotte

Wednesday Afternoon, 11 October 1967

Noah had lost the special glow that had always beamed from his face, surcharged as it was with youthful vigor and a light within that, she once told herself, emanated from his soul. At thirty-seven, he looked older than the years he had already lived. Something had died within him—some spark, some vital component that had anchored his optimism and his self-possession.

So she told herself as she scanned this revised face before her, its muted handsomeness worn down and made taut with its traces of deep-seated anguish and unremitting sorrow. Gray flecks of hair and haunted brown eyes gave him the look of a man of forty-five.

He was wearing a navy suit, a cobalt blue shirt, and a Paisley silk tie with gray ovals that were outlined by a deep blue hue with gray dots and set against a light blue background. She imagined that the meticulous care with which he groomed himself had become his way of holding his senses still and of maintaining the carefully-orchestrated structures of his current life.

"You have come, after all," she told him at the start of their meeting. "I thought you might change your mind. I thought you might have second thoughts about meeting a friend who has become a stranger."

"Nothing would have made me change my mind," he said. "I had to see you."

He, too, was carefully observing the face before him. It was her face, crowned by a sleek bouffant and made smooth with subtle cosmetics: pre-cleansing oil, thick eyebrows set wide apart and angled, blue eye shadow, and bold lip color. It was a face both glamorous and youthful. Today, she had the look of a twenty-seven-year-old woman. She was wearing a wool bouclé suit in a vibrant blue. Its boxy jacket had a fold-down collar and three sets of paired buttons for closure down the front. Bands of bright blue trim ran horizontally across at the bottom. The matching skirt had a classic A line with a side zipper. The color of her clothes complemented his own, as though there existed between them an unspoken collaboration—a natural affinity, an easy rapport, a long-established intimacy.

She had carefully dressed herself. She wanted him to see that her raven-haired beauty had flourished. She wanted him to believe that she was one of the extraordinary few who had been blessed with a life free of care and made even more blessed by her fame as a writer, by the earned fortune that she had added to her inherited wealth, and by a happy marriage. She wanted him see with his own eyes that she had found happiness without him. Before this meeting was over, she wanted him to understand that she had no inclination to look back at their troubled relationship or to look forward to a renovated association with him.

"I had to see you," he said, echoing his urgent remark. "I need you to help me. I need you to save my life."

"I've never saved a life before," she answered him. "But I'll help you if I can."

They were sitting in a booth within the most private corner of the main dining room in L'Espère. Nine or ten of her friends had spotted her as the maître-de guided her and Noah to their booth. They were reliable friends who would have stood by her even if she were committing a folly with a new, romantic gentleman. But they knew her well. She had, they believed, passed her years of romantic follies. Just as she was, so her friends were also caught up in the fervor and competition of their careers. They were thriving lawyers, artists, actors, and university administrators. Sighting her with Noah, they might imagine that he was her literary agent or a new publisher or her business manager. She was pleased to see them. Their presence, even though they were seated in other areas of this capacious room that seated a hundred guests, was going to help her to maintain her composure and to impart a contrived sympathy that Noah would accept as genuine.

Not only the passing sight of her friends held her to a proper course. The room itself with all its amenities drew her attention. Canvases with nautical themes brightened with a deeper resonance the rich cherry wood walls around them. The canvases were skillfully rendered prints of famous artworks that included Pierre-August Renoir's excited Normandy waves that were tossing their swirling energy toward the soft whiteness of clouds and the blue opalescence of the sky, Claude Monet's towering cliffs and hastening sailboats at Pourville, and Enrique Simonet's equally colorful boats—with gold, blue, and pink properties—sailing with supreme contentment on a quiet Venetian sea.

In the distance, on a platform near a panoramic window that looked out to the sun-burnished waters of Long Island Sound, a young, accomplished pianist—brown-haired and rangy, with brooding good looks and a long, thin scar that extended from the top of his right ear down to the lower part of his neck—was playing romantic ballads: "Moon River," "At Last," "Bewitched, Bothered, and Bewildered," and "Can't Help Falling in Love with You."

Nearer than that, men and women in stylish business attire, as affable as they were discerning and sophisticated, were sharing lunch and negotiating or closing profitable deals for their varied corporations. Waiters, quick-witted and precise, were passing to and fro with trays of cocktails and food service carts that carried a quiche Lorraine, containing tomatoes, tuna, black olives, green beans, and peppers; cider apple chicken with mushroom sauce; pork medallions with prunes; trout braised in Riesling wine; a zucchini and eggplant torte; Parisian dumplings; and a whole poached salmon trout with herbed mayonnaise.

She noticed all these things as her stay against confusion. To focus only on Noah, who appeared both remorseful and anguished, might have weakened her resolve to bring new punishment upon him. Watching him alone disconcerted her. In his letter, Noah had called himself a stranger. He was. The Fates had brought him low, and he was struggling to recover. Here and now, as she observed him through the haze of an absence of fifteen years, he was a ghostly after-image of the man that she had once regarded as her obsession. She did not know why he was suffering. But, no matter what or who had stolen his happiness, she would not pity him. She would, instead, work hard to make his suffering irrevocable.

"I knew you'd come through for me," he told her, a bit less tense once she promised to help save him. "That's why I'm here."

"I'm glad you're here," she assured him, crafty with her lies and with her plotting. "I like helping friends, whether they belong to the life that I'm living now or to the long ago past that I've already lived through."

She did not tell him the truth of her feelings. She had no interest in saving him or helping most people. Nor had she finished with the past. That thought made her pause. Her mind was plumbing a revelation as new to her consciousness as her willingness to accept its uneasy truth. She had never let go of the past. Ever since the violent failure of her relationship with Noah, she had re-lived all the hours and days and years that she had spent with him. She had allowed her hatred to fester, so that it pushed away the vague traceries of the passion and the love that she sometimes felt for him. Secretive and treacherous, she had pushed these feelings of ingrained hatred and ambivalent love down into the deepest recesses of her awareness. She had hidden those feelings even from herself, except for those moments when a friend from her university years reappeared to summon through a casual remark a happy memory of a campus dance they had attended with their hockey-playing boyfriends or of an exciting weekend they had shared with these same boyfriends in New York or in St. Moritz. Then, the recollection of her love affair with Noah Blake would flare the dark fragments of its long-ago reality for just a few moments, only to be suppressed by the adamant willfulness that held her to its chains.

If she was glad that Noah had come into her life once again, the pleasure of seeing him was devoid of affection. The pleasure that she was experiencing was the same pleasure that a vengeful spirit would enjoy, knowing that an enemy was placing his trust in her. Her hatred of this enemy, this Noah Blake whom Time or the Fates or Blind Chance had rendered vulnerable and grief-stricken, knew no boundaries. So she told herself as she listened to his words with sympathetic face and with comforting voice promised to rescue him if she could.

"I have so much to tell you," he said, right after she'd made that promise. "I hardly know where to begin."

Just then, two gray-haired waiters, skillful and deferential, brought them their meal. Noah was not interested in the food, delicious though it was. Nor was she. They ate sparingly, even as they permitted themselves to remark favorably upon the chef's proficiencies and the creative flair that he brought to their lunch: spinach-and-ham quiche, sea bass with mushrooms and cream sauce, and an orange mousse that was made from fresh orange juice, stiffened with gelatin, and served in hollowed-out oranges.

While they nibbled at their food, they drank two or three glasses of Veuve Clicquot. Noah was, she imagined, used to stronger drink. But, with her permission, he chose Champagne that deftly mated Pinot Noir and Chardonnay. Its golden glints and sparkling bubbles brought a subtext of celebration to this lunch that they were sharing with guarded cordiality. Only after Noah had drunk his second glass of Champagne and while they were eating small morsels of their food did he begin to tell her why he was there with her and what he hoped that she could do for him.

"First of all," he said, "I want you to understand that I am not an ungrateful man. We all know that life is a gamble and that most people have the cards stacked against them.

But I'm not one of those people. For most of my life, I've held the winning cards. I was born into wealth, and I've increased that wealth. The Blake & Tanner Corporation made the game easier. But there have been years when I have played it especially well. Both the corporation and I have made our association immensely profitable."

He paused in his telling to offer her a cigarette, even though they were in the midst of eating their meal. With a slight nod of her head, she politely declined. Only then did he lift a gold lighter to the cigarette that he had taken from a gold case and take a nervous drag on it.

"You haven't disappointed your father," she said. "He must be very pleased that you have become the son that he wanted you to be."

"Relieved might be a more appropriate description. I turned out not to be the black sheep, after all."

"Well, I'm not surprised that you and the world get along so well. The Fates have always granted you everything you want. They've always helped you to be a winner. They've given you everything that you wished for: a powerful father, a doting mother, an agreeable wife, and three loyal brothers."

"Not always," he said. "The Fates haven't always given me everything. They've taken from me, too."

"How did they do that?"

He started to tell her.

"They took away someone who meant the world to me."

He stopped speaking. His hand trembled as he took another drag on his cigarette. He grimaced. Sorrow held him in its grip. All of a sudden, he gazed at the Monet print on the wall near their booth. His gaze was, she felt, a strategy for displacing the bitter thoughts that were chipping away his manly self-control. For a minute or two, he gave his attention to Monet's towering cliffs and to the hastening sailboats that appeared to be vulnerable and may have been racing against an imminent storm. Whatever message he derived from the print did not comfort him. But this brief concentration on its colors and the implications of its narrative were, she imagined, holding his senses still.

She waited for him to pull himself together. She brought her attention to the food, so that she would not intrude upon the sadness that he was struggling to keep at bay. Quietly, she ate a few morsels of the quiche and took another sip of the Champagne.

When he resumed speaking, he did not mention the person that he had lost. She wondered whether one of his parents had died or, possibly, one of his brothers. Had he and Olivia had children and lost one of them to an accident or a terminal illness? He did not tell her. He was not ready to say the words that would tell her of the tragedy that had beaten him down. Instead, he chose to backtrack. He began speaking about his marriage.

"When Olivia and I first married, we were never especially interested in other people. The world existed for us alone. We were stereotypes of the self-centered rich. We didn't want to hear about other people's problems. We never helped anyone."

"Why are you telling me this?"

"I want you to know that we changed. You need to know that, so that you'll understand that we didn't deserve what eventually happened to us."

"Then tell me all of it. Tell me the way you need to tell it."

"For two years, we lived a wild and adventurous life. Whether we were deep-sea fishing in the Caribbean, hiking along the Larapinta Trail in Australia, hunting lions in South Africa, or skiing and tobogganing in Graubünden, Switzerland, we lived life to the hilt. Our friends were often celebrities and occasionally the CEOs of top-notch global corporations. They were as self-concerned and manipulative as we were. In the mid-fifties, Olivia and I danced at the President's Inauguration Ball in D.C. We partied at Maxim's in Paris. We reveled in a jazzy nightspot in New Orleans. We were reckless. We felt immortal. We were very happy. I was particularly happy because Olivia wanted to share with me all the things that I loved."

"You made a splendid life for yourselves."

"We did. For a while."

"Then something changed for you."

"Yes."

"Something that made you look at life in a new way."

"Olivia became pregnant."

"Did you want her to have the baby?"

"I did."

"Then you were still happy."

"Her pregnancy changed so much for us. We looked at ourselves in a new way. We thought we were very special. You'd think that nobody had done it before. We made this baby together. Not yet born, the baby was already influencing us to be better individuals. We stopped the heavy drinking. We quit the wild nightlife. We rearranged our lives. After my high-pressure days at the office, I enjoyed being at home with my wife. We added a special wing to our home. We worked with a builder and an interior designer to create a room for the baby that would be comforting and educational. We chose a soothing blue room, with walls decorated with paper animal portraits and colored letters of the alphabet. Already, we were thinking about the private schools that would prepare our son or daughter for an Ivy League college. My interest in the baby surprised me. Maybe the baby gave me the reason I needed to rid myself of the daredevil pursuits and careless adventures that were beginning to hound me with their body-assaulting consequences and their guilt-laden aftermaths. I needed to change. So did Olivia. We were out of control. We were living out the days and nights of superficial nonentities. We wanted to be more than that. In our dry season, away from the booze and the wildness, we had to admit that we didn't really like the persons that we had become. But the baby changed all of that. For our son or our daughter, we wanted to become the best people we could be."

She did not really want to hear about his life with Olivia, not when they'd been happy. But, pushing her food away from her, she gave him her complete attention. She was waiting to hear what had gone wrong.

"You're not the first couple that changed their ways because of a baby," she said. "But the change must have brought you and Olivia a special satisfaction. You had so much more to live for."

Stillness overtook him once more. Sorrow was churning inside him, poisoning his spirit and inhibiting his self-possession. It took him a minute or so to recover and find the words that would push forward the story he needed to tell her. When he did recover, his deep voice sounded as manly as ever, layered though it was with disappointment and melancholy.

"Yes," he answered her. "We had so much. Maybe we counted on the baby too much. The baby never arrived."

Her heart beat faster. He was about to tell her news that was dark and irrevocable.

"What happened?"

"Olivia miscarried. In the fifth month of her pregnancy. We lost our daughter."

She frowned, as though she were distraught and commiserating.

"I'm sorry."

He was telling her more. There was another loss that he and Olivia had endured.

"A year and a half later, she miscarried again. We lost a son."

Once again, she invoked a dolorous look to conceal the pleasure she was experiencing because Noah Blake had finally learned what suffering meant. Her words belied her thoughts. They appeared to comfort and to sympathize.

"Losing a child is a hard thing to bear," she said.

"It made us less certain. It made us older."

Her next words were nearly dismissive, cloaked as they were inside praise of his forbearance.

"You kept bearing it. You're here. You're carrying on."

"Yes," he said, unaware of her ambivalence. "We carried on. Olivia busied herself with charity work. In my free time, I coached a middle-school hockey team. But we never gave up hoping for a child of our own. Then, after Olivia and I brought our problem to a team of doctors at Johns Hopkins, things changed for us. The next time Olivia became pregnant, this amazing team knew what to do to protect the baby. Our son was born on the tenth of September in 1957. We named him Seth, and for nine years he brought us immense happiness."

"And now…?"

"A year ago, Seth died of a brain tumor."

She felt no sadness at hearing his news. Her hatred of him had dried up all her pity. Yet she carried forward her false show of sorrow. She wanted to hear more. She wanted to watch him grieving before her. She wanted to hear his words that told her that Blind Chance or the pernicious Fates had brought him low.

"How tragic it is for you," she said, "to lose a son at that age."

"He was the perfect son. He was so smart. Even in preschool, he excelled in math, science, and languages. He was taller than most of his schoolmates, and he was competing effectively with the best of them. He moved so swiftly when he was playing youth ice hockey. He learned so many skills and quickly, too. He was a wiz at skating forward and backward with the puck. He knew how to make tight turns and large turns and how to shoot forehand and backhand. And he was only six years old!"

Once again, Noah stopped speaking. His throat had turned raspy, and his voice stalled at the edge of tears. He held his lips tight and held his breath, too. His taut suppression of his grief subdued the storm raging inside him. Only then did he resume speaking.

"Seth was terrific at so many things. You should have seen him riding a Shetland pony or swimming in the pool at home. He had a sense of humor, as well. Even now, I can hear that joyful laugh of his when he played a prank on his best friends or when he was watching a clown at the circus."

Once again, he grimaced and then carried on. He was struggling fiercely not to show that he was a broken man.

"What a terrible loss," she said, her voice soft and soothing, as if she wanted to ease his hurt. "I am so sorry for you and for Olivia."

"We are sorry, too, and we'll never be rid of the sorrow, unless…"

He paused abruptly, uncertain now of the step to take next.

She coaxed him forward with a question.

"Unless what?"

He moved forward.

"Unless you help us."

"What can I do?"

He gazed into her eyes, seeking to confirm the empathy and the compassion that her words were promising him. She kept her glance upon him soft and elegiac. He believed in her glance. He believed that she wanted to hear more of his story and that she would find a way to help him, if she could. His words came more urgently now. There was an excitement in his voice and in the way he leaned toward her as he spoke. He wanted her to know more about him. He wanted to convince her that he was worthy of whatever help she was going to give him.

"Shortly after you and I parted," he said, "you gave birth to our son. I've never seen him. Believe me, though, when I tell you that there were many days when I wanted to see him. I wanted to reach out to you. I wanted to ask you to forgive me for hurting you. I wanted so much to see our son."

There was an angry edge to her next question. But she concealed that anger with tremulous regret that he had not corresponded with her.

"What stopped you? Why didn't you phone me or write me?"

"I didn't want to intrude upon the life that you had made with Steven. I didn't have the right. I assumed that the boy regarded Steven as his father. I thought it best to leave things the way they were."

"But now you think differently."

"I need our son. I won't be taking him away from you. I just want to make him part of my life at least some of the time. Bringing him into my life will be a tremendous thing. With him, Olivia and I can learn how to be happy again."

Only much later would she admit to herself the cruelty that she was invoking to destroy forever Noah's well-being and his inner peace. Only then, after the passage of many years and after their son had compelled her to confront the harsh truth, would she admit to herself that the outrage of being spurned by Noah had shackled her even as it had walled her inside a dark prison of her own making. So chained was she to her narcissistic grief that she refused to see or comprehend the grief of others. Her willingness to see would come later, when it was too late to remedy her wrongdoing.

On this October afternoon in 1967, she took pleasure in being cruel. She was equally impressed by the ease and alacrity by which she devised the lie that would damage and perhaps destroy Noah's hope and Olivia's, too. She lowered the pitch of her voice. She made her words sound hushed and regretful.

"I'm sorry that I can't help you. Our son, yours and mine, died in a skiing accident when he was eleven years old."

It took him a moment to understand what she had said. He looked startled and disbelieving. He gazed at her once more. It was a gaze that was even more penetrating than before. He needed to connect her mournful demeanor to the disquieting reality of her words. Her pretense of deep and abiding sorrow was all that he needed to understand that mischance, perpetual and unyielding, had crushed his last hope to have a son through whose veins his own blood quickened and thrived.

The desolation that he was experiencing stole not only his hope, but also his ability to articulate his feelings with crisp and confident words. He would recover his fluency after a moment. But his loss of hope for a son would be, she imagined, permanent.

His spirit instantly crushed by the cruelty of her false news, he could manage only a nearly inaudible mumble that let her know he had heard the words that told him his son Adam was dead.

"Oh," he murmured.

She wanted to inflict deeper wounds in him. She wanted him to suffer even more painfully. She wanted to remind him of his own cruelty in abandoning her and in refusing to claim Adam as his son. She chose matter-of-fact words that taunted even as they appeared to console.

"Maybe it's better that you didn't know Adam," she said. "You can't really feel a deep loss over someone that you never knew."

Her words, generated by her spurious empathy, were burning into his consciousness. When he answered her, confessional and morose, his brow was creased with grief, and his voice imparted the anguish that he was hard-pressed to conceal.

"I do feel the loss, deeper than you might imagine. I deprived myself of all the happiness I would have known when he was alive."

She tormented him further and, right after that, pretended to offer him a way out of his dilemma.

"Steven and I have a son of our own. His name is Ryan. His being with us, alive and well, has helped us find our way out of the darkness."

"It's a wonderful thing to have a son, alive and well."

"You and Olivia should try again. You're still young. You can have another son or a daughter."

"It's too late. And it's dangerous. The doctors have advised Olivia against having any other children."

"Then adopt a child. There are so many children around the world who need caring parents."

"Olivia doesn't want to adopt a child. She's convinced herself that we weren't meant to have a child. We've lost three of them. She doesn't want to risk being hurt again. I can't say I blame her. We'll just have to learn how to make the best of things."

"Well, we all have to learn that, for one reason or another."

"So we do," he said. "So we do."

That was that. She'd had her revenge. It had taken only an hour or two to inflict its pain. But that pain would last for the rest of Noah's life.

She enjoyed the orange mousse that the waiter brought to them. But Noah did not touch it. Instead, he ordered scotch, served without ice or any other mixer. Before they'd left the restaurant, he had drunk two more rounds of scotch.

When they left the restaurant, they appeared to be a married couple, compatible and relaxed in each other's company. The pianist was playing another love ballad, and the personable guests went on conversing, she imagined, about their latest business success or an offspring's imminent marriage or a recent vacation in the Bahamas, perhaps, or on the French Riviera.

When they left the restaurant and before she entered her Mercedes, which the valet had waiting for her, she turned to Noah. Though she maintained her friendly manner, her parting words were matter-of-fact and unsentimental.

"I don't suppose that we'll be seeing one another again."

Noah, heading for his Jaguar, turned back to her. He looked straight at her, pensive and rueful. Then, he forced himself to smile. He wanted to end their meeting with a happier thought.

"Maybe we will see one another," he said. "You never can tell what the future holds."

Despite his smile, his words sounded hollow and rehearsed. His heart was not in them.

With brisk movements, he turned from her. Without looking back and without any betrayal that he'd had a few drinks, he entered his car and drove away.

For weeks afterward, she felt buoyant and satisfied. To recover his happiness, Noah needed their son. But now, believing that Adam had died, he would never see him. He would never come to know and to love him. He would never have the heir for whom he had prayed. The desolation that he felt would keep burning in his soul. That same desolation would also live in his consciousness, furious and implacable. Forever.

PART TWO

OTHER POINTS OF VIEW

PART TWO

CHAPTER ONE

Steven

Tuesday Afternoon, 16 February 1971

"Block his jabs, but watch out for his right cross. Keep circling him. Don't back away. Throw right jabs fast and hard. Put all your power into that punch."

Moving with wily energy about the ring, refereeing and critiquing at the same time, Steven was issuing curt directions to his son Ryan. This younger son of his was having a hard time dealing with his brother Adam's bobbing and weaving in the ring that had been specially built for these competitions. He was also having trouble avoiding Adam's succession of rapid punches. Both of his sons were cautiously boxing each other. They were too cautious. They were holding back the fury that they always summoned when they faced other opponents. There was a part of him that did not want them to hold back. There was a twisted part that wanted Ryan to punch Adam so hard that he would knock him out.

"When Adam drops his guard, land a powerful right to his jaw."

He sounded like a tough-hearted drill sergeant bearing down hard on one of his recruits. He was barking out instructions. He was snarling a litany of corrections. They were in the spacious gym in the north wing of the tri-level home that he and Charlotte had built shortly after they were married. The north wing was an addition that, in his mind, became a necessity. He needed the gym to sharpen the defensive skills of the younger of the two youths he called his sons, though the blood that flowed through his own veins flowed only through Ryan's. His older son, Adam, from his embittered perspective not his son at all, carried the blood of Noah Blake, a man he regarded as an unwitting catalyst in the tautly harnessed rancor of his marriage.

He used this gym as a basic training site for his stoical and obedient sons. All around them, in the equally spacious areas that made the gym a place of grueling workouts and punishing exercises, were parallel bars and barbells, as well as ankle and wrist weights, pull-up belts, rowers, and treadmills. The place was Spartan and clean, and the atmosphere was military.

Adam, on holiday from his senior year at the same exclusive prep school where Ryan was a sophomore, had consented to be here in the ring with Ryan. But he did not really want to box with his brother. He loved him too much for that. Only when he had urged this older son of his to get in the ring and give his younger brother a chance to improve his skills did Adam consent. Ryan would be fighting in a boxing competition when he returned to their private school after the holiday break. Always accommodating and always loyal, Adam wanted to help his brother to win the school's boxing trophy. He also wanted to fulfill his father's wishes. He needed to know that he was pleasing the father whose love he quietly sought. He was that father, and he had in these recent years withheld the love he had once shown him, unconditionally and honestly.

Adam was eighteen. He was tall, rugged, and confident about all things except his relationship with him—the man who pretended to be his natural father and who had for several years shown him the affection that Noah himself might have offered him. Adam looked like Noah, dark-haired, handsome, and rangy. He sounded like him, too, with a voice both husky and articulate. He was stronger than Ryan and more experienced as a boxer.

Here, in the gym, Adam was mostly feinting the fast punches and right jabs that he brought to this mock fight with his brother. He did not want to hurt him. He did not want to humiliate him in any way.

But Ryan was not a novice in the ring. He had been boxing at his private school since he was eight years old. Now, at sixteen, he had mastered the essentials of the combat sport. He had learned how to stand defensively, with his legs shoulder-width apart and how to lead with the left foot and fist for most penetration impact. He kept both feet parallel and his left heel off the ground. His coach at school had taught him how to hold his left fist vertically, about six inches in front of his face at eye level. From that coach, Ryan also learned to hold his right fist beside his chin and to tuck his elbow against his ribcage to protect his body.

The coach taught him much more than that. But he was not Ryan's only boxing teacher. When Ryan was home during winter and spring recess from school and during part of his summer vacations, he—his willful and ambitious father—kept testing his resilience and his courage. He reviewed with him all that his boxing coach had taught him at school, and he taught him a few strategies that he had not yet learned. He showed him the importance of jabbing an opponent as a way of setting up heavier and more powerful punches. He showed him, too, that a straight punch thrown with the right hand carried an unforgiving power. From a guarded position, the boxer throws his right hand from his chin and with a right cross smashes into his opponent's face. He also showed Ryan how to throw a hook or a semi-circular punch to the side of his opponent's head and how to throw an uppercut by shifting his torso slightly to the right, dropping his right hand below the level of his opponent's chest, and thrusting that hand upwards toward his opponent's chin or torso.

He was determined that Ryan would outbox every opponent. He pushed him into rigorous boxing drills, and he arranged boxing matches between Ryan and some of his athletic buddies.

Ryan was solidly built. At sixteen years old, he stood six foot, one inch. Weightlifting, swimming, ice hockey, and mountain climbing had made his body strong. As he was growing into his manhood, he gave evidence on many occasions that he would move through even the harsh experiences of life with self-assurance and tough-minded physicality. But there were other times when he allowed his good-natured spirit and his deep-seated empathy toward others to override the toughness. It was then that his son's conduct roused his fatherly anger. To burn that sensitivity out of him, he invoked these harsh and militant drills. He meant to make Ryan fierce and callous and hardened. He wanted him to overcome all his opponents. He wanted him to eclipse even Adam, whom he accepted as his blood brother, not ever having been told that Adam was Noah Blake's bastard and that he—Steven Bennington—had rescued him from the scandal and the misery of being regarded as illegitimate.

"Bob and weave! Bob and weave!" he shouted as he himself moved with wily dexterity around the ring, shadowing every move of his sons. In this instant, he was calling out to Ryan. "Block his punches!"

Ryan parried Adam's next punch and then turned on him with his own series of punches. By chance, he landed a hard punch to Adam's jaw that brought Adam down, reeling as he was with surprise and dizziness.

Ryan cried out, instantly remorseful and apprehensive.

"Adam!"

He knelt beside his brother and, grabbing him by the shoulders, lifted him to a sitting position.

"I'm sorry," he said. "I'm so sorry. Are you hurt?"

A bit woozy, Adam managed to smile.

"I'm all right," he said. "You caught me off guard."

"I didn't mean to," Ryan said. "I don't want to hurt you. Not ever."

"It's okay, brother. We're still friends."

Adam permitted Ryan to help him up and to walk with him to the stool in his corner of the ring. There was no animosity in the quick glance he gave his brother. He appreciated him more than ever, this never-failing advocate whose hero-worship, brotherly love, and kind-hearted nature he valued above the proven mettle of even his loyal friends.

He, their conflicted father, noticed all these things. There was a part of him that respected the genuine camaraderie that existed, steadfast and invincible, between his sons. But his discontented heart and his cynical awareness of the influence that Noah Blake still held over Charlotte even after all these years held him in their chains. Disdainful and belligerent, he scoffed at the sympathy that Ryan was extending to Adam. He hurried over to his sons and pulled Ryan away from Adam.

"Save your pity," he said. "Adam got what he deserved. He wasn't paying attention."

His sons, knowing how easy it was to enrage him, said nothing. Instead, before Ryan returned to his corner of the ring, he met Adam's steady gaze. They needed no other language to verify their loyalty toward each other.

That was their usual response to his tyrannical conduct. Their taut stillness was the response that he anticipated and, with a sadist's distorted outlook, enjoyed for a minute or so before his self-hatred hurried back to kick aside his ambivalent perversities.

On this morning, though, Adam responded in a manner that surprised him.

After he dismissed his sons from their workout, never abandoning his army sergeant's toughness, he watched Ryan hurry away to shower and dress. He noticed his younger son's confident gait and his ingrained buoyancy that came alive the moment that he had turned away from his father and was swiftly moving into an afternoon with neighborhood friends who were also on holiday from their schools.

But Adam did not leave with him. Instead, once they were out of the ring and standing in the hallway that led to the locker room and the shower stalls, Adam began speaking to him with clipped words and brusque intonations that stopped him, the hardhearted father, in his tracks. His brown eyes were searching his face. His words were probing and accusatory.

"You don't like me."

"You're talking nonsense," he told him, blunt and self-defensive. "You're talking like a fool."

Adam held firm. He wasn't going to back away from this confrontation.

"I'm telling you what I see and what I feel."

"You're imagining things."

"I want to know why you hate me."

"Drop it, Adam. You're way out of line."

He turned and made a wily retreat from Adam. Instead of heading for the locker room, he left this north wing of the house and made his way toward the garage. He intended to find solace by driving his Ferrari, testing its speed and its horsepower along seemingly endless roads that were as smooth as they were solitary. As he maintained a swift gait, he had the sense that Adam was watching his every move. When he looked back to the north wing, he saw Adam standing outside the exit door from the gym. His imposing muscularity and his brooding demeanor made him appear angry and dangerous. That look gave him fatherly unease. Adam, he imagined, would have enjoyed meeting him in the ring, boxing with his fiercest powers the father who took pleasure in withholding his love and denying him the praise that he had earned by succeeding in all the essential areas that define a son's excellence.

He turned his glance away from Adam and kept walking toward the garage, which was located in the east wing of his home. Whether the thought of fighting him had really crossed Adam's mind, he could not say. But Adam's troubled gaze stayed with him through the rest of that day. He had to admit, reluctantly, that the image of his son boxing against him in the ring disconcerted him. The sadness that attended him exposed the feelings that he had tried to hide, not only from Adam, but also from himself. Confused and conflicted, he still loved this older of his sons. But he no longer was free to express those feelings. His bitter heart and his rage against his wife's ongoing affair with Rick Blanchard and her professed love for Adam's father shackled his will. Anger and hatred had made him their prisoner.

For today at least, there would be no more boxing. He was pleased that his son Ryan had prevailed in his fight against Adam. He wanted Ryan to prevail in all contests in which Adam stood as his opponent. The blood that flowed through Ryan's veins was Bennington blood. Despite the Bennington name that he carried, Adam's blood was Noah Blake's blood. He would never be a true Bennington.

So he told himself once again, while the enmity that was festering in the most secret corner of his consciousness scalded his mood and disarranged his contentment.

It had not always been so. For the first fifteen years of his marriage, he had known the familial happiness that all reputable husbands and fathers experience. In so many ways, Charlotte had made their adventure of being together seem exciting and original. If theirs was a marriage of true minds, the truth resided not in authentic passion or in the conventional niceties of marital bonding. The truth lay within the experiment they were carrying forward to discover whether they could learn to love each other without devising self-serving plots or perverse betrayals. Faithfulness to a single partner had never been a virtue that roused their interest. In their sexual relationships, they had always preferred a variety of partners. They had soon grown weary of even the most thrilling partners. Their young narcissism and their craving for different sensations drew them invariably toward new partners and new places. But, after he rescued Charlotte from the scandal of her unmarried pregnancy, she suppressed her wilder impulses. She tried to fall in love with him, even as she struggled to elude the ghostly presence of Noah Blake that haunted her still. In those first years of their marriage, she never mentioned Noah. Gradually, he came to believe that she had gone past her dreams of him. Her wifely behavior began to convince him that he was winning her love, after all. She accommodated his every need, not only in bed, but also through all the wonderful activities, uneventful and nondescript or essential and extraordinary, that sustain and enlighten a marriage.

First of all, she shared her work with him. Though her literary agent guided her through the completion of each of her novels, Charlotte brought the manuscripts to him before she allowed anyone else to see them. She valued his input.

She saw him as a prototype of the readers for whom she was writing. They shared many productive discussions of what was working effectively in her latest novel-in-progress and what needed to be clarified or even discarded. As a writer, Charlotte thought for herself. She was not afraid to invoke daring narrative strategies. Nor did she hesitate to subvert the tropes of literary masters from the past. She was brutally honest in her assessment of the human condition. The world that she created through her fast-paced fiction was often dark and unforgiving. Her protagonists were usually trapped by their own unsavory deeds or violated by pernicious friends or destroyed by unscrupulous strangers. There was an ingrained honesty in her writing that, he eventually perceived, she refused to bring into her own life.

In these happy years, he taught Charlotte to fly a Cessna 172 Skyhawk, and he guided her through a rigorous trek up Mount Washington, the highest mountain in New Hampshire and in all of the northeastern United States. Together, they worked with a university professor to attain a fluency in German, French, and Italian. So well did they excel, that they were able to travel through Berlin, Paris, and Rome with proficient ease. In many other activities, they reveled in their mutual proficiencies. On winter holidays with their two sons, who had by that time entered their early teens, they skied and snowboarded in Lausanne. They ice-skated in Graubünden. For one wild and remarkable hour, they rode Thoroughbred polo ponies, roan-colored with powerful limbs and crossed with the agility of Criollos, on a frozen lake in St. Moritz and played a swift game of polo. In various summers, they snorkeled in Tahiti, they kayaked on the perilous white waters of the Kitka River in Kuusamo, Finland, and they explored the Ajanta caves in Aurangabad, India, with their rock-cut sculptures of Buddhist deities and their vivid paintings of the past lives and rebirths of the Buddha.

"My life has become a great adventure," Adam declared to Charlotte and him the morning after they had hunted down a bear in the forests of Montana during the autumn of 1968. Though they were spending most of their nights in a hunters' lodge that provided every amenity, they'd managed to rough it a few days and nights, along with their hunting guides, when they used sturdy tents as their home base and rode in fast-moving jeeps while tracking a giant bear, perhaps, or a mountain lion.

"Sometimes," Adam informed Charlotte and him on that hunting expedition, "I feel that I'm living out a terrific dream and that the two of you have made it all possible."

"I feel the same way," Ryan said. He was glad to echo his brother's understated elation.

Hearing the spontaneous joy in his sons' remarks, he believed that, after years of tortuous searching, he had finally discovered the happiness that was going to last for all the remaining days of his life. He was supremely contented. Only in the uneasy dreams occasionally disturbing his sleep did he imagine that some shadowy figure whose face and form he could not decipher was stealing away his happiness.

In this same happy period, Charlotte won a few of the more prestigious awards for three of her novels, and he found enormous success as a hard-driving vice-president for his father's fast-food corporation and as a canny investor on Wall Street. Their unbridled ambition and an insatiable desire to win every challenge they confronted propelled every one of their victories. For fifteen years, the conniving Fates or envious Chance tolerated their happiness.

Then, during the autumn of 1968, only a few months after their hunting expedition in Montana, everything changed for Charlotte and him and, with ricocheting damages and psychological injuries, for Adam and Ryan, too.

During that October, *Time Magazine* published a cover story about the huge audience that Charlotte's latest novel was attracting. In the gallery of photos that were anchored to the glamorous subtext of the magazine's essay, Charlotte appeared with various celebrities who had attended a gala dinner party that her publisher had hosted in an upscale Manhattan restaurant. The gala honored not only Charlotte, but also four other authors who had signed lucrative contracts with her publisher. Film stars, Olympic athletes, and television anchors greeted her as a more-than-ordinary luminary whose talent and fame shone as brightly as their own. New York producers of popular musicals and prize-winning dramas, Washington-based senators and Wall Street brokers, and ambassadors from London, Paris, Berlin, and Hong Kong also consented to be photographed with her. She was the golden girl of all the best-selling lists. With her lovely bones and immaculate skin, her slim figure, and the fashionable wardrobe that she wore with inherent authority, Charlotte embodied the self-possession and playful insouciance of the most dazzling of the celebrities. No matter that her wardrobe replicated the styles of Audrey Hepburn and Jacqueline Kennedy. Everything that she wore, she made new and original. With Oleg Cassini and Hubert de Givenchy advising her, she became her own style. In that year, she was thirty-eight years old. With the subtle application of cosmetics and with a chic hairdo, she appeared to be a decade younger. Her sensuality, exuded like a delicate perfume, enhanced rather than diminished her decorum. Fashionable women approved her choices. The literati, with their exclusionary arrogance and their rigid standards, applauded the power of her prose and the timely themes that complicated and quickened her narratives.

Time Magazine's cover story validated Charlotte's fame and her burgeoning talent as a novelist. That October issue represented the pinnacle of her success. It also exposed, for his eyes only, the dangerous fault line in their marriage. The danger derived from her friendship with Rick Blanchard.

After his divorce from Olivia Tanner, Rick had led the carefree life of a wealthy playboy. He was not interested in marrying anyone else. Being a playboy had become his stock-in-trade, an erotic pastime that he shared with women as adventurous and as self-serving as he was.

Among the gallery of photos that *Time* had used to illustrate Charlotte's celebrity, as well as that of the four other writers, were three that showed her with Rick Blanchard. Never was she photographed alone with him. Each time that they were photographed in the same frame, the camera caught them in the midst of other guests, smiling or chatting, reflective or exhilarated. Yet, though they had positioned themselves within the animated tapestry of current power brokers, old money, and start-up moguls, the camera always captured them standing with easy intimacy next to each other.

At first, he suppressed his doubts of her fidelity to him. After fifteen years of being married to one another, he took her faithfulness for granted. He never imagined her to be ideal. His realistic view of the world did not permit him to expect moral perfection in anyone, including himself. Human beings were a carnal and predatory species. They always had been. They always would be. He was not aware that Charlotte's celebrity had improved her character. Rather, that celebrity had persuaded her to tamp down her capacities for scheming against her friends, for subverting the wellbeing of potential adversaries, and for betraying the trust that they—he and Charlotte—had cautiously built into their marriage. In their university days, he had admired Charlotte's free spirit. He had been drawn to her savvy dismissal of the safe conventions that inhibited originality and punished rebels. In those days, she called a spade a spade. With him, she rarely cloaked her motives with half-truths and pernicious aims. She admitted that she was a self-centered adventuress. She was a seeker of experiences that she would find only at the cusp of danger. She was a weaver of plots that often paired her with men as devious and as self-serving as she was. She was outrageous. She was fallible. She was secretly vulnerable.

He began to love her because of all the rebellious things that she did. His desire for her, influential and distended, deepened and intensified each time that he was with her and all the times when he was not. That he was willing to love her, tarnished though she was by her past promiscuity and her faithlessness, did not surprise him. He had no interest in acquiring a wife who wore her morality on her sleeve or who found pleasure in suppressing her mate's healthy impulses. He preferred a woman who had already excited her life with numerous romantic attachments. Such a woman was not afraid to test the wildness of her nature or to pair herself with a formidable man who lived life to the hilt. So he believed when he was a man in his early twenties who had not yet initiated all the adventures that kept testing and renewing his individuality.

His marriage to Charlotte was both a test and an adventure, for her as well as for him. Their union challenged them to become adventurous in a different way. They had to enter unknown territory that required clear-sighted honesty and mutual goals. They had to dare themselves to be faithful to each other. In the first fifteen years of their marriage, they accepted and passed all the tests. They overcame every desire to break free of the conventional rules of marriage. Yet they never felt constrained by those rules. On the contrary, they turned their marriage into a creative enterprise. They made so many of their days spark with different activities, new friends, and frequent travel. They brought maturing energies to their careers, and they guided their sons into intellectually stimulating school programs and equally formidable athletic competitions.

Everything in their marriage was going supremely well until the publication of that *Time Magazine* article.

He had felt reasonably certain that the photographs that paired Charlotte with Rick Blanchard did not presage any danger to his marriage. If that were the case, if Charlotte were really involved in an affair with Rick Blanchard, she would have taken steps to conceal their relationship. Rick's presence at the gala that celebrated the success of Charlotte's latest book was probably a chance happening. He was there, undoubtedly, to pay tribute to the CEO of The General Electric Corporation whose book about Wall Street was attracting good reviews and strong sales. Rick was enjoying immense success as a vice-president in that corporation.

So he told himself, struggling all the while to perceive his imagined scenario as harmless as it was plausible.

His unwillingness to confront Charlotte with his misgivings was, he admitted to himself later, a fault line in his marriage. He did not trust her to tell him the truth. For seven days and seven nights, suspicion goaded his dark thoughts. He brooded about her past infidelities. He recalled her penchant for superficial trysts, and he dwelled upon her long-ago affair with Rick. During this period, she was often away from home, busy with her book tour that brought her through all the major cities in the United States and into a few cities in Europe, too. At the same time, he busied himself with his own thriving career and tightly harnessed his suspicions. When she returned, inspirited by the success of her book and caught up by the sheer joy of being so completely alive and youthfully lovely even at thirty-eight, he set a team of detectives on her trail.

"She's meeting Rick Blanchard once or twice a week," the younger of the detectives reported to him.

His name was Tyler Madison. He stood at five foot, eleven inches, and he was immaculately groomed. Dressed as he was in his navy double-breasted suit and his expensive shoes, he might easily have been taken as an ambitious executive from Boston or New York. He had curly black hair, penetrating brown eyes, and a scar that left its vague traces across his right cheek—a memento from his years as a goalie for a college hockey team, perhaps, or from a skiing accident. He was no more than twenty-seven or twenty-eight years old. Yet his experience of the world had already jaded his disposition. From his perspective, nobody looked innocent. Everybody carried incriminating backstories.

He—Steven Bennington, a privileged man who was about to lose the happiness that he had cultivated for the last fifteen years—understood Tyler Madison well. Each of them shared a realistic view of the world and a canny awareness of its moral compromises and its casual betrayals. As they sat in the privacy of his Manhattan office after all of his staff had left for the day, he listened carefully to everything that this Madison fellow was telling him. Hearing his words, imparted without a pause or any show of emotion, he was more disappointed than surprised. At the same time, he noticed Madison's coldhearted detachment as he brought out a folder of reports, neatly typed and tersely describing each occasion when Charlotte met Rick Blanchard. Always, he was to learn, they disguised their meetings, whether they appeared in close proximity at a public gathering or whenever they hurried away to more remote locations to enjoy their trysts.

"During the past six weeks, while your wife has been touring with her newest book, she has met Rick Blanchard five times," Madison said. "During the weekend of October fourth through the sixth, they stayed in her parents' Newport home, which, as you know, is unoccupied after the summer."

"What were they doing in Newport, besides sleeping with one another?"

"They drove to a horse farm about a mile from the Scotts' property. They rented two Pinto horses and spent a couple of hours riding along the trail there."

"Was anyone with them?"

"They rode together, apart from any of the other couples or the family groups making their way along the trail. My two agents, a former marine and a pretty blonde, were among those couples. They took plenty of photos. I'll show them to you in a few minutes. My agents even waved to them and called out a 'hello' when they passed near them. By then, Blanchard and your wife had dismounted and had paused to look at a meadow of late-blooming chrysanthemums, daylilies, and lupin. Blanchard was caressing your wife and then kissing her. He began whispering romantic words to her, and she responded by returning his kiss. They appeared to be very happy."

"What else do you have to tell me?"

"In Newport, they attended an international boat show at the yachting center. In fact, Blanchard piloted his own yacht in a race that involved seven other boats. Of course, your wife served as Blanchard's co-pilot in that race. They were lucky. They came in second. If they'd won the race, their faces would have appeared on the front page of Newport and Providence newspapers."

"They're lucky, all right. They're lucky I don't kill them."

"You don't need to kill them. You've got the goods on them. You can turn this thing to your advantage."

"Maybe. Maybe not. Anyway, tell me everything else I need to know."

"On Tuesday, the fifteenth of October and Wednesday the sixteenth, they stayed in Blanchard's cabin in Maine. I set a different pair of agents on their path. Once again, my assistants passed as a good-looking couple, and they were also athletic. Blanchard and your wife spent some time skiing on Shawnee Peak in Bridgton. Later, they drove to Portland, about an hour away from the Peak, and they dined at a fine restaurant there. On the following day, they took a long walk inside the woods near Blanchard's cabin. They dined at a steakhouse that was located about a half-hour's drive from the cabin. Other than that, they spent plenty of time inside the cabin. My assistants noted in their report that Blanchard and your wife appeared to be a couple who'd been married for many years and who were still very much in love with each other."

"Is that it?"

"There's more."

"Tell me quickly. Get it over with."

"On Wednesday afternoon, the twenty-third of October, they appeared at an art exhibit in Philadelphia, though they arrived and left separately. Later that evening, they stayed in Blanchard's penthouse in a gated section of the city. During the week of the fourth of November, while your wife was on the Pacific Coast making television and bookstore appearances for her novel, she and Blanchard spent a few days at a posh hotel in Hawaii. They booked separate suites on the same floor, but they spent the nights in his rooms."

"They were very sure of themselves. Too sure. Maybe they didn't care if they were caught."

"Could be. More likely, they believed that they could beat the odds. Chance was on their side. It wasn't very likely that they would run into any of your New York or Connecticut friends in any of the places that they chose for their meetings."

"Newport. Maine. Philadelphia. Hawaii. Was there any other place?"

"There was. On November thirteenth and fourteenth, they shared a weekend in Paris. They visited art galleries. They attended a wine festival. They danced in a popular nightclub. They stayed in a five star hotel and enjoyed all the amenities there, including a spa, a swimming pool, a casino, and an elegant ballroom."

"That's enough. I don't need to hear any more."

Now Madison brought out his album of photos. Whether they were skiing or horse riding, swimming or dancing, Rick Blanchard and Charlotte looked years younger than they were. The pictures made clear that they had rediscovered their love. A special radiance had taken hold of them. They were each other's rescuers, and their reawakened passion for each other was an unanticipated lifeline that the wily Fates or their own scheming had granted them.

"My team and I took plenty of pictures. We have photos that show Blanchard and your wife in all of the places where they met. We were three couples carrying forward our detective work, but never in the same location. My girlfriend and I covered the Paris assignment. The second couple followed your wife and Blanchard to Hawaii. The third couple tracked them in Philadelphia. The six of us easily passed as honeymooners. We were able to get close to them and to get all the pictures we needed. The most intimate ones show them kissing on an Hawaiian beach, dancing in a jazzy nightspot in Paris, and—most incriminating of all—sleeping together in Hawaii and Philadelphia."

He quietly studied the photos, turning page after page of the album in quick succession as if he were viewing a montage of images in a movie or a series of snapshots that were being used as evidence in a police report. Some blowups of the photos emphasized Charlotte's lips pressing upon the right corner of Rick's mouth; Charlotte's seductive glance at Rick as they sat at a tony bar; Rick's large, proprietary arms clasping Charlotte's waist as they danced an old-fashioned two-step with its hip-to-hip position and its hopping movements; and Charlotte's gleaming skin, supple breasts, and exhilarated face mated with Rick's muscular physique and excited demeanor as they ran hand-in-hand and naked across the tawny sands of a beach toward the wind-swept, moonlit waters of the Pacific Ocean.

Even after the passage of three years, he remembered the telltale photos as clearly as if he were studying them now, here in the quiet of his after-hours office. Tyler Madison, with penetrating stare and ingrained detachment, was observing his reaction to the photos while he sat opposite him in a comfortably upholstered chair a few feet away from his desk.

He, Steven Bennington, the cuckolded husband, yoked his rising fury to a taut stillness. He summoned a fake detachment. He found matter-of-fact words to close his meeting with Madison.

"You and your team have done a good job," he told him. "Now I'll take over."

Madison rose from his chair, exchanged a few words about the bill, and left quickly. He was used to making quick departures. He was slick, all right, with a street-wise smartness pushing him forward. He had no interest in witnessing the violent repercussions of his detective work.

There were repercussions, but the violence was reined in, curbed, and held in check with the promise of more violence, looming and imminent.

When Charlotte returned from her book tour, he refrained from showing her the album of incriminating photos. For six days, he waited. He wanted to observe her contrived lightheartedness when she was with him and to hear her smoky-voiced lies as she told him how much she had missed him and how she had been yearning to be with him, here in the comfortable privacies of their home. She was used to lying. She had made a game of becoming different Charlottes to appease the expectations of her readers and to draw the genuine praise of new friends and the favorable surprise of friends of long standing. Hers was a complicated artifice. The masks she wore often muted her glamour in favor of a contrived authenticity that linked her name to community and global charities, to her success as a wife and a mother, and to her occasional rescue of friends besieged by baleful adversaries. She invoked her glamorous incarnations for the international parties and ballroom dinners that required her to hobnob with government officials, royal families, and topnotch moguls that could enhance his career as well as her own.

On one of these occasions, when they were dressing to attend a lavish premiere of a Broadway musical and the equally lavish party afterwards, he brought out the album of photos that revealed her intimate association with Rick Blanchard.

Charlotte and he, her secretly aggrieved husband, were spending the week at their Manhattan home. Nobody else was there. Adam was busy with his first year at Yale, and Ryan, now a junior, was away at his boarding school in Connecticut. The housekeeper and her daughter, who came in three times a week to maintain the orderly upkeep of the place, had completed their work for the day and had left the house shortly before four o'clock.

When he entered her bedroom, he had already finished dressing. His black tuxedo, with its satin lapels and pleated trousers, as well as the white pleated wingtip shirt and black bow tie, intensified the formality of his manly gait even as they disguised the contained fury that impelled him forward. Charlotte was adjusting her diamond earrings and reviewing in the long mirror at the side of a Louis XVI armoire the glamorous image she embodied while wearing a black chiffon evening dress. On this evening, she took little notice of him, but she offered him, nonetheless, a bright smile and a quick-witted remark about her incipient narcissism. The smile and the remark were her stock in trade. They were meant to disarm him.

"This lily is gilding herself," she said. "She's nearly ready to meet the curious eyes of tonight's other pleasure seekers."

He had often come into her bedroom when she was applying blush to her cheeks or mascara to her eyelashes or a discreet gloss to her lips. He'd always arrive with a grin that casually accommodated his equally quick-witted rejoinder.

"You're golden without the gilding," he'd say, intending to prod her from her cosmetics. "So let's hurry away and set the night spinning."

This brief exchange, or others that simulated its lightheartedness, would influence the mood for the evening ahead of them.

But tonight he offered no witty remark or lightness of heart. Instead, while suppressing his anger inside a tight-lipped silence, he placed Tyler Madison's album of photos on the desk of the vanity before which she now took a seat.

Finished with her cosmetics, she opened the album with casual-seeming curiosity. After scanning a few of its pages, she closed the album and rose from her chair to face him. She contrived a smile. She sensed his anger, muted though it was. She meant to dispel his doubt of her with a blithe manner and a flash of vivacity.

"It doesn't mean anything," she said. "Rick's an old friend. He's a valuable resource. He sparked me up when I'd grown weary of my busy schedule."

He moved closer, hovering over her—rancorous, though not yet threatening.

"You didn't ask me to join you. You asked him, instead."

She looked directly into his eyes, wary but not yet afraid.

"I needed to be away from us for a while. I needed a change. I needed to be with someone other than you."

"I'm your husband. Doesn't that make any difference?"

She turned away from him now. She wanted to distract him by busying herself with the fashioning of her appearance. She took hold of a hairbrush from her vanity and walked toward the long mirror at the side of the Louis XVI armoire. She surveyed the flow of her dress and, satisfied that she wore it with her usual flair, began brushing her hair. She protracted her movements so that her care of her appearance subverted the importance of what he was telling her. He was probing her mind, and she didn't like it. She resented his asking her whether his being her husband made any difference to her.

"Of course it does," she answered him with well-calibrated poise. "But I wanted something I couldn't have with you. I wanted to be young again. I wanted to re-live the excitement of being with Rick."

Once again, he moved closer. He was standing behind her. He caught sight of himself in the long mirror. In an instant, his brooding face and his tall and muscular virility had become threatening.

"You love him."

Wary yet matter-of-fact, she kept brushing her hair.

"No. But he's good for me in many ways."

He took hold of her by her shoulders and swung her around. Startled, she did not resist his hold on her.

"You're in love with him."

"No."

He slapped her, all the while pinioning her so that she could not escape the clasp of his left hand upon her shoulder. Not only her face, but also her trapped body recoiled with the impact of the slap.

"You're in love with him."

She began struggling against his hold upon her, even as she kept lying, breathless now and calculating her next move. She went on lying to him. She believed (he imagined) that, if she kept lying, she might send his doubts scattering. She might dissuade him from the truth.

He slapped her harder.

She was screaming now. The slap threw her head backward. Her face became flushed with the red marks flaring across her right cheek. The clasp of her necklace opened, and the string of diamonds fell upon the carpeted floor. Still she protested his handling of her and his accusations. Rebellious and insistent, she yelled out her lie.

"No."

He slapped her even harder. Her whole body recoiled and went limp from the power of the slap. Her hair became disheveled. Blood trickled from the left corner of her mouth. She would have fallen to the floor if he had released her from his imprisoning hold.

He waited until she found her breath once more. Then, as if it were a chant weaving its mischief and its revenge, he threw out the same accusation.

"You're in love with him."

"No!"

He was shaking her and, at the same time, lifting her slender body away from the floor and watching it dangle under the power of his grip.

"You like when he fucks you."

"Stop it! Stop it!" she cried out to him, her wavering voice no stronger than a sobbing appeal. "You'll ruin everything for us."

He released his hold upon her, pushing her away from him as though he were discarding an unwanted possession. She fell against the back of the upholstered chair near the vanity desk and slid onto the floor.

"You're a tramp," he said. His voice was a raspy whisper now.

He was weary of her and of himself. He had forfeited the tight control that had almost always defined who he was to himself. He loathed the Steven Bennington that he had become in this hour. He knew that he must do everything to retrieve the Steven Bennington whose stoic disposition had always served him well. But, despite the self-hatred that gave him a fleeting pause, he once again gave vent to his anger. With his grating whisper, he taunted Charlotte further.

"You were a tramp before I married you. You'll always be a tramp."

She did not answer him. Instead, she stood up, while using the chair to ballast herself. Then, right after she recovered herself, she took her seat before the vanity mirror and began repairing the damage that his violence had wrought upon her. She was no longer sobbing. Nor did her brown eyes look upon his mirrored image with fearful appeal or muted hatred. Stillness came upon her while invoking hardened detachment and claiming as her own the face and body that she was carefully restoring.

The calm that was giving her back her self-possession goaded, rather than pacified, him.

"Admit it!" he sneered. "Admit that you love Rick Blanchard!"

She did not answer him at once. She focused, instead, on applying new makeup that covered her bruised cheeks and neck and on refreshing her lips with another layer of gloss to conceal the nearly imperceptible cut at the left corner of her mouth.

Only when she stood up and rearranged her dress as she peered at herself in the long mirror by the armoire—only then did she respond to his heated complaint. She told him what in his heart he already knew. She spoke the words that he did not want to hear.

"I don't love Rick. I don't love you, either. I love Noah Blake. I've never stopped loving him. He's the only man I'll ever love."

She turned to him so that their eyes could meet. She was telling him the truth. She did not flinch before its stern, conflicted reality. But, though he tried to disguise the pain of the deep wound she was inflicting, he did flinch. He winced. Disheartened and nearly broken, he turned away from her without uttering another word.

Everything that had been meaningful between them was over.

Later, he was to wonder whether her admission of loving Noah surprised even herself, so tortured and ambivalent were her feelings toward the man who had abandoned her.

For a few weeks, he made their New York brownstone his home base. Charlotte returned to Greenwich. He busied himself with his career and avoided her. The thought that his sons, at recess from their school during the holidays, would be returning to their home in Connecticut compelled him, finally, to deal with the wreckage of his marriage. He and Charlotte conferred with their lawyer, Garrett Finlay. When he looked upon her then, there in Garrett's meticulously appointed office, he no longer loved her. Nor was there any love in her eyes for him. In those three meetings, neither of them made a scene. They were accepting the way things were for them. There was serious talk of a divorce.

But they did not divorce. Garrett made it clear that they had too much to lose. His parents and Charlotte's, too, warned them about the consequences, as harsh as they would be irrevocable, if they abandoned their marriage. Charlotte's conservative readers might turn away from her popular novels if she divorced her husband. Divorce would also undermine his leadership role in the Bennington Corporation.

Although they did not divorce each other through the courts, they devised their own kind of divorce. They lived in the same homes, but not as man and wife or even together. They added a wing to their Greenwich home and an additional floor and entrance to their New York brownstone. They came and went as they pleased. They gave the impression that their long-established marriage was still flourishing. On all the important holidays and during the summers, they consented to be in one another's company so that they could maintain a stable environment for their sons. But they no longer shared each other's bed. From time to time, Charlotte renewed her trysts with Rick Blanchard, and he began seeing other women. They were seductive strangers whom he paid well. They offered him exciting temporary nights that left him feeling hollow.

Each day, his hatred for Charlotte deepened. She had committed a crime against him and against their sons.

Willful and adulterous, she had destroyed his happiness. She had undermined the authenticity of their being together as husband and wife. Together, they fabricated a scenario meant to persuade their sons that all was well between them. They were ideal parents. He was a loving husband, and she was his faithful wife. Sometimes, he wondered whether Adam and Ryan saw through the charade that he and Charlotte were playing. His doubts intensified his unhappiness. He had cast himself into a prison of his own making. He could free himself only if he brought truth back into his home.

He felt lost. He saw no way out of his dilemma without damaging his career and hurting Ryan, the son whose blood was the same as his own.

Then, one afternoon in May of 1970, a television anchor named Caitlin O'Hara interviewed him for a national television news program that was profiling the most influential business executives in The United States. He felt like a man being reborn. Her titian hair, light-skinned beauty, and slender figure thrilled him. Being in her company quickened his pulse, not only during the interview when they were being filmed in a television studio, but also at the business lunch they shared the following day while they were in the company of her colleagues. Later that month, after she interviewed him about the success of the Bennington restaurant franchises in Europe, Asia, and South Africa, he once again shared lunch with her and her colleagues. He learned that she was twenty-seven. She was not married, but a year earlier her fiancé, a war correspondent and a television anchor, had been killed in the crash of a military helicopter in Thailand while he was covering the Vietnam War for CBS. He also learned from her close friends that she was still grieving for the man that she loved and that she refused to enter a relationship with any other man.

It was at this time, only nine months ago, that he began devising a plan to break away from his sham marriage. He wanted to wait until Ryan was in college and old enough to deal with his parents' divorce.

He did not care how Adam might feel. Adam was his son in name only. For a few minutes, while he was racing his Ferrari along the deserted roads that stretched away from his Greenwich home, he relived his stern treatment of him that had occurred only a half hour earlier in the boxing ring of their home gym. For more than two years now, he'd been punishing the boy for being Noah Blake's son. He wanted to push Adam out of his life.

Yet there was a part of him that loved and respected the boy. The memory of their strong bond still lived within the shadowy corners of his consciousness. He wondered how long it would take to destroy Adam's love for him. He imagined that, if he continued to mistreat him, Adam would one day go out of his life and never look back. He wondered, too, how he would feel if that ever happened.

PART TWO

CHAPTER TWO

Noah

Wednesday, 8 October 1975

And a Memory of August 1965

And Spring 1962

Anguished and perspiring, Noah awoke from a dream about Seth. It was a variation of his many dreams about the son he had lost nearly a decade earlier. This time his dream called back an afternoon in August 1965. At that time, Seth was nearly eight years old. Two months later, he and Olivia would learn that their son had only a year to live. But on the bright summer day that his dream allowed him to experience as though it were happening for the first time, he and Seth were riding their favorite roan-colored Arabian bays along the horse trail that stretched across the wide expanse of the flourishing green land behind the summer home that he and Olivia had built near his parents' place at Saranac Lake. Once again, he heard the murmuring chant of the wind, and he saw the sunglow splendor of undulating fields of scented grasses and the ascending emphases of Adirondack hills.

He was riding side by side with Seth, observing his ease and confidence as he rode his horse. His son had been riding since he was four years old. He was always dressed protectively in a hard hat and a chin harness, in long sweatshirt and comfortable breeches, and in boots and gloves. He noticed on that day and in this dream ten years later, that Seth was sitting with the weight of his body in the center of the saddle. He was allowing his hip joints to be open and his legs positioned as close as possible around the horse's sides. At the same time, he was relaxing his arms at the shoulder and elbow so that he could move with the movement of the horse's head. He held his hands correctly with palms facing each other and thumbs uppermost. Without using his arms, he clasped the reins by wrapping his fingers around them and almost closing his hands to make a fist. It was as though arms and reins belonged to the horse, the better to follow its motion.

They had been riding at a leisurely pace while enjoying the late August warmth and the pleasure of being together on a summer day when they were both free of school or business obligations. But, after twenty minutes, Seth wanted his ride to be more exciting.

"Dad, I'll race you to the edge of the forest," he exclaimed. "That way, we'll make this ride very special."

"All right," he called out to him, caught up in the free-spirited lift of the moment. "We'll have a race. Let's go!"

Instantly, he and his son asked their horses to go forward into a canter on the left rein. As he did, so did Seth sit deep and press his left leg on the fine leather band contoured about the belly of the horse to keep the saddle in place. Then, once again he and his son made the same moves. With a squeeze of the right leg back behind the leather band, they asked their Arabian bays more actively to go forward into a canter.

Seth and his horse shot ahead of him.

He saw, as a vivid memory printed forever upon his mind, how skillfully his son collaborated with the kinetic energies of his horse. As he came cantering behind his son, he could see the Arabian bay lengthening out its body and neck and fully extending its legs as his son powered over the winding trail. Riding with the seat taken out of the saddle, Seth tucked his upper body in behind his horse's neck and extended his arms forward as with each stride the horse stretched his neck forward. He fused the outline of their forms. That afternoon, he was riding with shorter stirrups to make it easier for his weight to be lifted out of the saddle. Through the reins, he was always keeping contact with the horse's mouth in order to help balance him. Onward and more swiftly he went galloping.

So, also, did he—proud father of his son and instructor of all his outdoor activities—ride swiftly onward, cantering and galloping toward the forest that was looming up out of the August mist. Teeming apple orchards, colorful brush, and wild flower fields went flashing by him. Adolescent youths harvesting a passing field and a rugged man driving a tractor over a southerly hill leaped into his vision and just as quickly scattered away. On and on he galloped, while trees and hills soared, wavered aloft, and disappeared. Even the radiant sun tilted, and the cloud-laden sky darted, loped, and vaulted. So it seemed to his excited senses as he rode swiftly toward the forest, always keeping in his sight his son's fast-moving race toward the edge of the woods.

Minutes later, when his son reached the entrance to the woods, he was caught by surprise. Seth did not pause there to bring their horse race to a close. He did not push his lower leg forward while still squeezing both legs against his horse's sides. Nor did he brace himself against the stirrup, shorten up his reins, and push the hand that held one of the reins into the horse's neck. He did not use his other hand to keep a strong hold on the second rein, as the horse started to slow down. Seth did none of these things. Instead, he raced along the clearing into the woods.

He quickly followed his son.

But only for an instant did he see his son, riding his roan-colored bay even more swiftly toward the receding distance, before he disappeared in the midst of a towering array of white ash trees, with their fluttering green canopies and late summer promise of autumn bronze, gold, and copper. Nor did he see him when he reached a circuitous turn in the clearing and passed by ornamental cypresses, their early leaves already tinged with blue-gray and yellow-gold hues. Riding now in search of his son, he heard as a faraway sound the strong, slurring notes of a tawny-colored ovenbird. He witnessed as blurring motions or animated flares upon his senses the sprint of a horseshoe hare and the scurrying motion of a red squirrel. He saw a whitetail deer leaping with athletic ease into the shaded, receding space that was the forest path beyond him. Still he rode briskly forward, his keen eyes looking for his son or for any sign that he and his Arabian bay had powered through the area.

But there was no sign. There wasn't the slightest evidence that Seth had ever arrived there. Even when he dismounted and, while leading his horse into the deep folds of the forest, he searched all the byways and the unexpected intricacies of the trail, he could not find him. Then darkness came upon him, covering the sky and the forest and the trail that twisted its paths before and behind him. Maddened by the thought that his son was lost to him forever, he cried out his rage and his sorrow.

"Seth! Seth! Where are you? Call out to me. Let me hear you, so that I can find you."

Only the wind answered his cry, though, and the darkness that hid his son inside its murky prison and covered everything else rose, nebulous and daunting, into a towering wall that he could neither fathom nor scale.

Then, once again, he cried out his rage and called to the son who never answered him.

"Seth! Seth!"

Heavy sobbing ripped out of his throat, and bitter tears and beads of perspiration trickled down his weary face. His anguish, prevailing and deep-seated, pushed him out of his dream. Exhausted and defeated, he opened his eyes to find the early morning sun weaving its light across his bedroom. Another day was beginning. Seth would not be a part of it. Nor would he be a part of all the other days that he, the father whose grief would never be assuaged, was condemned to live. Unchained from his dream, he understood with clarified awareness that his son had never been lost in the woods. He had died of a brain tumor. No matter how angrily his fatherly cry disturbed his dreams or cut through the reality he inhabited, he would never find Seth along the winding horse trail in a forest or on the smooth turf of a soccer field or at home in his comfortable room where, as a boy of seven or eight, he was building models of famous airplanes after studying their intricate designs. Seth had died, and he could not come back to him.

He was alone in his bed. There was no wife beside him to whom he could whisper his grief or ask for comforting words. He and Olivia slept apart. Their uneasy dreams and restless tossing and turning made them tense and jittery, lost as they were inside their unappeasable sorrow. No longer were they able to solace each other during the nights when their dreams of their son overtook their sleep and stole the tenuous peace that sleep had brought them.

He hurried out of his bed and hastened to impose an orderly pattern upon his day. He showered and shaved and dressed for a busy slate of appointments with corporate executives and government officials. He chose a navy suit that Oleg Cassini had designed for him, a white Armani shirt, and a Pierre Cardin silk tie with navy, cobalt blue, and teal blue stripes. He was determined to look his best. At forty-five, he did not possess the youthful good looks that he had carried with him until grief and alcoholic addiction overtook him. Nor did a once-inveterate narcissism propel his every move. But grief had not cancelled his self-awareness, and a grueling recovery from alcoholic addiction had allowed him to reclaim his mental acuity and his knack for making profitable business deals. He also reclaimed some of the faded handsomeness that he had worn with philosophic acceptance before Seth died. He knew the importance of appearing self-possessed and dynamic. He knew as well that the clothes he wore enhanced his identity as a formidable and authentic leader. They suggested a well-ordered life and a clear-minded attention to detail. Except for the dreams of Seth that still haunted his sleep, he had recovered his health through daily exercise with a trainer at the exclusive gym where he was a member and through a trove of meaningful activities that included playing goalkeeper for a businessman's soccer league, skiing along the rugged, wintry slopes of Vermont and Maine, sailing his yacht on summer-bright Saranac Lake, playing the drums in a local jazz combo, and flying his Cessna Skymaster in air racing shows in Cleveland, Ohio, and in Newport, Rhode Island.

On this October morning in 1975, he put a special briskness in his pace as he hurried downstairs to greet Olivia at the breakfast table in the spacious kitchen of their New York brownstone. He wanted to elude the cloud of melancholy that was hovering near him as though it were a permanent residue of the unhappy dream that had troubled his sleep. He needed a clear head and absolute focus to meet the day's challenges. At nine o'clock, he was scheduled to meet with the major stockholders in the Blake & Tanner Steel and Aluminum Corporation. After that, a conference with the president of the Steelworkers Union was on his agenda. At eleven, he was going to join a meeting with the New York City Opera Guild about their fund-raising program for the 1976 season. At noon, he would head to the airport for a flight to Washington, D. C. At three o'clock, he would be participating in the President's task force to create more apprenticeships that enabled young men and women to learn essential job skills.

On his way to the breakfast table, his thoughts turned to Olivia, despite his tenuous resolve to avoid reviewing the past turbulence of their relationship. Their having survived those unhappy years did bring him solace. But the fear of falling back to their self-destructive ways always hovered near him. Nevertheless, they had recovered some of their lost happiness. They had learned to accommodate themselves to tattered expectations and to failed dreams that had burned their roots to the sockets. In these recent years that they had lived through, Olivia had made a friend of the light-heartedness that willfully keeps at bay the guilt and despair that had been plaguing her. Now, as he descended the stairs while on his way to the breakfast room, that part of his past flashed its quick imagery upon his private seeing.

At that time, in the spring of 1962, Seth was five years old and, apparently, in excellent health. Olivia loved her son as much as he did. But their love for each other had dimmed. Its light had become a small, dying flame. At thirty-two years old, he had felt trapped by his marriage. Olivia no longer excited him. He craved a younger partner who would ignite new fires within him and whom he would pay well for the passionate hours they spent together. Rosemary was the first of his secret girlfriends. Nicole, Pamela, and Monica were among the others, whose names he had already forgotten. In different ways, they were all lovely and statuesque. He favored brunettes and redheads, because they did not replicate the blonde sensuality that Olivia had in earlier times made both erotic and genteel.

"You and I can have a good time, honey," he would tell each of these women on the evenings when they first met at an exclusive salon or in the private rooms on the second floor of a supper club or in his penthouse on Sutton Place that none of his relatives or friends or even Olivia knew that he owned. "Ours can be a very amicable relationship. You get to fly with me in my private jet to a hideaway in Jamaica or Tahiti or St. Moritz. We'll have a great time together. You can help me feel tremendous again. I can help you with gifts of diamonds and Jaguars and plenty of cash. There will be no regrets afterwards. There will be no yearning for a permanent bond. There will be no feeling that lasts beyond the time we spend together."

"Sold!" said Rosemary, with her sly wit and seductive manner. He admired her even more because there was no love in her heart for anyone except herself.

"I promise to forget you, too, even when I wear the diamonds and drive the Jaguar," Nicole told him. He grinned when she spoke the words, because her haunted eyes and fake insolence belied her words.

"You lay all of your cards on the table," Pamela said, her words both careless and abrasive. "I like that in a man. I know where I stand with him. I know what he wants me to be when I am with him. I know what he becomes. We're two sly animals in rut."

Those women had played the game well. Only Monica made trouble.

"You want me not to feel," she said. "But I can't do that. Of course, I feel. I may even fall in love with you. Where's the harm in that?"

Her blue eyes gleamed within the oval face that her pale skin, upturned nose, and full lips made very beautiful, indeed. Her delicate manner and her sometimes-tremulous voice suggested a vulnerability that she was unable to conceal.

"Oh, there's much harm in it," he answered her. "Don't fall in love. Don't break the most important rule of this game that we are playing."

"I'll try not to," she answered, eager to please him.

"Try very hard," he told her, as he brushed his lips against her lips and drew her into his bed.

They met eight or nine times after that. They had skied in St. Moritz. They had spent an exhilarating weekend in Paris, when he was attending a symposium of business leaders. They swam in Tahiti a few months later, and they attended an Octoberfest in Berlin a few weeks after that.

Always, Monica had been careful not to mention the word "love" when she was with him. But her furtive glances, her grateful caresses, and her prolonged climaxes when he made love to her revealed the soulful passion she felt for him. In spite of himself, her love lifted his spirit. If he had let himself go, he might have confessed to her that he loved her, too. But he did not let himself go. He did not reveal the truth of his feelings. Instead, he stopped seeing her. He refused to take her phone calls. The doorman did not allow her to enter even the foyer of his secret Sutton Place apartment. On two or three occasions, the security guard escorted her from the Blake & Tanner Building which was located within the hubbub of Wall Street.

Soon after that, Monica discovered his Sutton Place address. She wrote a note to Olivia, telling her about their frequent trysts and declaring that he was planning to marry her after he divorced Olivia.

That evening, when he returned home anticipating some solace from a challenging workday, Olivia confronted him with Monica's note.

"I thought you had quit seeing other women," she said, accusatory and furious. "I thought you were leveling with me. I thought you were being true."

He did not back away from Olivia's fury. Nor did he beg for her forgiveness. His cynicism and his arrogance, still working their blunt powers in those days, pushed him forward.

"She doesn't mean a thing to me, " he said. "I paid her for her service. I never mentioned the word 'marriage.'"

Further incited by his hardheartedness and by his careless regard of his adultery, Olivia stepped closer to him and slapped his face again and again.

"Bastard!" she shouted. "Lousy bastard!"

When she started scratching his face with her long fingernails, he grabbed hold of her wrists and pinioned them to the sides of her slender figure, with its muted sensuality and its inherent elegance.

"Enough," he told her. It was a declaration, a command, and a warning.

Olivia began to sob. Her eyes were brimming with tears, and her face wrenched by her anger and her sorrow.

"Why?" she asked. Her voice was soft and raspy now. "Why?"

He stared at her, making direct eye contact. His eyes made no appeal for her forgiveness. Nor did they convey any remorse. Yet their razor-sharp appraisal of her conventional response and his tough-minded acceptance of the moment gave no quarter to her feminine pride or her gratuitous hysteria. Men betrayed their wives every day. What of it?

"I wanted to go to bed with someone else. I wanted to feel new. I needed to feel young again."

"Doesn't our marriage mean anything to you?"

"Of course, it does. You are the most important woman in my life. You've given me a fine son. You've made our home a haven of culture, refinement, and good times. You're the loyal wife that makes her husband shine whenever you are in his company. I've given everything of myself that I can give as your husband. You know that. If, once in a while, I give something of myself to other women, it's nothing important. It never lasts. It doesn't mean anything."

"You're being selfish. You are destroying our marriage."

"You're over-reacting."

"What if I treated our marriage as carelessly as you do? What if I took a secret lover?"

"Go ahead. But do it only if it will make you feel better. Sometimes, new partners teach us how to fall in love again. An open marriage can sometimes ignite new passions between a husband and his wife."

"I don't want to take another lover," Olivia said. "I want only you."

Her words moved him in ways that surprised him. Suddenly, it was important that he did not hurt her.

"That's a tremendous thing to tell me," he said, while caressing her shoulders and studying her blue-eyed gaze. He kept his voice low and intimate. He did not want to make any promise that he could not fulfill. But, in spite of his self-absorbed disposition and his devil-may-care callousness, her forthright confession of her love and her pledge of fidelity worked their influences upon him.

"I'll try to live differently," he said. "I'll try to want only you."

"We can learn to be happy together," she said. "We used to be. We can learn all over again."

"Of course we can."

Now, while drawing upon a thought that they used to express whenever they were about to test themselves in a new experience, she chose words that might spur them on to a renewal of their fidelity.

"There's adventure in that."

For three months, he stayed away from other women. Determined to rouse his need of her, Olivia invoked new intensities of glamour and sensuality. Their lovemaking grew passionate once more. Together, they revived their need of one another. They felt like young lovers who were acquainting themselves with genuine ecstasy for the first time.

Then, in a careless hour, he forfeited all the rewards that his fidelity had brought him. At a formal dinner party that took place within his brother Todd's sumptuous home in Martha's Vineyard, he met Sandra Lancaster, a voluptuous woman with whom he had slept many times during his university years. Though she had never married, she had taken many lovers, including European royalty and powerful United States senators and judges. That evening, the film star of popular westerns who had escorted her to the party was enjoying the adulation of several female guests even as he discreetly arranged a rendezvous for the following evening with the richest debutante there. Sandra did not seem to mind. She had grown bored with her cowboy. She was far more interested in the excitement that she might find in the company of one of her former lovers.

Time had been kind to her. In this season, a summer tan gave her back some of the earlier years that she had already lived. Her bouffant hair, cool brown eyes, and gleaming smile also served her well. They replenished and intensified the fashionable image she carefully cultivated. That evening, she was wearing a peach embroidered chiffon evening gown that complemented her tall, slim figure. An hour earlier, she had made a stunning entrance at this sumptuous party that had drawn into its environment impressive foreign royalty, government officials, and prominent scientists. Many of these guests had taken note of her arrival. Men allowed the spell she cast to work its powers upon them. They imagined sequestered meetings and promiscuous copulating. Women peered at her with instant approval or with the subtle envy that masks itself within quiet admiration. When she entered the ballroom, a white satin cape lined in peach had enhanced the beauty of her gown.

Right then, there on the terrace, the white cape was nowhere to be seen. She had, he imagined, left it at the banquet table where she had been sitting for a few minutes before she began dancing with men both young and older. The cape had worked its magic as she entered the ball. She had no further need of it.

While she stood close to him on the terrace, he felt suddenly buoyant and new. The thought occurred to him that they made a good team. Her carefree manner, poised discreetly on the cusp of abandon, pleased him. It matched his cynical view of the world. If they had been married, Sandra would not have complained about his casual affairs with other women. She would have been too busy choosing temporary lovers and discarding them after a few weeks or months. She was a renegade that loved experiencing illicit pleasures and making freewheeling choices. In all these way, she was like him. He regarded her as his equal.

He watched her watching him. She was taking his measure. She was deciding what the years had taken from him and what, at thirty-two, they had given him.

He was wearing a summer tuxedo, with its off-white jacket that had black satin facing upon its lapels and satin stripes down the side of black trousers. A white shirt and a black bow tie completed the formal look. In his own eyes, he looked the way every man in his class wants to appear. He looked as he was. He looked successful.

"You still look a bit of terrific," Sandra told him. "But you also look as bored as I do. Let's go for a walk on the beach. The night is still young and filled with possibilities. Let's be rebels once again. Let's make the night spin faster."

He had been standing alone on the terrace, smoking a cigarette and drinking his fourth or fifth round of scotch. The moon was casting its luminous glow upon the wind-stirred waters, across the tawny sands of Todd's beachfront property, and over the multi-colored foliage that surrounded his home. The light of the moon also cast its glow upon the shrewdly calibrated artifice of Sandra's glamour. It illumined his face as well, but only partially, suggesting a divided self that pulsed with mystery, concealment, and ambiguity.

Already feeling drunk, a little, he was quick to take up Sandra's invitation.

"I'm game," he said. "Let's get excited together."

She laughed just before she lightly kissed his lips. Her elegant hand traveled across his chest and came to rest upon his crotch. Instantly roused, he grabbed hold of her svelte body and, pulling her toward him, returned her kiss with a raw urgency that superseded the teasing and superficial nature of the kiss that she had offered him.

When he pulled away from the kiss, he smiled and watched her reaction.

She was smiling, too. She was pleased that she had roused him.

"You haven't changed, I'm happy to say."

They left the terrace quickly and hurried to a deserted part of the beach. There, they undressed and tossed their clothes in a rumpled pile along the sands that stretched all around them. Right after that, he took hold of her again and planted a fierce kiss upon her ruby lips.

"Now," he whispered. "Let's do it now."

She lightly laughed. Her smoky voice became even more teasing and exhilarant.

"Not yet," she said, while she pulled away from him and ran off to the breeze-quickened Atlantic waters.

He swiftly followed her. His head was reeling a bit because of his drinking. But he had not lost his keen-eyed awareness or the lascivious rush upon his senses as he beheld the raw promise of her nakedness.

They swam in unison, alternating front crawls, sidestrokes, and backstrokes. The warm summer waters quickened his senses. He felt fully alive again. He reveled in this night swim with Sandra. It was a fantastic game they were playing. He was at last freed of all the obligations that chained him to their rules. He was master of his fate, with no meddlers to obstruct his journey or to impose their will upon his choices.

When they left the water and returned to the beach, they made vigorous love. Sandra's face brightened because of the pleasure he was giving her. Her eyes gleamed, and her breathing grew excited. He stroked her faster and faster and waited until she climaxed before he shot his sperm inside her. Only afterwards, months later when he recalled this night, did he realize that the pleasure he took from Sandra involved more than sex. Their being together was an act of rebellion. For that half-hour, he had broken free of the rules that made his life a prison. It would take years for him to understand that not the rules, but his willfulness had made the prison. His selfish aims and his unforgiving nature defeated him. Most grievous of all were the punishments that Blind Chance eventually inflicted upon him.

After that night with Sandra, four years were to pass before Seth died and before Olivia became lost for a second time inside her madness. But it was the night of the banquet at his brother Todd's summer home that started the downward spiral for him and for Olivia. Though none of the guests had left the merriment of the party to walk along the secluded part of the beach where they might have discovered him enjoying sexual intercourse with Sandra, those same guests noticed Sandra's rumpled gown and the beach-sand in her hair when she returned to the ballroom. Although they perceived that she was alone, they saw, nevertheless, that a private exhilaration attended her. A quarter of an hour afterwards, when he made his way back to the bar, which was located in the north corner of the ballroom, the guests there studied his disheveled tuxedo and whispered that the tawny sands of the beach also covered his hair.

One of the guests, Spencer Jackson, a supercilious CEO of a pharmaceutical corporation known for his rigid and conservative views, did more than whisper.

"What in heaven's name has happened to you?" he inquired. "You look a bit tossed about."

He quickly answered him, devising a lie that was as smooth as it was extemporaneous.

"I drank one scotch too many. So I took a walk along the beach to get some fresh air. It was the right thing to do. The breeze revived me. But I was wobbling all over the place. I slipped and fell into the sand."

Jackson chuckled. He was enjoying what he thought was his discomfort.

"Well, if I were you, I wouldn't try to dance," he said. "In this ballroom, wobbling is not allowed."

Reed-thin and six foot five, Jackson patted him on the shoulder and hurried away from the bar.

Jackson and the other guests were not the only ones who noticed him. Olivia had noticed, too, at the very moment that he was hurrying away from the ballroom with Sandra. Had he not been a bit intoxicated, he might have left the ballroom without Sandra and, minutes later, met her on the beach. But on that troubled evening he drew upon the willful and incautious behavior that had often propelled his trysts and his betrayals. He allowed Sandra to take his arm and to laugh with complicit intimacy as they made their exit from the dance.

When she noticed that he was leaving with Sandra, Olivia was dancing with a French diplomat. She went on dancing with the diplomat and, right after that, with other cosmopolitan men that included corporate executives, a Dutch ambassador, and a mogul from Hong Kong. Even when he returned from his tryst on the beach, sated and disheveled, she maintained the congenial persona that heightened her glamour and that endeared her to all of her friends. On this morning thirteen years later, as he descended the stairs to join her for breakfast in their home on Sutton Place, he recalled that Olivia gave no clue that she had seen him leaving the ballroom with Sandra on his arm. When he asked her to dance, she readily accepted and moved with smooth precision as he led her into a waltz. Her eyes shone with love for him. There was a lilt in her voice as she shared pleasant words with him. She was vivacious. She was exhilarant. She was a model wife. Only in retrospect did he understand that she was playacting for all the guests who had seen him hurrying off with Sandra and who were now observing Olivia with careful eyes and silent approval of her self-command.

Even when they sat together at the dinner table, Olivia remained a vibrant presence. Drawing him into the conversation that included the energetic repartee of a neurosurgeon, a Hollywood glamour queen and her latest husband, and a Texas oil baron, she spoke of their recent vacation in the Bahamas, as well as the plays they had seen in New York, the Metropolitan Opera gala they had attended there, and their purchase of a painting by Mary Cassatt. He, in turn, shared memories of rafting and kayaking in the Southern Alps, driving his Alfa Romeo in the Grand Prix races in France, and flying his new Piper Cub from a private New York airport to an air base in Quonset, Rhode Island.

During the rest of that long weekend, he sensed no tension in his exchanges with Olivia. Even on that Sunday afternoon, when they played a set of doubles with Sandra and her film star cowboy as their tennis opponents, Olivia stayed affable and gracious. If she noticed Sandra charming him with witty remarks or holding his arm intimately when she appeared to slip while making her way out of the sun-glowing tennis court in the east wing of his brother's property or kissing him with sensual urgency when, on the following morning, she hastened away to a flight that was bound for California, Olivia gave no evidence of being disturbed or even vaguely jealous. She even allowed him to plant a kiss upon her cheek just before he guided five-year-old Seth through a swimming lesson in the heated pool that was located in the south wing of his brother Todd's property.

Ellen Templeton, Seth's governess, was there with them. Brown-haired and blue-eyed, she was a genteel young woman whom Seth adored. She was also the epitome of decorum. Always, she maintained a formal and respectful manner toward him, the father of the boy that she cared for with genuine affection. He wondered whether the rumor of his extra-marital affairs had reached her ears. Whatever the case, Miss Templeton was happily married to a rugged Air Force pilot currently stationed in Vietnam. With his son's governess, he had invited no complications, all of which he was certain she would have rebuffed.

On this vacation Monday, the four of them there in the pool were especially exuberant. He felt that Olivia was pleased that he was giving some attention to Seth, whom he had mostly ignored during their visit to Todd and his wife Isabel. Miss Templeton glowed with a special happiness, because her husband was arriving home on leave after being away in a combat zone for a year. Seth was beaming with energy all through his swimming lesson and even more so when Todd's six-year-old son and four-year-old daughter joined them in the pool. Those hours in the pool stayed with him all these years afterward. With Seth and Olivia and the others, he had rarely felt so free-spirited and so filled with joy. All of them reveled in their lap swimming, and they reveled again and again playing volleyball and other water games such as jousting while on inflatable rafts and trying to swim to the other side of the pool without being tagged by a fast-moving sentry.

For the rest of that week, he felt heartened by the apparent accord between Olivia and him. If she was aware of his latest indiscretion with Sandra, she willed herself to forgive him. But a few days after they returned to their own summer place at Saranac Lake, the anger that she had been suppressing flared out of her, disquieting and vehement. The cause of her fury was the diamond necklace that he had bought for Sandra. He had attached a note to the gift that asked Sandra to accept the necklace as a memento of their escapade on the beach. The jeweler had inadvertently sent the gift to Olivia.

On that evening in late August, they were dressing for still another party that a friend from his university days and his new wife were hosting at their summer compound three miles away. He was looking forward to the party. Sandra would be there, along with the promise that they might once again share the secret pleasures yoked to small rebellions that revitalized the senses and that recovered for an hour or so faded aspirations and lost dreams. But while he was placing his gold watch on his wrist and, right after that, adjusting his bow tie, Olivia hurried into his bedroom, her frantic gait and the frown that creased her forehead as if it were a jagged gash signaling her displeasure.

With a furious gesture, she threw the necklace upon his dresser and with it the note that he had addressed to Sandra.

"Is this how you pay your whores?" she screamed.

He went on adjusting his tie.

"I've told you before. These things don't mean anything. They last for an hour, and then I forget them."

"Liar! Liar! I'm sick of your lies!"

"Get hold of yourself, honey. Miss Templeton and the servants will hear you."

"They already know the kind of man you are."

"At least, they don't scream about it."

"They're not married to you, you bastard!"

Her fury pitched now at the rim of hysteria, she hurried from the room.

Olivia will get over it, he told himself, as he put on his jacket and placed his wallet within an inside pocket. But, when he entered her bedroom, hoping to calm her so that they could go on to the dinner party that awaited them, she was not there. He walked casually down the hall into Seth's room, expecting to find Olivia with their son. But she was not there. Miss Templeton was reading a story to Seth as he lay in his bed, already drifting into sleep.

Upon seeing him, Seth came fully awake and reached out to hug him.

"Enjoy the party, Daddy," he said.

He hugged his son with fatherly warmth.

"I plan to enjoy everything," he told him. "Now get a good night's sleep. I want you to be ready for a day of sailing with me tomorrow."

Seth beamed.

"I'll be ready, Daddy," he said. "I'll go to sleep right after Miss Templeton finishes reading the story to me."

"Good boy," he told him.

He turned to Miss Templeton and asked her whether Olivia had appeared earlier to say good night to their son. Whether Miss Templeton was aware of Olivia's quarrel with him, he could not say with any certainty. To his eyes, she was the same Miss Templeton that he always anticipated. With her calm and respectful manner, she informed him that Olivia had already left for the party. Only then did he understand with a vague apprehension that he had better prepare himself for a complicated and even unpredictable evening. Nevertheless, he counted on Olivia's inbred decorum and his own casual-seeming stoicism to carry them safely through the next hours. With these thoughts feeding his optimism, he left the house in his Alfa Romeo.

He had driven only a few miles when the flashing lights of two police cruisers compelled him to stop. A rugged police captain was signaling him toward an alternate lane. The lane in which he had been traveling on that dark country road had been cordoned off. Beyond the flashing lights of the cruisers he saw a crash-wrecked car. Or, rather, he saw only part of the car because of the lights that blinded his clear seeing and the darkness that, like a mushrooming cloud, rose around him.

The police captain continued to signal him toward an alternate lane. But something, some canny instinct, kept him from moving forward. At that moment, no one else was driving through the darkness of that road. But, only minutes earlier, Olivia had to traverse this road as she made the drive to the party. The thought made him pause. Instead of driving onto the alternate lane, he turned off the ignition and stepped out of his car. He held his senses tight, resisting the apprehension that was rising within him. He walked toward the police captain and, even before arriving at the place where that hardened man was standing, he spoke the words that might negate his premonition or at least clarify what needed to be done.

"Is there anything I can do to help?"

Just then, as he approached him, he saw that the police captain was none other than Jake Masterson. He was a trusted friend. They had often hunted red deer in South

Dakota and fished for marlin in Florida. On this troubled night, they recognized each other in the same moment.

"Noah," Jake said. "It's good that you're here. It's your wife. She's had an accident."

Jake led him into the darkness that was dispelled in part by the flashing lights of the cruisers and by the headlights of the ambulance that he had not seen earlier. A few hundred yards beyond the ambulance, he saw that Olivia's BMW had crashed into a guardrail. He guessed at once that his wife, angry and disoriented because of their quarrel, had been speeding. She lost control of her car, and it hurled itself into the air, flipped, spun off the highway, and crashed into the guardrail. From where he stood, held back by a blunt-faced police lieutenant and by "Do Not Enter," "Stop," and "Detour" signs, he saw that the front of Olivia's car was smashed up, that the driver's door had been torn away, and that all the windows were broken. Moving closer because Jake was guiding him beyond the barrier signs, he saw two young medics lifting Olivia out of the car and placing her onto a stretcher. She was unconscious and moaning.

The thought that she was dying impelled him to hurry forward. He was careful not to intrude upon the work of the medics. Yet, once they placed his wife on the stretcher, he inched his way to her side.

"Olivia. Olivia," he called to her while keeping his voice steady and gentle.

As far as he could tell, she did not stir awake. But the movement of her swollen lips and the flicker of her eyelids told him that, as though she were far away, she could still hear him. Nevertheless, she could not speak the words that she had a mind to tell him.

He noticed the vivid red blood staining her hair and the deep gash upon her forehead. He noticed, too, her uneasy breathing and, just before the emergency medics strapped her onto the stretcher, he became aware that her supple body had gone limp and was still bleeding.

Seeing Olivia so vulnerable and possibly finished, he felt desperate and guilty. Though he was not a religious man, he found himself praying that she would not die. If she died, he would regard himself as her murderer.

For the next three days, her life hung in the balance. Surgeons treated her concussion, repaired her fractured arm and her broken pelvis, and subdued her life-threatening internal injuries. After three surgeries, she lay in a coma for twelve hours. Only when she regained consciousness did she give her doctors some evidence that she was going to survive her traumatic injuries. By the end of that week, she was eating solid foods again, and she was conversing with the close friends and relatives who were allowed to visit her. She spoke to him as well, her voice concealing its melancholy within a show of good cheer and a quiet forgiveness of his infidelity.

Her doctors had not yet told her that, because of her grievous injuries, she would never be able to bear another child. A week later, when they did tell her, she wept. The accident had taken a vital part of her womanhood. As gently as he could, her primary surgeon reminded her that, because of her history of miscarriages, she would probably not have given birth to another child even if there had been no car accident. But his honest words did not allay her grief. Irrevocable mischance and her willful actions had destroyed the possibility of her bringing another child into the world. Only when her doctor reminded her that she had been blessed with a healthy son did she cease weeping.

"Yes," she said. "Thank God for Seth."

Upon her release from the hospital, though, she fell into a deep despair. She was, she told herself as well as him, no longer a complete woman. Only thirty-two, she could no longer give birth to another son or to the daughter that she had always wanted. For the next six months, she was in and out of a Connecticut sanitarium.

Gradually, with the counsel of a female psychiatrist, she appeared to rally. When she returned home, apparently recovered and revitalized, she never alluded to his affair with Sandra. In fact, she behaved as if his infidelity had never happened. She busied herself, instead, with her role as an ideal wife and mother. She worked with interior decorators to bring into their home a revised stateliness that anchored itself to a pristine modernity. She chaired a prominent committee that raised millions of dollars for underprivileged children in the United States. She brought leaderly acumen to other committees, including the New York Opera Guild and a national scholarship fund for underprivileged students. She hosted lavish parties for their New York and Connecticut friends. In league with him, the fallible husband whose faults she now quietly accepted, she gave Seth a few swimming lessons that complemented his instruction and, again with him when he was not traveling out of the country on business and also with an accomplished riding instructor, she taught the five-year-old boy how to ride a pony. They spent life-affirming summers at their home at Saranac Lake in the Adirondacks. They wintered with his brothers and their families in St. Moritz and in Lausanne, and during that season, they entertained a wide circle of friends at their penthouse on Sutton Place.

Always, their Seth was the unknowing catalyst in whatever happiness he and Olivia fashioned out of the renovated scenario that was their marriage. Always, Seth's presence fortified their conviction that, despite his past infidelities and her tattered belief in him, they had succeeded in building a family.

But after Seth died three years later, Olivia once again fell into despair. This time, she stayed in a sanitarium for nearly a year. When she came back to him, he vowed to himself that he would never again betray her. Her stay at the sanitarium had been auspicious. She left there feeling reborn and self-determining. In that year, he helped her, too. He pulled a few strings and guided her onto the staff of Erika Lind's renowned fashion house. After her years at Pembroke in Brown University, she had studied at The Parsons School of Design in New York. Her extraordinary gifts as a couturier were now bringing her praise as well as fame.

At times, he felt that she was more interested in her career than in her relationship with him. He felt relieved. Their love for each other was, after all, no longer passionate. After their son died, they had settled into a quieter bond that navigated the familiar territories of habit, that suppressed disappointment and heartache, and that shunned the unexpected or the problematic. Within the quietude of that bond, they worked hard to disguise the emptiness of their relationship. Their immersion within their world of powerbrokers and dealmakers deflected their attention from each other. The fast pace and glamorous ambiance of their careers provided the adrenaline rush that each of them craved. They felt reborn, redefined, and rescued. Their success in a competitive and brutal world dispelled the unease that would otherwise have haunted them because of her inability to give him another child and because of the unforgiving consequences of his infidelity.

Nevertheless, Olivia still regarded his being there as essential to the contrived happiness that sustained her. He was the buffer against the loneliness that might overtake her during those hours when she was not caught up in the hubbub of the fashion world or in the merriment of a lavish party or in the challenges of her committee work. He was her shield against the despair that hovered nearby, always threatening to take hold of her despite her continuing alliance with helpful psychiatrists.

He wondered whether her refusal to adopt children was part of a stern punishment that she was meting out to him. A son and a daughter might make all the difference for their troubled marriage. Their becoming the lifelines for two healthy children might awaken dormant capacities for nurturing loved ones and restore the broken promises that once made their marriage seem valid and inevitable. He sometimes told himself that Olivia and he would be better off apart from each other. If they made a clean break of it, she might go forward to make an alliance with a man who could rescue her from her suppressed bitterness and her tautly harnessed despair. He, in turn, could marry a life-loving woman who would give him a son as well as a daughter. But in his heart he knew that Olivia did not want to break the chains that bound them together. If he left her to remake his life with another woman, she might kill herself. He did not care to live with the guilt that would then overtake him.

Theirs had become a symbiotic union. As self-possessed as she was in her career and with her friends, she still required his guardian presence. Possibly, she needed him to be there so that she could inflict upon him her subtle penalties and her more hurtful punishments because he had so often been unfaithful and because he had goaded the fury that led to her car crash and to the surgeries that prevented her from having children. His staying with her may have had more to do with his need to be punished rather than with his continuing love of her.

So he told himself as he descended the stairs and made his way to the breakfast room in his New York penthouse at seven-thirty on this Wednesday morning of October eighth in nineteen-hundred seventy-five.

On this particular morning, Olivia looked radiant. She was wearing a dark Brunswick green woolen suit that featured large wool shank style green buttons and was fully lined. So she explained after he praised the look of it and complimented her on wearing it so well. That the suit was one that she had designed made his praise even more important.

"I'm very pleased that the buyers liked it as much as you do," she said, "when they saw it last spring in New York, Paris, and London during previews of the Erika Lind autumn collection."

This morning her voice carried a special exhilaration. What influenced her excitement were the hours that lay before her. Those hours were drawing her into the final preparations for a sumptuous dinner party that Erika Lind, her boss and one of the most famous couturiers in the world, was hosting at The Waldorf Astoria the following evening. Not only the international buyers of the clothes that she and her colleagues designed would be there. Manufacturers, retailers, production partners, warehouses managers, and wholesale representatives were also taking a prominent place on the guest list. She placed a special value upon all these people, because they were essential to the success of each new line of clothes that her house had designed. Other noteworthy guests would be there, including matrons and debutantes from their privileged class, as well as their husbands and boyfriends; style-setting film stars with their latest leading men; foreign ambassadors and their wives; and the New York governor and his wife.

"Promise me that you will return from Washington by four tomorrow," she said. "Give yourself plenty of time to shower, shave, and dress. We mustn't be late. We have to be at the Waldorf by seven, so that we can greet all of the guests as they arrive."

"You can count on me," he said, as he touched her cheek with a kiss before taking his seat at the breakfast table.

This morning, his casual smile charmed her.

"I always count on you," she said. "And you always come through for me."

"Of course I do," he answered her, self-assured and buoyant. "I always back winners."

For just a moment, she studied his brown-eyed gaze upon her. She saw that he wanted to please her. She understood that he had chosen words that would give her a boost. She appreciated the effort that he was making. But, with a sly wit and a clear-sighted view of her capacities, she selected words of her own that identified the primary agent of her success.

"Do you know why I win most of the time?" she asked him without waiting for his reply. "I count on myself first of all."

She was telling him that she could not really count on him, at least not first of all. She had her reasons. His past transgressions had fractured her trust in him. He could admit the truth of that, without resenting her. That she had found success on her own pleased him. It might be the preface of a new cycle in which she would be strong enough to go forward without him or inspired enough to walk side by side with him and with two adopted children. With these thoughts in mind, he raised his glass of orange juice and, while allowing it to touch her own, proposed a toast.

"Here's to winners," he said.

They chatted about prosaic things as they ate their breakfast, such as their hiring a new gardener for their summer home at Saranac Lake; their securing tickets for a popular Broadway musical; and their sponsoring the New York debut of a gifted classical pianist. For those brief moments, Olivia captivated him with her charming remarks and her insightful opinions. When he left the table, he carried with him a renewed confidence that eventually

Olivia would agree to the adopted children. They might adopt children who were Irish, Welsh, or Norwegian. He had studied the roots of his family. The Blake family of which he was a member appeared first of all in twelfth century Norway and Wales and, shortly afterwards, in Ireland. He wanted children who would carry forward some links to the Blakes' historical background, however tenuous those links might be.

His morning went swiftly. He conferred effectively with corporate stockholders, a union president, and board members of the New York Opera Guild. But when he was driving to the airport, the bitter truth that, at the age of forty-five, he had neither a son nor a daughter rose up once again to disturb his self-awareness. Instantly, it cast a cloud over him, despite the bracing overture to the day that he had gratefully experienced.

But then, quite unexpectedly and within the next half hour, the cloud lifted.

In the VIP lounge of the airport, he met Steven Bennington, who was also traveling to Washington, D.C., on business for his corporation. He had not seen him since their university days. Around them, within an Art-Deco setting, an understated camaraderie prevailed, moored to discreet conversation and to a rigid decorum that he associated with his own class. These multi-national travelers were sipping imported teas or drinking brandy-laced coffee or enjoying scotch, bourbon, and vodka. Waiters were moving with smooth agility about the wide space of the room, carrying trays of sandwiches and pastries. He could hear the momentary tinkle of glasses and the muted clatter of dishes. He could also hear fragments of business talk, nostalgic reminiscences of extraordinary travels, and sophisticated remarks about exhibits of Gauguin and Van Gogh masterpieces at the Met. Always, the vague roar of jets that were arriving or taking off on distant runways rode upon the air.

As he and Steven sat in a booth drinking coffee and sharing news about their lives, he noticed that Steven looked very happy and far younger than his years. His buoyant manner seemed genuine. After they spoke of their continued love of racing cars, purebred horses, and ice hockey, he let Steven do most of the talking. He wanted to know the specific causes of his happiness and, if possible, become privy to the strategies for taking hold of his own share of happiness. He nudged him forward with a remark about his buoyant manner and a question about the blue print or game plan that influenced his good fortune.

"You are so alive," he told him. "I've never seen you so happy. What have you done to keep it—your happiness, I mean?"

"Well, for one thing, I'm making loads of money," Steven said, confident and personable. "I also have a terrific wife."

"So it has worked out for you and Charlotte. I'm glad to hear that."

Steven paused, surprised by his remark and a bit uneasy.

"Oh, not with Charlotte," he said. "It hadn't worked out with Charlotte and me for a long time. We were divorced two years ago."

Now it was his turn to pause. Suddenly, he felt intrusive. But he quickly found the correct words to say.

"I didn't know. I'm sorry."

"Don't be sorry," Steven answered him. "I've found me a wonderful new wife. She was Caitlin O'Hara before I married her. She's a television anchor and a very smart woman. She knows how to keep me jumping through hoops. I love every minute that I'm with her. She has a warm heart."

"Well, then, it's great to hear that you've pulled it off. You have a very happy life. These days, that makes you quite a rarity."

"Oh, don't give me too much credit," he said. "Blind Chance favored me while I was stumbling through the dark."

He changed the subject. He wanted to know about his son.

"How is Ryan?"

At the mention of Ryan's name, Steven beamed.

"He's doing very well. He's a sophomore at Johns Hopkins. Eventually, he wants a career in government."

"That's a worthy aspiration."

"I heard that you and Olivia had a son. How's he doing?"

Stillness overtook him. He held his breath. He gritted his teeth. He struggled to keep at bay the anguish that was hurrying back to claim him. Only then, after he held his senses still, could he speak the essential words that he needed to tell Steven. When he did speak, he tried to keep his voice matter-of-fact and stoical. But the slightest quaver hinted at his unappeasable sorrow.

"Seth died of a brain tumor nine years ago."

Steven frowned. His gaze softened. There was pity in his next remark and a desire to know more about his marriage to Olivia.

"How sad for you. Do you and Olivia have any other children?"

"No. We weren't lucky in that way."

"It must be very hard to lose a child."

"You've been through it. You've known the grief. You lost Adam. Though I was never part of his life, I lost him, too."

Now his words not only made Steven pause. They also puzzled him.

"What are you talking about?"

"Adam died when he was eleven years old. That's what I was told."

"Adam is alive."

He could not speak. He could not trust the words that he thought he heard.

"Did you just say that Adam is alive?"

"Yes. Who made you think that he is not?"

His mind was reeling. He sounded as though he were far away as he offered Steven a reply that told him very little.

"I was misinformed."

"Charlotte."

Once again, his mind seemed to be playing tricks. He hastened to ask questions that might resolve his doubts about the astonishing news he thought that Steven was bringing to him.

"Is it really true? Is Adam alive?"

"Very much so."

He could not speak. A sob rushed out of him, and he placed his hand over his brow so that Steven might not notice that he was weeping. But Steven did notice and was visibly moved. Then, after brushing away his tears and after Steven offered him a lighted cigarette, he accepted it while his hand was shaking and quickly took a drag on it. A tremor came back to his voice again as he quietly spoke the words that validated the news that he had heard.

"I have a son who is alive. It's a tremendous thing. My finding him in this way."

"So it is," Steven said, somewhat awed perhaps by this display of emotion from a man that he had always regarded as hard-hearted and callous. "So it is."

He pulled himself together. He needed to assure Steven that he had a realistic point of view about the relationship that he might create with Adam.

"I know that you've fathered Adam through all the years of his life," he said. "He loves you and respects you. That will never change, even if I were to enter his life. I hope that you will allow me to do that. I would like to bring Adam into my life, too."

"I don't think it has anything to do with me. I'm all for it, of course. You should look him up. He'll be interested in knowing that you are his father."

"Is that on the level? Do you think that he and I can become friends?"

"You know what they say. It's never too late."

"Maybe. Maybe not."

"I haven't been the best father to him," Steven admitted. "I've given him a rough time. At times, I've been worse than a drill sergeant. He still believes that I'm his 'real' father. But my relationship with him may be damaged beyond repair."

He perceived now that there must be a backstory involving Adam, Steven, and Charlotte. Maybe he would learn about it later. At the moment, it did not seem important.

"You're the dad that he's used to. That will never change."

"It could, if you do the right things."

"I'd do everything possible to make it work."

"I'm not certain, though, that Adam needs a father now. He's being graduated from Yale next May. He's engaged to a lovely girl. They'll be married in June, and they'll honeymoon in South America. Then, they'll be busy at Harvard Medical School."

"I know I won't count so much. The important thing is that he's alive and well. I have a son. Nothing could be better than that."

"I'll arrange a meeting. I'll be there, too, so that I can cushion his surprise at discovering that you are his biological father."

"I can hardly wait," he said, while his doubts of Adam's acceptance began assailing him.

PART TWO

CHAPTER THREE

Adam

Thursday, 23 October 1975

Adam was surprised that his father was so eager to bond with him during homecoming weekend at Brown University. He had seen his father no more than a half dozen times in each of the two years since his parents were divorced. He had not experienced the suppressed dismay or the anguished abandonment that he might have had to endure if his parents had divorced years earlier, when he was a vulnerable boy who needed the protective feeling of their presence. He might have felt a grievous loss or a stinging betrayal if they had divorced when he was in his early adolescence, constrained by his need of their love and by his awareness that he was a stranger to himself and to all the other persons who were his trusted friends or his amiable acquaintances. But he was twenty years old when his parents were divorced. That year, as a junior at Yale University, he had long since learned how to negotiate his way into the world. Self-assurance, a tall and athletic physique, and burgeoning popularity kept at bay his disappointment about his conflicted relationship with his father and his emotionally muted kinship with his mother.

A year later, still at Yale, he had defined who he was in even more formidable ways. His success on soccer fields and in boxing rings, as well as in equally competitive classrooms, quickened his belief in his varied and life-affirming capacities. His travels with enterprising university friends and sometimes with his brother Ryan during winter and summer recess from school brought him into even more adventurous terrains. He had explored the glacial valleys, sub-Antarctic woodlands, and alpine landscapes of the Torres del Paine in Patagonia. He had observed Andean condors, with their wingspans exceeding ten feet, dancing in the thermal updrafts of Peru's Colca Canyon. He had scuba dived with trained dolphins in the Bahamas. With a Sherpa team guiding him and his friends, he had climbed the south side of Mount Everest in Nepal. He had kayaked on the white waters of the Hurunui and Buller Rivers in New Zealand. He had mountain-biked across the Jebel Sirwa Mountain Range in Morocco. Riding on an Appaloosa in northwest Wyoming, he had cantered along open plains that wound through aspen forests, clambered up rocky gorges, and crossed rushing streams that poured out of vast mountains.

These more recent years of defining who he was to himself and to others had inspirited him with steel-true determination to break free from all the adversaries who had meant to thwart his progress and his happiness. One day, he might forgive the pair of wily classmates who had attempted to foil his victories on the playing fields and in the classroom. But he would never again trust the ambitious jock (Thompson was his nickname) who had "accidentally" fallen against him while they were descending a staircase in their dorm, causing him to wrench his shoulder on the day before an important soccer match. Nor would he ever trust the temporary roommate (Bronson was his last name) who had tossed away his World History term paper and declared afterwards that he had mistakenly discarded it with the rough drafts of his own paper. He had played successfully in that crucial soccer match in spite of his injury. He had also managed to draw upon his research notes and quickly produce an excellent term paper for his World History seminar.

But it was not those two university adversaries who had shaken his trust in other people. In every school that he attended, he had found it easy to make many friends who shared an easy and loyal camaraderie with him. It was, instead, his parents who had disturbed his conviction that they would always be on his side as long as he followed the rules, worked hard, and activated his best capacities. Though his mother applauded his successes, she was rarely involved with his life at school or with the choices he made for the life that he cultivated when he was away from school. She was more concerned with her career as a novelist and with her efforts to maintain the fame that her novels had brought her. His father was a different matter. In his elementary and middle school years, he believed that he and his father were making an extraordinary bond with each other. His father was a nurturing spirit who patiently guided him through his earliest experiences with horse riding, boxing, swimming, soccer, kayaking, and rock climbing. In those years, his father regarded him as a son worthy of being loved and being treated with gentle empathy. So it seemed to his keen-minded, boyhood awareness.

By the time he was a full-fledged adolescent, though, his father's caring regard of him had altered. Suddenly, without explanation, his father became a tough-minded taskmaster. He pushed him into punishing regimens that were, he insisted, necessary if he wanted to excel as an athlete or as a self-possessed youth who was acquainting himself with the wider world. For all those hard years, he listened to his father. He strove to meet with special proficiencies every one of the challenges that his father set for him. He told himself that his father's intentions were both honorable and realistic. The world could be a rough place. As a reliable son whom his father had prepared well for its lacerating betrayals and its rigorous expectations, he could claim life-shaping victories only if he learned to set the bar high for his goals and for his achievements. He must avoid self-pity. He must learn to withstand discomfort and to live with pain. He should maintain a stoic demeanor that bonded with militant self-control and dispassionate reasoning.

He could not deny that, while imparting these stringent rules, his father had helped him to become a strong-minded individual who kept augmenting his leadership qualities and his well-honed aptitudes. But the positive influences his father's instruction had wrought upon him became complicated by its harsh terms and its ambivalent motives. Not until he was a senior in his prep school did he begin to understand that his father wanted to punish him, though as an always-dutiful son he had done no wrong. Then, as a youth of seventeen, his unhappiness compelled him to admit that his father did not love him. Nor, he was convinced, did his father even like him. He did not understand why. But when, at last, during his final months as a prep school senior, he confronted him with this truth, his father scoffed at his perceptions.

"You're imagining things," his father told him. "You're seeing dark motives where there are only good intentions. Besides, I don't want you to be a softie. You've got to be tough on yourself and tough on others if you want to get anywhere that's important in this world."

He might have believed his father if he had praised his successes once in a while and offered him an occasional, fatherly pat on the back or a bracing hug. But his stern manner, his barely suppressed anger, and his furtive scowls reinforced his belief that his father neither liked, nor loved him.

During these three years and more, while he was studying at Yale, he never mentioned to his closest friends his problematic relationship with his father or his parents' divorce. He kept his silence even on those infrequent occasions when his soccer or rowing buddies mentioned the tangled scenarios in their privileged homes. Recently, though, months after he fell in love with Claudia Lisi and she with him, he mentioned his troubled feelings about his father. With her long, brunette feather cut and big flicked hair, her soft brown eyes and olive complexion, and her round face and long, slim figure, she was the epitome of natural beauty that touches with glamour even a high-collared shirt, navy blue flare jeans, and platform shoes. Her gentle manner enhanced her keen-sighted awareness and a mind that explored with originality both the sciences and the humanities. When he expressed his disaffection with his father, Claudia offered him words that were meant to ease his doubts about him.

"Your father may be one of those men who find it difficult to express the softer side of their natures. When you were a child and seemed very vulnerable, your father didn't hesitate to praise you and to express his love for you. But, once you became an adolescent, he used a man-to-man approach with you. It wasn't what you wanted, but he apparently believed that a no-nonsense approach would keep you on a steady and disciplined course."

"You are probably right," he told her. "But he made himself a stranger to me."

They were walking hand in hand along the campus green. The October sun had brightened everything around them. The leaves on the giant elms, tinged as they were with red and gold; the topiary of a doe and her fawn; the comfortable benches filled with students reading their books; and the limestone path on which they were sauntering as they headed for the library—all these images gleamed upon his sighting them. They lifted his spirit, at least a little. Only the frown that creased his brow intimated his unease at this talk of his father.

Noticing the frown and sensing his discomfort, Claudia had more to say.

"Maybe you expect too much from your father," she said, her words both understated and intuitive. "If you do, you will always be disappointed."

Her words solaced him for that day, at least. Upon further reflection, though, he believed that Claudia's words told more about her kind nature and her willingness to imagine the hidden good in the puzzling behavior of fathers and mothers. Those words could not negate his father's barely suppressed disdain of him. Nor could Claudia's words explain his father's unwillingness to be in his company except for a few times each year after his parents' divorce. His father had often invited Ryan and his latest girlfriend to vacation with him and his new wife at their ski lodge in Maine during winter recesses from school or on cruises that brought them to the Bahamas as well as to Alaska during the summer. Once in a while, his father invited him, too, belatedly, but on those occasions he always found reasons that he could not join the group. With a bitter heart, he surmised that his loyal brother Ryan had prodded their father to include him in the summer and winter celebrations. He did not feel deprived. Instead, he was relieved that he would not have to endure his father's struggles to affect a paternal interest in him or to negotiate a new and authentic bond with him.

For all these reasons, he was surprised when his father invited him to the Homecoming Weekend at Brown University. His father's new wife, Caitlin, would not be attending, because she was in an advanced stage of her pregnancy with their first child. Nor was Ryan going to be there, because of his busy slate of exams and his obligations to his football team, on which he was a quarterback. His father had also invited Claudia. But she, too, was busy with exams and with a recital sponsored by the Yale Music Department, for which, as a gifted classical pianist, she would be playing a Brahms' concerto.

So, with carefully harnessed feelings, he accepted the invitation.

No sooner had he done so, than his father threw out words that took him off his guard.

"We'll have a great time," his father promised him. "I'll show you off to all my college friends. I'm counting on your making your usual, first-rate impression."

He could not believe what he was hearing. The words, carrying forward both enthusiasm and praise, astonished him. He could not imagine that his father's attitude toward him had changed since their last meeting. Yet these friendly words subverted the hard-hearted persona that his father had maintained for so many years whenever he was in his presence. Now, what quickened his curiosity about the invitation was not first of all the anticipation of his father's continued ambivalence toward him. Nor was it his own troubled feelings that he wanted to test and, possibly, to explore. Rather, he wanted most of all to observe and to decipher the tremendous change that his father's friendly words had expressed.

The three-day weekend at Brown took on a swift pace. The distinguished faculty and many enterprising students played hosts to hundreds of parents and alumni. There were football games and swim competitions; performances of classical dance, classical music, and modern jazz; seminars about the Space Age and nineteenth-century American poetry; a festival of student films; and a lavish banquet. He attended all of them, though not always with his father. Usually, he teamed up with friends from his prep school years who were now students at Brown and with Claudia's sister and her husband, who were beginning their careers as assistant professors in the Department of Comparative Literature. Whenever he was with his father during this weekend, he was careful to make a favorable impression upon the Wall Street bankers and brokers, the corporate executives, and the international moguls who had maintained their friendship with his father since their university days. He knew the value of power links. Though he and Claudia were headed for careers in medicine, he might one day need the friendship of one of those bankers or CEOs.

During this weekend, he shared rooms with his father in a private club within the university campus that offered them a stately setting and many amenities. Very late on that Saturday evening, after they had allowed themselves to be caught up in the day's spirited events, his father made a remark that suggested not only his street-wise realism, but also his momentary nostalgia and his shrewd understanding of what he could take from the world and what the world might not give him. They were walking through the reception room of the club a few minutes after midnight. Throngs of people were still partying in the distant festive rooms he and his father had just left, their voices quickened by the joy of being together. A band was playing in the ballroom, and a woman was singing a love ballad. But nobody else was in the reception room to which they had made their way except a desk clerk. Noticing that they were alone there, his father surveyed the look of the room and allowed himself to smile. It pleased him to reacquaint himself with the cathedral ceiling, the oak paneling, the richly upholstered sofas and armchairs, and the canvases of John Singer Sargent, Mary Cassatt, Thomas Hart Benton, and Winslow Homer. He invited him to observe as well. He wanted him to understand that this expansive room and many of the other rooms had figured in important episodes in the earlier part of his life and that of his mother.

"While we were students at Brown," he said, "your mother and I attended some lavish parties here and more than a few elegant dinners."

He tried to look at the room in the same way that his father saw it. Yet he guessed that, since his father's university days, the room and all its furnishings had been carefully refurbished or at least conservatively renovated. What his father was remembering must have once existed beneath the various alterations, as if the room were a large canvas that had once yielded images that were similar and yet different, so subtle were the changes that the years had wrought upon it. With penetrating eyes, he gazed upon his father and at the same time called to mind the photos he had seen of him when he was a student, here at Brown.

"You must have been very happy in those days," he said as he followed his father around the room.

For that instant, his father looked away from the oak paneling, the amply upholstered chairs and sofas, and the vivid paintings and turned to face him as he replied to his conjecture about the happiness that he had experienced during his university days. His father's gaze was just as direct as his own and his voice sounded matter-of-fact and understated.

"Sometimes I was happy," he said. "Not always. Nobody gets to be happy always."

A stoical expression touched his father's demeanor. He had trained himself well to withhold any words that might reveal too much about his feelings. Instead of exploring those feelings with him, he quickly changed the subject.

"You and I have had a fine weekend together," his father said. "But I've been saving the best for the last. Tomorrow morning, at the breakfast that officially closes this homecoming holiday, I'd like to introduce you to a special friend of mine. We were in the same class here at Brown. I hope that you will like him."

Having said so, his father hurried up the stairs to his room. He followed him and, on his way to his own room down the hall, called out a quiet "good night" to him. Alone in his room, his thoughts did not dwell upon the classmate that his father mentioned. Instead, he thought about the enjoyable time that he had spent with his father. He was both grateful and surprised that his father had shown him affection that was layered with respect and friendship. His thoughts turned to Claudia, too. If he was grateful for his father's expression of friendship, he was elated once again by the blessed chance or the happy fate that had sent Claudia to him. No sooner had his head touched his pillow, than he fell asleep. He slept deeply and well. It was a rare kind of sleep that comes only to those who allow themselves to believe that, at long last, they have made happiness a negotiable friend.

On the following morning, he joined his father for breakfast. He was not taken aback when his father explained that they would be having their breakfast in a private room, rather than in the banquet hall that was already crowded with hundreds of homecoming guests. His father preferred to dine within the comforts of a room that sealed him away from the hubbub of excited and demonstrative people.

"Besides," his father explained, "I'd like you to meet my special classmate in a quiet setting, away from the crowd and all the fanfare."

As they entered the private breakfast room, he saw at once that a table had been prepared for them by a sun-touched bay window that looked out upon a tree-lined street and impressive brownstones. He saw as well, sitting there at the table, a long-limbed gentleman who was peering out the window, his profile partially concealed by the rays of the October sun that cast a haze around him and by the young waiter who, with accomplished movements, was placing a vase of fresh yellow and red roses in the center of the table. Only after an older waiter guided his father and him to the table did he see his father's friend more clearly. The man that he saw was middle-aged and, though a generation older, resembled himself. In fact, the resemblance was uncanny. He wondered whether he was a relative that had been living out of the country or a Bennington who had lost favor with his father's family.

He had no time to consider his supposition. As soon as they took their seats, his father introduced him to this stranger.

"Adam, I'd like you to meet Noah Blake. He was my soccer mate here at Brown and a top-notch competitor whether we were in a boxing ring or on a ski slope."

He held out his hand to Mr. Blake, who quickly clasped it. The hand was large and felt warm. It held his hand for only a moment, yet the press of it was firm and its friendliness seemed instantly to be authentic.

"I'm so pleased to meet you, Adam," Mr. Blake said. "I've heard some very good reports about you."

Mr. Blake's voice was deep and emphatic, but a tremor hinted at his tension or, possibly, his uncertainty. In spite of his smile and his buoyant remarks, he seemed like a man who had been touched by grief that would not let go of him. It was only a guess that might be spawned from a false impression. But even Mr. Blake's smile seemed drawn from a repressed melancholy. So he imagined and right afterwards dismissed his too-quick appraisal when he noticed Mr. Blake making a smooth recovery and settling into amiable conversation about the weekend football game in which Brown defeated Dartmouth, the excellence of the Brown theater company and their performance of Shakespeare's *Twelfth Night*, and the thrill of piloting his new Learjet only a week earlier.

His father came into it now, eager to share anecdotes about the places where each of them had traveled, though not with one other and not at the same time. They spoke of skiing in St. Moritz, of attending bullfights in Mexico, of kayaking in Finland, and of racing Ferraris in the Indianapolis 500.

But always Mr. Blake drew him into the conversation.

"I'd like to know all about you," he said, beaming at the prospect of his friendship. "I'm sure you have been living a fantastic life."

"No more than yours," he answered him. "Your work brings you across the globe. There's adventure in that."

Mr. Blake smiled, once more at the edge of nervousness. He wanted to make a good impression. He wanted to be liked. He wanted, most of all, to be honest with him.

"I regard my business trips as work," he said, "but at times they have a way of turning into adventures."

He was not interested in speaking about himself, though. He wanted to know all about *his* travel, about his pre-med program at Yale, and about his plans after Yale. He was especially pleased when he told him about Claudia.

His father observed them quietly as they conversed. He was deliberately staying out of their exchange of words. Apparently, he wanted them to get to know one another.

All this while, two young waiters kept serving them an excellent breakfast that included orange juice, waffles and blueberries, scrambled eggs and bacon, buttered toast, and coffee.

He was enjoying himself. His father's friends had always recognized his merit, but none of them had ever made him think that he was extraordinary. Mr. Blake's respectful attention to him was lifting his spirit. From the band on his left ring finger, he saw that he was married. He wondered whether he had a son.

"You've shown such an interest in me, sir," he said. "I'm wondering whether you have a son of your own."

Hearing his remark, Mr. Blake became suddenly tense and fell silent.

His father shared that tension and was about to offer a makeshift reply to deflect attention from his friend's reluctance or inability to speak. But Mr. Blake did speak up, his words gone ragged and raspy.

"My son Seth died when he was nine years old."

He hurried to make amends for alluding to a subject that was so hurtful to this friend of his father.

"I'm sorry that you've lost your son," he said. "I've been wondering why you seem different from my father's other friends. Now I think I know why. I've been sensing the unhappiness that you try to hide."

Mr. Blake froze. He could not speak. He pressed his lips tightly together. A frown creased his brow, and his brown eyes looked haunted.

His father came into it now.

"Mr. Blake *is* unhappy," he said. "But you and I can help him to get back some of his happiness. That's why I wanted you to meet him."

His father's remark puzzled him. He never before had asked him to rescue one of his friends. Besides, Mr. Blake was a total stranger. He observed Mr. Blake with studious attention, though he directed his words at his father.

"How can I help? I've never met Mr. Blake until today. I don't know anything about him."

Now Mr. Blake came into it. He tried to be brisk and encouraging, but tension weighed down his every word.

"You'll learn everything about me that is important," he said. "It won't be hard to get to know me. I've been told that I grow on people."

He probed further. There was a missing piece here, some fragment of the puzzle that connected itself to this meeting with Mr. Blake.

"Why me? Why do you think that I can help you?"

Hearing his questions, Mr. Blake fell silent. The silence might have become awkward, but two waiters returned to their table at that instant to pour more coffee into their cups and to replenish his father's plate with more scrambled eggs and bacon. His own plate needed no replenishment, nor did Mr. Blake's.

The questions also made his father pause. He did not resume eating. Instead, he directed his hardened glances at both of them. He was taking their measure. He was calculating the gravity of their tension and the challenge behind the questions that sought to know why Mr. Blake thought that a university student who was a stranger could be of any help to him.

Then, after observing his perplexity and Mr. Blake's stillness, his father directed his next words to his friend.

"You'd better tell him, Noah," he said. "Don't back away from it. Telling him is the reason you're here. Tell him why you think that he can help you."

Prodded by this advice and casting aside his hesitation, Mr. Blake directed his clipped and understated words at him, the university student that he had met not even an hour ago. A matter-of-fact openness quickened his explanation of why he was seeking his help.

"Because you are my son, and because I'm the father who never claimed you."

The words startled him. They roused his disbelief. He turned for an explanation to the man who had always fathered him.

"Is this true?"

His father told him what he needed to hear.

"Yes, " he said. "Your mother is your natural mother. But I am not your biological father. I became your father when I married your mother, a couple of months before you were born"

He treaded cautiously now. Anger was stirring within him, and a door was opening onto a dark corridor that he had not expected to enter.

"Why didn't you ever tell me?"

His father—the man that he'd always called his father— did not answer him at once. Instead, he sipped his coffee and then busied himself with the lighting of a cigarette.

Mr. Blake also brought out a cigarette and lighted it. He took a drag on it and for a moment looked as if he was about to speak. He peered at him and noticed the dismay that had overtaken him. Before Mr. Blake could choose words that might dispel that dismay or that might appease his uncertainty and, in the same instant, break through the silence, his father found the words that explained why he had concealed his true lineage.

"Your mother and I thought it would be better for you not to know anything about your biological father."

He was more than dismayed. He felt cheated.

"Why not?"

Mr. Blake hurried in to clarify the matter. He was imparting more than an explanation. He was offering him a confession. His words sounded bitter. He imagined that, long before this day, this sorrow-laden man had compelled himself to become his own judge and jury. He had found himself wanting. Once more, he was declaring himself guilty.

"I'll tell you why they never mentioned me. I'd made it clear even before you were born that I didn't want any part of you."

"And now, after all these years, you want to be my father. Just like that."

"Yes. If you'll let me."

The words spilled out of him. Though he kept his voice low and, with taut proficiency, harnessed his anger, he told Mr. Blake how it was with him. While he spoke, he sometimes looked toward his father, implicating him in this response to Mr. Blake's petition.

"I'm a Bennington. I've always been a Bennington. This gentleman seated across from me, whose name is Steven Bennington, has always acted as my father. Maybe he was playacting all the time. Maybe that's why he treated me roughly. But he's been my father for all of the years that I've lived. He always will be my father. That will never change."

"No, it won't change. I understand that. I'm not asking you to change it. But I am asking you to let me come into your life. At least some of the time."

"It's a bit late for you to ask that."

His words, harsh and unforgiving, unsettled Mr. Blake. He noticed once more this troubled man's vaguely anguished expression, and he heard more clearly the tremor that wavered across his words.

"Yes, it is late," he managed to say. "But I hope it's not too late."

Whether it was too late, he could not say. Precisely, at that moment, the older waiter approached them to advise his father that his New York office was telephoning him.

"If you would like me to bring a phone to your table," the waiter said, "I shall be happy to do so."

"I'll take the call in my room," his father said, as he rose with limber ease and hurried away from the table, though not before excusing himself and leaving them with a remark that was both pertinent and encouraging.

"The two of you could use some time alone," he said. "You need to find out where you stand with each other."

The minute that his father hurried away, an awkward silence came hovering by him and by Mr. Blake. He began to pick at his breakfast, though he had no appetite for food. Mr. Blake followed his lead. The return of the young waiter was a godsend. He freshened their plates with hot scrambled eggs and bacon. His being there gave him time to observe with furtive interest Mr. Blake's impressive features. His was a lived-in face. It was a face that carried traces of quiet courage, deep-seated anguish, and an ongoing battle with despair. His resemblance to this man was uncanny. For all he knew, he might look the same way twenty years down the road.

He struggled to suppress the pity that he suddenly felt for this stranger. He did not want to be on this man's side. He did not want his meeting with him to go easy. Not caring that one of the waiters was headed toward their table with cups of sliced pears, strawberries, and apples, he threw forth a spate of heated words that were as probing as they were accusatory.

"Why didn't you want me when I was born? Why have you waited so long? Why have you come to me when I have no need of a father?"

Visibly recoiling from his anger, Mr. Blake fell silent once again. He refrained from speaking until the waiter had placed the cups of fruit near each of the plates that contained their breakfast. Only after that did he offer reasons why he had failed to acknowledge him as a son.

"Because I was selfish," he said. "Because I was uncaring. Because I didn't understand what a tremendous gift was being offered me."

So wretched did Mr. Blake appear as he spoke those words that the sight of him, unhappy and petitioning, roused his pity in spite of his resentment and his animosity.

Quickly, he found blunt words that pushed back even a vague sign of this pity.

"I don't need another father," he said. "I'm not sure that I need even one. I've learned to depend upon myself."

"But I need you. Please give me a chance."

"I don't know that you deserve a chance. You were cruel to cast me away for all the years when I might have learned to love you as my father."

"Sometimes, people are cruel without understanding how much they are hurting others."

"I suppose that I should be used to cruel people. My mother was cruel because she hid you from me. My father was cruel because I wasn't really his son."

"Give me a chance. Please. Let me try to make amends for all the years when I should have been your father."

"It's too late."

"Only if you think so. Only if you don't give me a chance."

Once again, Mr. Blake's words sounded ragged and raspy.

The furrowed brow, the nervous drag on a cigarette, and the repressed forlornness disturbed him. He thought it ironic that he was refusing this offer of the same paternal affection that Steven Bennington, the man that he accepted as his father, had often withheld from him. The words disturbed him as well because their very sounds drew from him the pity that he had struggled to keep at bay. His sudden willingness to solace this stranger surprised him. Ambivalent and conflicted though he was, he did not want to push this stranger out of his life now that he was asking to be a part of it. So he offered him a promise.

"Maybe," he said. "Maybe I'll try. At least, you'll see that I tried."

At that very moment, his father returned. He looked even more buoyant than when he'd left the table. His business call must have gone well. He not only seemed pleased. He also sounded jaunty.

"How goes it with you two? Truce? Retreat? Alliance?"

"Mr. Blake and I are still negotiating," he said. "We are just beginning."

Mr. Blake brightened at the prospect.

His own face did not brighten. One day, possibly, his bitter heart might allow him to pity this man who so belatedly sought to be his father. But he doubted that he could ever bring to their relationship the love and the trust that he would have offered him unconditionally had he been a part of his life ever since he was born. He could not forgive him for his abandonment of him.

He could not forgive his mother, either, for keeping him apart from his biological father when his being there with him would have mattered. He felt an equal bitterness toward Steven Bennington, the man who had offered him a father's guidance that was leached of any show of affection. Only time would tell whether he could learn to forgive the three of them. Only the years that waited ahead of him knew whether he could conquer his bitterness and learn to forgive the three strangers who claimed to be his parents.

PART THREE

AFTERWARD

PART THREE

Charlotte

Saturday, 8 November 1975

Her party was over. It had been a lavish dinner party, orchestrated by a renowned chef and his catering firm and by her aptitude for drawing to herself influential guests, the most popular entertainers, and the immense success that she was currently enjoying. Among the forty-six guests were literary and talent agents, publishing CEOs, and television and film executives. Bankers and lawyers were also there, as well as stockbrokers and other Wall Street magnates, and a few of her neighbors who made their homes in equally opulent penthouses that overlooked Central Park. Her sons were there: Ryan, with his latest girlfriend, and Adam, with his Claudia. Rick Blanchard had flown in from a business deal in South Africa, accommodating her desire to be viewed as a woman who still inspired romantic attachments.

She had urged Rick to be a part of this festive evening that meant to celebrate her as she launched a new phase in her busy career. She was on her way to the West Coast, where for the next four months she would be working with an important film director on the screenplay adaptation of one of her novels. At this glamorous party that had unfolded its pleasures all evening, she did not care to be seen as a woman without an escort. Her being paired with immensely successful Rick enhanced her image, without subverting her carefully muted sensuality or diminishing the genteel appeal that drew legions of fans to her books. She thought it was appropriate that she team up with Rick. They went back a long way. They carried similar baggage, including memories of the damage that they had inflicted upon others, the scars that they carried from their volatile attachments to other people, and their inveterate wiliness. Always, she and Rick came back to each other, without ever pretending that their long-standing alliance would persuade them to marry. In a special sense, they were already married, so solid was their bond and so incisive their understanding of the individuals they represented. They were linked by their mutual self-centeredness and by their casual promiscuity. Toward their friends, they could be kind at least some of the time. Toward adversaries, they were always unforgiving.

Rick's being here at her party had lifted her spirits. Without realizing it, he had helped her to create a lighthearted persona even though she did not feel lighthearted. In fact, she felt angry and betrayed because of Adam's unexpected alliance with Noah, the man who had abandoned her when she was pregnant and who had told her to get rid of the baby. She had not deferred to his will. She had given birth to a son, and he had become Adam, a healthy human being who had known only Steven Bennington as a father. She heard the news about Steven's bringing Adam to meet Noah at Brown University's homecoming week right after she returned from her book tour. Adam phoned her from his dormitory at Yale. He mentioned his meeting with Noah only incidentally, after he had spoken of the October success of the Yale rowing team, on which he was a captain; his interview with the admissions team at Harvard Medical School; and his ski trip to Maine with Claudia. She had praised him and his team for their rowing victory. She had encouraged him about his interview at Harvard. And she had expressed a genuine pleasure upon hearing about his skiing with Claudia. But she had refrained from commenting about his unexpected association with Noah. She wanted to see him face to face when she pleaded with him to reject the overtures of friendship that Noah was making. She needed to implore Adam in person not to become involved with Noah or to invite him to the July festivities that would celebrate his marriage to Claudia. She intended to speak with Adam after the party had ended and after all her guests had gone home.

Nevertheless, she approached the party with an unease that shadowed the exhilaration she compelled herself to express. Fortunately, none of her guests detected her unease. Nor did her effective concealment of her troubled feelings surprise her. Pretense was her stock in trade. Besides, there were many things about the evening that amused and delighted her.

Her guests had admired the renovations that her team of architects and interior designers had made to the three-story atrium and to the undulating carpeted staircase that led them to the expansive dining room, with its sky-mural ceiling; its faux-marble-finished walls; its pair of long, mahogany banquet tables; and its amply upholstered chairs.

The chef and his assistants had created an exemplary meal that included terrine of rabbit in rosemary aspic, salmon in Champagne sauce, and cookie wafers layered with raspberries and Chantilly cream.

After dinner, some of the guests had sauntered into the double-height library and noticed the revised catwalk and the new, built-in shelving with glass doors and elaborately carved ornamentation. The ladies had commented favorably about the nineteenth-century Aubusson carpet there, the damask on the sofa, and the striped fabric on the club chairs that stood behind the sofa. Other guests had strolled onto the glass-encased, heated terrace, where they observed pale gold pillars, hardy autumn greenery, fashionable tables and chairs, and the Manhattan skyline. Eventually, all of her guests made their way into the ballroom, all the while remarking on the changes: the French chandeliers, the satin curtains, the apricot-hued furnishings, and the second-floor mezzanine.

By that time, her party was in full swing. A band that often played at posh supper clubs in New York, Chicago, and San Francisco was accompanying a svelte blonde chanteuse and her tall, dark-haired husband as they imparted romantic fervor and melancholic subtexts to popular ballads. Long-married couples and new, amorous partners gave themselves with easy assurance to the rhythms of waltzes, foxtrots, and sambas. All her guests were doing their part to make the evening both enjoyable and special. Wives carefully monitored their husbands' drinking. Single women tempered their seductive inclinations. Bachelors subdued their prurient impulses. Her guests knew her well. They took care not to invoke her displeasure, especially on this evening when they were here to celebrate the million-dollar contract she had made with a Hollywood studio and when journalists from *The New York Times* and *Architectural Digest* were covering the splendor of the occasion and the pristine restoration of her sixteen-room townhouse.

She had paid special attention to Adam. She wondered whether his emerging bond with Noah might become an unhappy intrusion upon her own relationship with him, the first of her two sons. In those moments when she was being completely honest with herself, she had often admitted that she had never been especially close to him. She did not care to be motherly in any conventional way. Nor did she want to smother Adam with the excessive affection and the incipient adulation that bound him to an unhealthy allegiance to her needs and trapped him inside uncertainty and remorse if he chose to have opinions that differed from her own. She could not abide weak-willed men. If, for some important reason, Adam chose to think for himself, so be it. She had not complained when he made a stronger bond with Steven, whom he rightly accepted as his father. Steven's militant bearing and his intuitive awareness of the rigorous tests that would foster Adam's rugged masculinity counted for a great deal. Adam was making his journey into the world with a steadfast belief in himself and with a realistic expectation that he might maintain a formidable place in its varied environments if he brought to his experiences of them a tough-minded resilience and the ability to recover from disappointment and loss.

Long ago, the thought crossed her mind that Adam might have been aware that in subtle and sometimes surreptitious ways she had always favored Ryan, the son whose father was really Steven. If that were so, Adam never appeared disconcerted when he was in her company with Ryan. His bond with Steven meant more to him. It was the bond of a loyal son who would do everything he could to please the father that he loved. She never resented that bond. On the contrary, the adamant strength of it pleased her. Without Adam's knowledge, his unwavering bond with Steven represented her triumph over Noah. The man who had deserted her years ago would never know the love of this, his first son. The loss of his second son, the boy named Seth, had crushed Noah's spirit. Even now, she imagined that he was struggling to recover the hope and the happiness that the Fates had taken from him when Seth died. It had given her pleasure to imagine that, in spite of his valiant attempts to find new meaning in his life, Noah would never again be happy.

From the time that he was a boy of seven or eight, Adam's uncanny resemblance to Noah kept her from establishing a warmhearted bond with him. So intense was her ambivalent hatred of Noah that the image of him that was replicated in the face and the body language of Adam disturbed her equanimity. Only when she learned of Seth's dying was she satisfied. Having witnessed Noah's despair, she felt triumphant. She had lived to see how wretched he was. She had lived to deny him access to Adam, the son who might have rescued him from his despair.

Now the unexpected was happening. Adam was creating a bond with Noah, after all. She would try to put a stop to it. Strong of will and eager to help the downtrodden and the despairing, Adam would go his own way, no matter what she said. Nevertheless, she would appeal to his sense of justice. She would urge him not to alter Noah's situation. Blind Chance or the implacable Fates had wrought stern punishment upon Noah. Let that punishment go forward, with its lacerating remorse and its endless anguish. Adam would listen to her. Whether he would act upon her willful petitions was another matter. Perhaps, he would discover that his own thoughts about Noah did not lie that far afield from hers.

So she imagined, as she directed her attention to Adam and to Claudia, the sensible young woman with whom he planned to spend the rest of his life.

She was not surprised to find that Adam and Claudia were ideal guests. They had been so in the past. Tonight, they were especially impressive. Adam looked handsome in his black tuxedo, and Claudia looked radiant in her blue chiffon gown. At the start of the evening, when they joined the festive gathering in the atrium, sipping Champagne and beaming with elation, and later when they were seated at the dinner table, they had chatted amiably with so many of their fellow guests. Now, here in her resplendent ballroom, they continued to do all the right things. They joined in a spontaneous songfest. They toasted a New York senator and his bride. They put at ease an ambassador from Scotland and his reticent wife. They danced an eightsome reel that included Ryan and his girlfriend and the ambassador from Scotland and his wife, as well as Rick and her. They conversed with Yale classmates and with other friends from earlier days. In short, they did their part to spark the evening.

When the party was over and her guests had gone home, she was very pleased. In fact, she allowed herself to feel at least momentarily elated because her party had been a resounding success. She was pleased, too, that Rick had decided to spend the weekend with her before he flew back to South Africa and before she embarked on her extended visit to the West Coast. With these thoughts in mind, she made her way into the privacy of the library, where Adam and Claudia as well as Rick were waiting to speak with her.

Rick was nursing a scotch while he leaned into a comfortable sofa. Claudia was perusing Daphne du Maurier's famous novel *My Cousin Rachel,* and Adam was standing by the panoramic window, peering at the November moon that cast a spectral glow upon the stunted trees, verdant shrubs, and elegant topiaries in the terrace garden.

When she entered the spacious room, she affected a breezy manner. She was determined to conceal her tension and to play upon the casual assurance that put her friends at ease and enhanced her image as a woman of the world.

"Let's celebrate," she said. "My party has been a delightful success. I owe no small thanks to the three of you. You made all the right moves. You chose all the right words. You impressed. You regaled. You sparkled."

She was carrying a tray of drinks to them. She might have prepared the drinks at the bar that stood in the south corner of the room. But to do so would have deprived her of her carefree entrance and the pleasure of watching them look toward her with various measures of surprise and good will.

"I take it that you are giving us five-star ratings," Rick said, while leaning still into the comfortable sofa.

"What I'm giving you is a fresh tumbler of scotch."

She brought the drink to him and studied his smiling face, still handsome despite its cragged traceries and its well-worn weathering. She saw that he was enjoying her exhilaration, even though he suspected that her entrance was a performance. He knew her well. She was up to something, and he had instantly decided that he would enjoy finding out what her game was.

"Well, bully for you," he said. "You know the way to this man's heart."

"I do, indeed," she said. "That's one of the dividends of a long-term friendship."

He laughed.

"You sound like my broker."

"Of course I do," she answered him, still lighthearted and effervescent. "Brokers and I think alike."

He leaned forward, grabbed her by the waist, and drew her closer to him. She had all she could do to balance the tray of drinks. She noticed then that Rick was at the cusp of being drunk.

"Give me a kiss," he said, not caring that Adam and Claudia were there in the room with them.

He rose from his place on the sofa and waited for her to make her move. Without any hesitation, she brushed his lips with a fleet kiss and quickly turned away, though not before choosing new words that would keep him on her team.

"I'll give you a real kiss later," she said.

She hurried forward to the place where Claudia was standing by the floor-length bookshelves, reading du Maurier.

"Champagne and du Maurier go well together," she said.

Claudia looked pleased.

"Even better when we toast each other," her future daughter-in-law said.

"That's exactly what we're going to do."

Now she hurried toward the terrace window, where Adam was taking one last glance at the gleam of the moon before he turned to her again to accept bourbon on the rocks.

"For you, Adam," she said. "A drink to keep your heart warm."

He accepted the drink with thanks and, with his keen-minded gaze, carefully observed her. Often enigmatic and always in search of the truth that lay beneath her artifice, he appeared to be judging her every word and even her smallest gestures. That had been his way ever since his childhood. Even then, he knew that she was withholding herself from him. Yet he never petitioned her for acceptance. He was more interested in winning the approval of Steven, who had carefully fathered him. His refusal to petition her for her motherly love impressed her. There was, she felt, a suppressed hardheartedness inside him waiting to be released. He would do well in the world. Experience would make him bitter and even arrogant. Eventually, it would leach him of sentimentality and of pity. So she hoped, understanding how ruthlessly the world treated the weak and the trusting.

Whether he had guessed why she had asked him to stay after the party, she could not say with any certainty. But she heard a knowing irony in his response to her plan to open this meeting with a special toast. He made his response in the form of a question that was merely rhetorical rather than inquiring.

"An after-party celebration?"

"More like a conference," she replied, without skipping a beat. "We need to talk."

Her words intrigued his interest. They quickened Claudia's curiosity as well. She returned the du Maurier to the bookshelf and joined Adam in the center of the room, where they sat across from Rick in club chairs and watched her lift her glass of Champagne. They and Rick, too, followed suit. In unison, the four of them raised their glasses and saluted each other.

"To winning," she said. "Let's not accept anything less."

She watched Rick savoring his scotch and quickly swallowing all of it. Adam and Claudia merely sipped their drinks, and she barely touched hers. She needed to keep her wits working on her behalf. She wanted to persuade Adam to accede to her wish that he not invite Noah to the grand wedding that was to take place in the height of the summer. She planned to use all the subtle tricks of her deviousness and all the disarming nuances of her sophistication to win Adam's allegiance, at least in this one matter that was so important to her.

Silence took hold of Adam now and Claudia and Rick, too, just for an instant, as they waited for her to explain why, a few hours earlier as her party was beginning, she had called them to this meeting.

She did not keep them waiting long. Instead, she began to tell them why she had asked them to meet her in the library.

First of all, she directed her words at Adam and Claudia. She imparted a congenial manner and maintained a perfect control.

"I'm asking the two of you for a favor. Before you decide whether you will grant me the favor, though, you will have to search your hearts. You will have to share my point of view. You will have to see things as I do."

With penetrating gaze and merely a hint of the skepticism behind that gaze, Adam studied her carefully, without giving any clue that he could ever see things as she did. Nor did his next words offer any promise.

"What is it that you want us to see?" he asked.

"A problem, and the cause of it."

Claudia came into it now. As she spoke, she observed her with a new gravity.

The thought crossed her mind that her son and his fiancée must have already discussed his new relationship with Noah. Wherever Adam stood in this problem of Noah, Claudia would stand with him, not as an echoing expression of the words he had shared with her, but as the strong-minded young woman who did her own thinking and came to her own conclusions. Independent and forthright though she was, she nevertheless shared most of Noah's opinions. She would have to persuade Claudia, as well as Adam, about the rightness of her harsh judgment of Noah. She felt that she had made a good start by not telling them at once her reason for drawing them into the library at two o'clock in the morning. She had roused their interest. She had chosen the right words. She had stirred their guessing the moment she had mentioned, without declaring its specific nature, the problem that was trailing her.

"It must be a serious problem," Claudia said, "since you've called us to this meeting."

"It is serious," she answered her, while she selected with rigorous care the words that might make them her advocates. "What's so annoying about it is that, for so many years, I've taken steps to avoid it. I never imagined that some wild chance happening would work against me. The problem is here, and it's all too real. "

"Well, don't keep us in suspense, honey," Rick said. "Give it to us straight up. We'll rip your problem apart. That's a promise."

He rose from his place on the sofa and headed for the bar. He poured himself another tumbler of scotch and, once again, swallowed it with pleasure. Instead of returning to the sofa, he sat on one of the bar stools and went on observing her with a well-calibrated melding of street-wise awareness and sharp-edged cynicism. In her heart, she knew that he wanted no part of her family problems. Nevertheless, his being there with her created the impression that, in this matter of Noah Blake, they were strong allies. Whether Adam and Claudia could read him as acutely as she did, she could not say. But, though Rick had distanced himself from the meeting that was unfolding, she called out to him while recognizing him as an essential presence.

"I'm glad you're on my team, Rick, though I'm not surprised. You've always been a loyal friend. But it's Adam and Claudia to whom I am making a special appeal."

Hearing her words, Adam remained silent. He detected a plot.

Claudia covered for him by asking an appropriate question.

"How can we help?"

Without a pause, she spoke matter-of-fact words to her son and his fiancée that were anchored to polite expectation and restrained entreaty.

"You can help by not inviting Noah Blake to your wedding."

Instantly, Claudia glanced toward Adam, her silent language of eyes and stillness prodding him to speak.

Adam swiftly answered her, the mother whom he had so often ambivalently regarded.

"I can't do that. I want Noah to be there."

Her words became more excited now.

"He was never your father. He doesn't belong at your wedding."

Adam would have none of it.

"He does belong, because he *is* my father, even though he's made his claim belatedly."

His curt words pushed her to implore him further. She affected a quaver in her voice, and her eyes became misty. She made her plea even more urgent now.

"Steven is your father," she said, "even though you do not share the same blood. He's your father because of the many years that he has given to you. He was there for you through all the years of your boyhood, whether he was coaching you in boxing or rowing or lacrosse or in the proper use of a Winchester rifle. He was there for you when you were sick and when you were happy."

She wondered whether Adam saw through her contrived appeal. He would not budge. He refused to be influenced by her beseeching manner or by the heartless plan that she was trying to impose on him. He knew the score. He had spent hours analyzing Steven's character and Noah's, too. So she imagined.

"Steven gave me many things," he said. "But he didn't give me his love. Not completely. Not when I really needed it. Not after he found out that you were seeing Rick on the side. Not after you told him you loved only Noah. You should have reminded him that you also hated Noah."

She deflected his remark, with its abrasive and knowing subtexts. She understood now that Steven must have told Adam about the plots that she had devised against Noah. Nevertheless, she defended Steven once again without mentioning her promiscuous relationship with Rick or her ambivalent feelings about Noah.

"You owe Steven a lot."

"Of course, I do. That's why he'll have a special place at the wedding. But I want Noah there, too. I'm not leaving him out."

She stayed in control, but her quiet words were unyielding. Her hatred of Noah was boundless.

"He's come too late. He doesn't deserve your acceptance."

Even-tempered and resolute, Adam held firmly to his own point of view.

"It's never too late for a man to admit that he's made a mistake. It's never too late for him to ask for forgiveness."

The anger that she had harnessed all through the evening flared out of her now.

"What about me? What about my feelings? Noah Blake abandoned me because I was pregnant. He didn't care that I was going to be scandalized because I wasn't married. He didn't care about you. He didn't want you to live."

Adam did not answer her at once. Instead, he lowered his head with pensive deliberation. He might have been an aged judge weighing the evidence of a witness for the prosecution. In that moment, while waiting for his next words, Claudia glanced at him with the admiration and trust that intensified their bond. Only after that did Adam respond to the virulent testimony against Noah. He stayed firm. He stayed steady. His voice conveyed absolute conviction.

"What Noah did was wrong," he said. "He was everything that you accuse him of being. He was heartless, uncaring, and selfish. But all of that happened years ago. These recent years have put him through hell. He's a broken man. He's lost the son that he *did* claim and nurture and love. His wife can never give him any more children. He never expected to meet me, because you told him I was dead. He's called me a gift from God. I can't turn away from him. I pity him. I want to help him. Some day, after I get to know him well, I may even forgive him."

She could not bear the words that he was telling her. She could not keep back new declarations of her anger. Rick at the bar and Claudia at her place near Adam observed her with their own degrees of dismay and comprehension as she lashed out at Adam.

"You are being as heartless and as selfish as Noah. You don't care about my feelings."

Adam's gaze remained direct and uncompromising, with no trace of sentimentality or inclination to be chained to her grievances. He saw who she was, despite her efforts at concealment.

"I do care," he said. "I care very much about your feelings. It will be better for you to let go of your hatred and your need to avenge yourself against Noah. Your hatred has made you its prisoner."

In that instant, she saw with bitter clarity how much her plotting against Noah had cost her. She had lost Adam's trust. She had lost it long ago. Her subtle detachment from her son through all of his formative years and her refusal to forgive Noah cast a dark shadow upon her.

Willful and perverse nonetheless, she once again protested Adam's words. Those words were challenging her to free herself from the hatred that was imprisoning her.

"You are cruel to say so. Do you realize how cruel you can be?"

"Yes," he answered after a moment's reflection. "I can be very cruel. You and Noah and Steven have taught me well."

www.ingramcontent.com/pod-product-compliance
Lightning Source LLC
Chambersburg PA
CBHW070739190726
48292CB00002B/344